HEATHCLIFF
AROUND
THE WORLD

by Geo Gately

TOR

A TOM DOHERTY ASSOCIATES BOOK
NEW YORK

This is a work of fiction. All the characters and events portrayed in this book are fictitious, and any resemblance to real people or events is purely coincidental.

HEATHCLIFF AROUND THE WORLD

A Tor Book
Published by Tom Doherty Associates, Inc.
49 West 24th Street
New York, N.Y. 10010

ISBN: 0-812-50910-2

First printing: November 1989

Printed in the United States of America

0 9 8 7 6 5 4 3 2 1

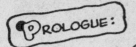

PROLOGUE:

THIS STRANGE ADVENTURE BEGINS AS MANY HEATHCLIFF STORIES BEGIN...

AND WITH IGGY'S WORDS, HEATHCLIFF BEGINS WHAT HE THINKS WILL BE A USUAL DAY...

SEE YOU LATER, HEATHCLIFF, BE GOOD NOW!

HE TAKES THE SHORTCUT THROUGH HOGAN'S ALLEY THAT HE USUALLY TAKES...

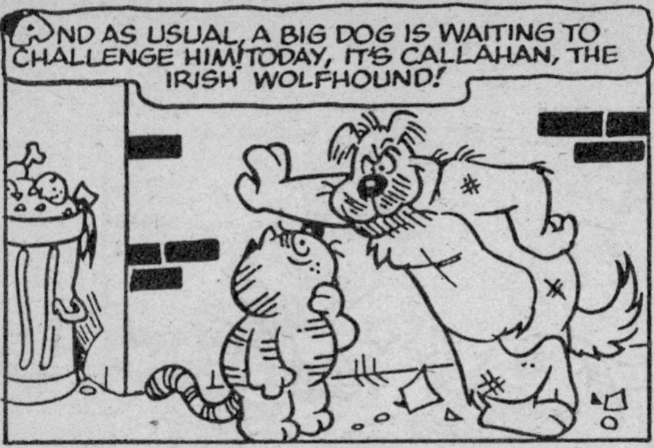
AND AS USUAL, A BIG DOG IS WAITING TO CHALLENGE HIM! TODAY, IT'S CALLAHAN, THE IRISH WOLFHOUND!

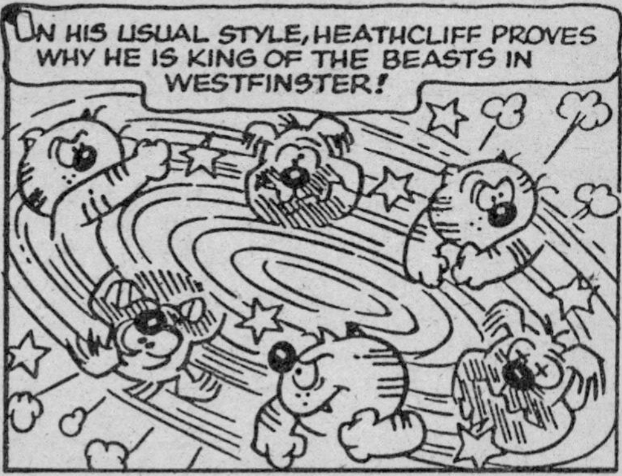
IN HIS USUAL STYLE, HEATHCLIFF PROVES WHY HE IS KING OF THE BEASTS IN WESTFINSTER!

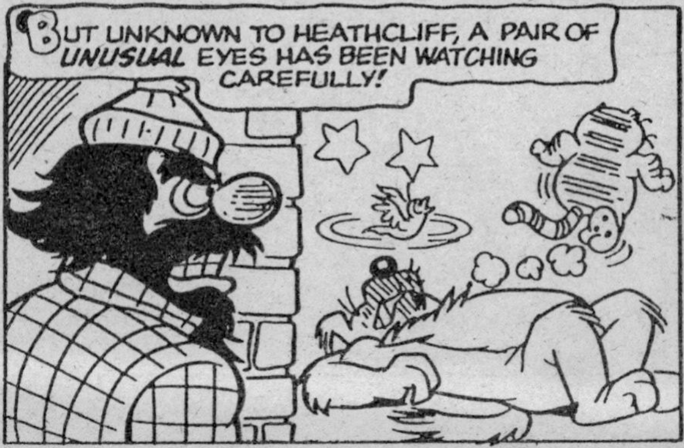
BUT UNKNOWN TO HEATHCLIFF, A PAIR OF *UNUSUAL* EYES HAS BEEN WATCHING CAREFULLY!

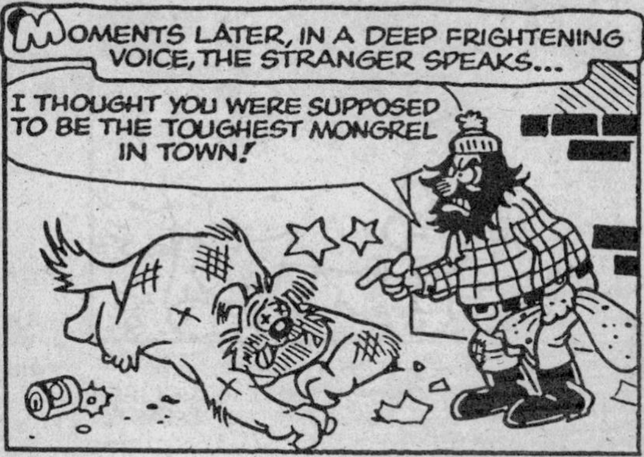
MOMENTS LATER, IN A DEEP FRIGHTENING VOICE, THE STRANGER SPEAKS...
I THOUGHT YOU WERE SUPPOSED TO BE THE TOUGHEST MONGREL IN TOWN!

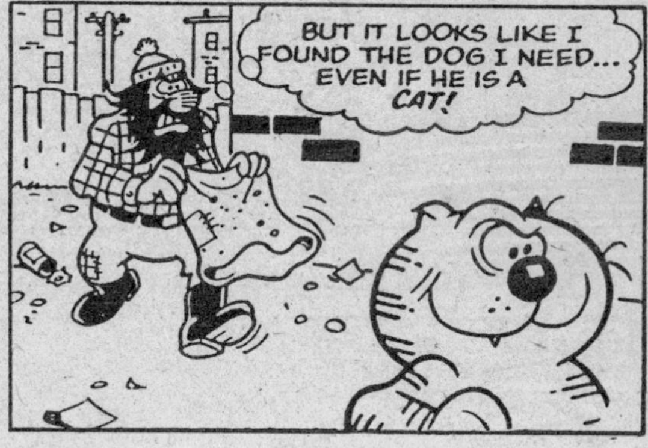
BUT IT LOOKS LIKE I FOUND THE DOG I NEED... EVEN IF HE IS A CAT!

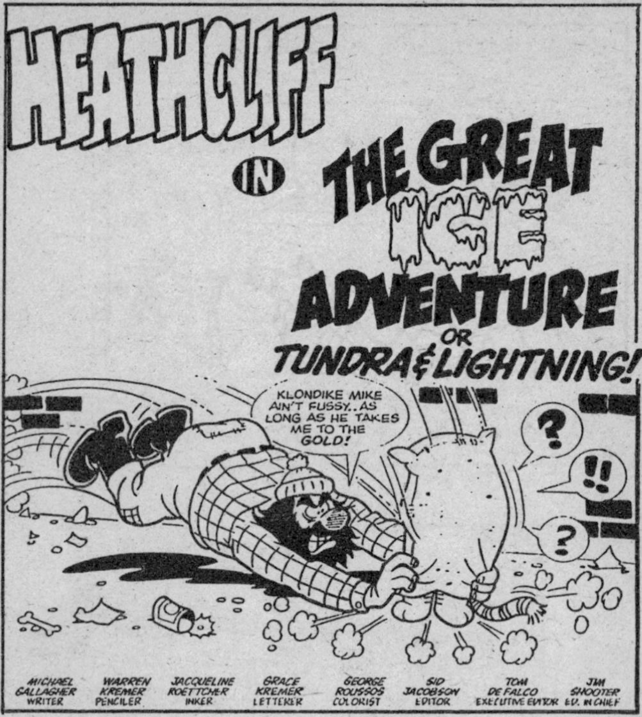
HEATHCLIFF
IN
THE GREAT ICE ADVENTURE
OR
TUNDRA & LIGHTNING!
KLONDIKE MIKE AIN'T FUSSY.. AS LONG AS HE TAKES ME TO THE GOLD!
?
!!
?
MICHAEL GALLAGHER WRITER
WARREN KREMER PENCILER
JACQUELINE ROETTCHER INKER
GRACE KREMER LETTERER
GEORGE ROUSSOS COLORIST
SID JACOBSON EDITOR
TOM DE FALCO EXECUTIVE EDITOR
JIM SHOOTER ED. IN CHIEF

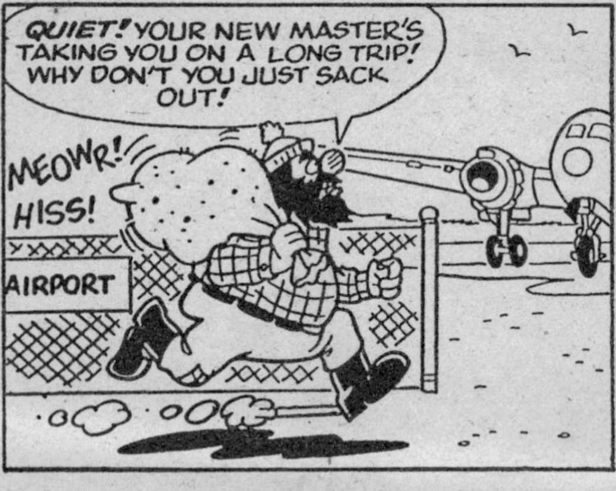
QUIET! YOUR NEW MASTER'S TAKING YOU ON A LONG TRIP! WHY DON'T YOU JUST SACK OUT!
MEOWR!
HISS!
AIRPORT

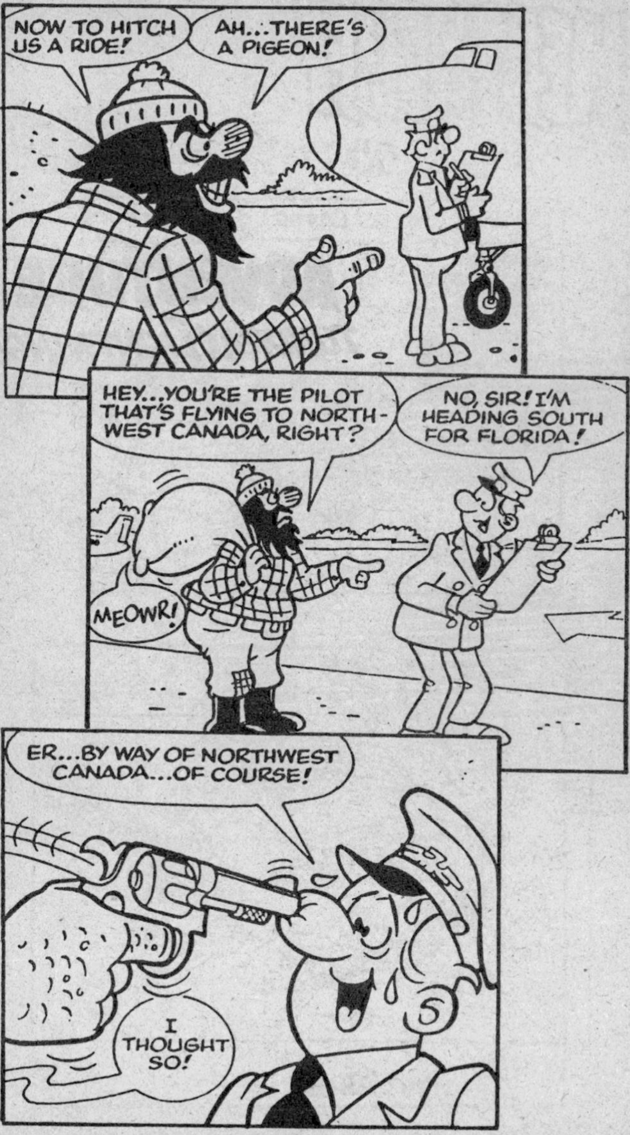
NOW TO HITCH US A RIDE!
AH...THERE'S A PIGEON!
HEY...YOU'RE THE PILOT THAT'S FLYING TO NORTH-WEST CANADA, RIGHT?
NO, SIR! I'M HEADING SOUTH FOR FLORIDA!
MEOWR!
ER...BY WAY OF NORTHWEST CANADA...OF COURSE!
I THOUGHT SO!

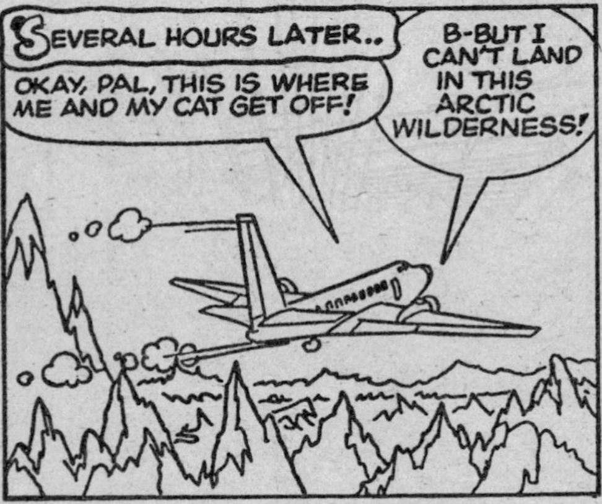
SEVERAL HOURS LATER..
OKAY, PAL, THIS IS WHERE ME AND MY CAT GET OFF!
B-BUT I CAN'T LAND IN THIS ARCTIC WILDERNESS!

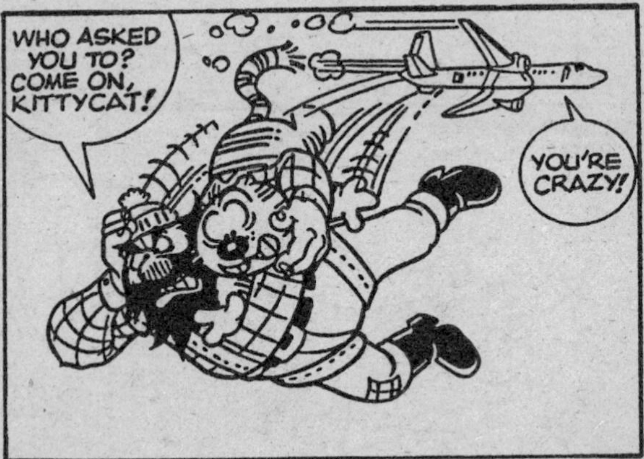
WHO ASKED YOU TO? COME ON, KITTYCAT!
YOU'RE CRAZY!

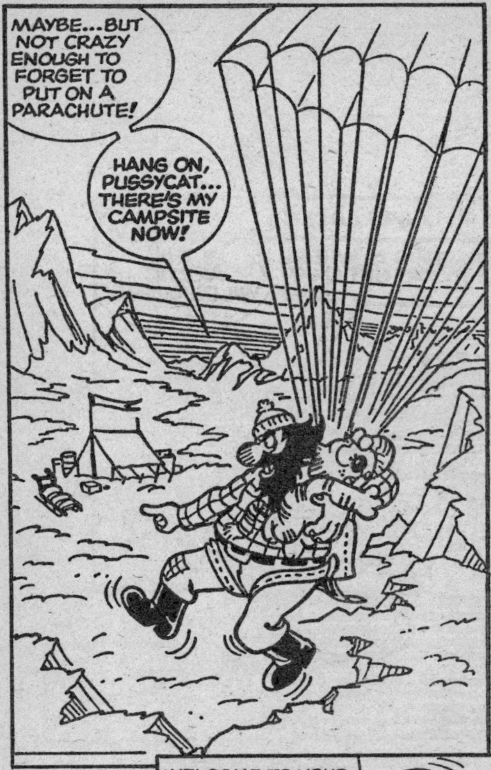
MAYBE...BUT NOT CRAZY ENOUGH TO FORGET TO PUT ON A PARACHUTE!
HANG ON, PUSSYCAT... THERE'S MY CAMPSITE NOW!

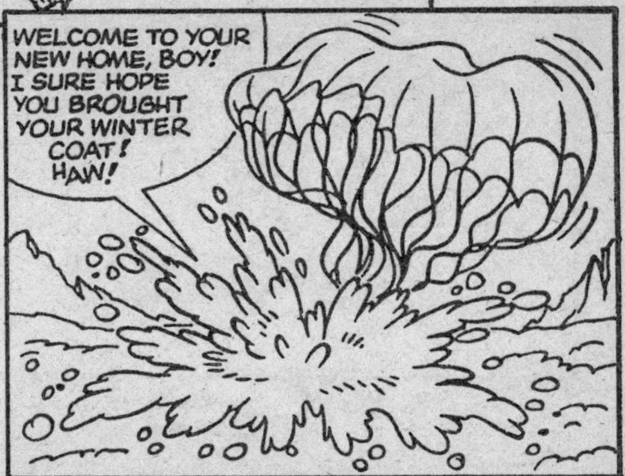
WELCOME TO YOUR NEW HOME, BOY! I SURE HOPE YOU BROUGHT YOUR WINTER COAT! HAW!

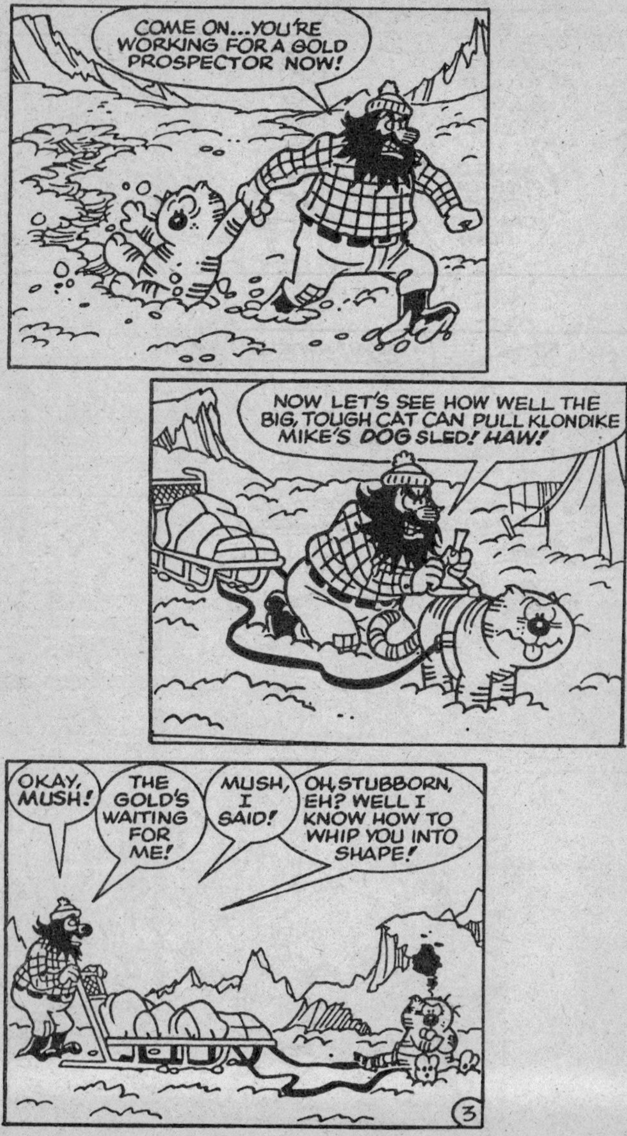
COME ON...YOU'RE WORKING FOR A GOLD PROSPECTOR NOW!
NOW LET'S SEE HOW WELL THE BIG, TOUGH CAT CAN PULL KLONDIKE MIKE'S *DOG* SLED! *HAW!*
OKAY, MUSH!
THE GOLD'S WAITING FOR ME!
MUSH, I SAID!
OH, STUBBORN, EH? WELL I KNOW HOW TO WHIP YOU INTO SHAPE!
3

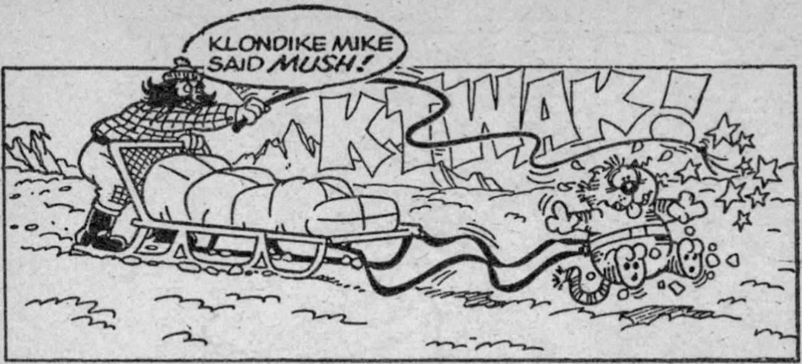
KLONDIKE MIKE SAID *MUSH!*
KTWAK!

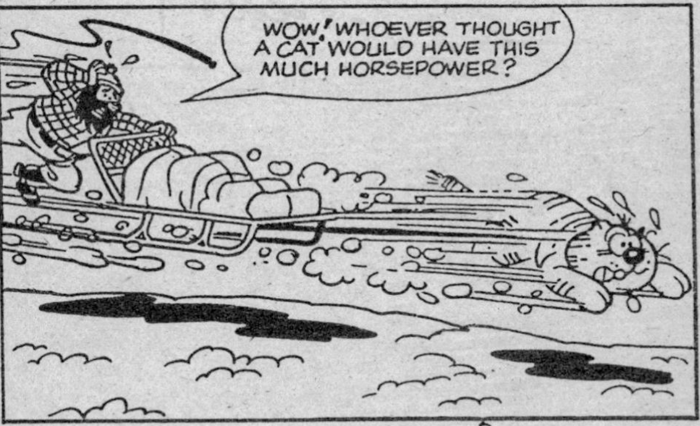
WOW! WHOEVER THOUGHT A CAT WOULD HAVE THIS MUCH HORSEPOWER?

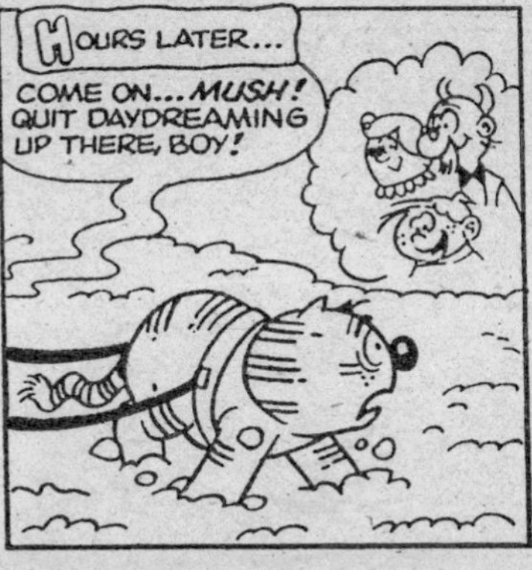
HOURS LATER...
COME ON... *MUSH!* QUIT DAYDREAMING UP THERE, BOY!

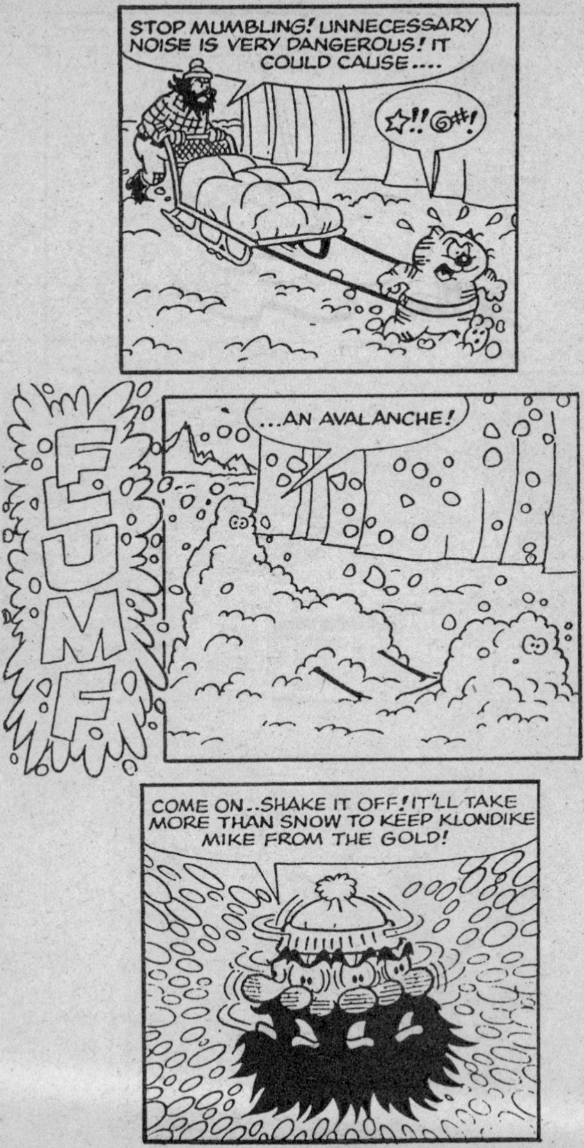
STOP MUMBLING! UNNECESSARY NOISE IS VERY DANGEROUS! IT COULD CAUSE....
FLUMF
...AN AVALANCHE!
COME ON..SHAKE IT OFF! IT'LL TAKE MORE THAN SNOW TO KEEP KLONDIKE MIKE FROM THE GOLD!

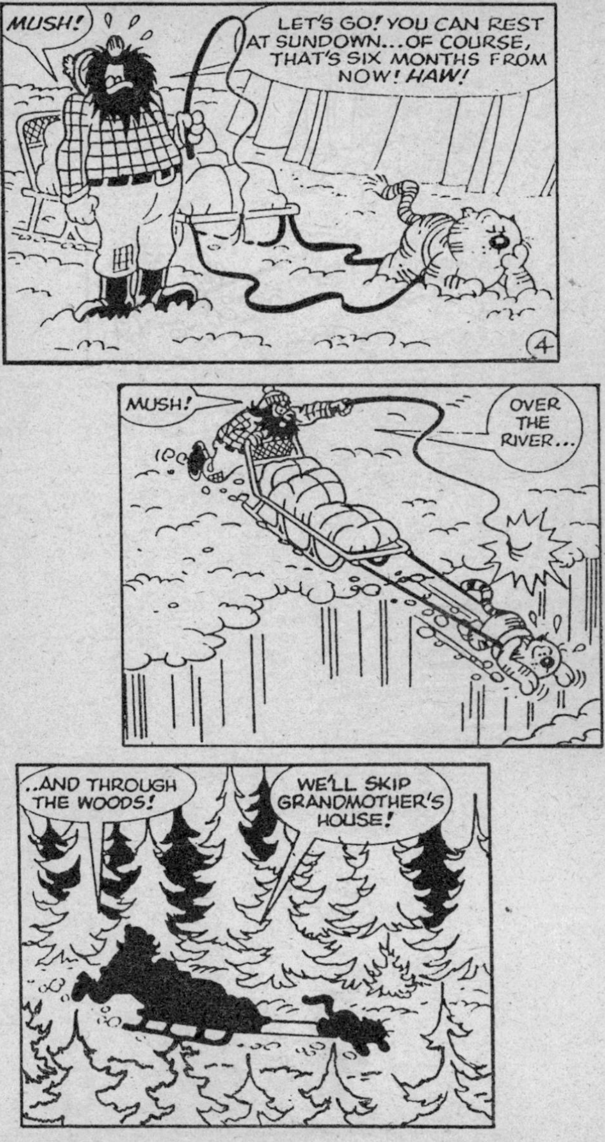
MUSH!
LET'S GO! YOU CAN REST AT SUNDOWN...OF COURSE, THAT'S SIX MONTHS FROM NOW! HAW!
4
MUSH!
OVER THE RIVER...
..AND THROUGH THE WOODS!
WE'LL SKIP GRANDMOTHER'S HOUSE!

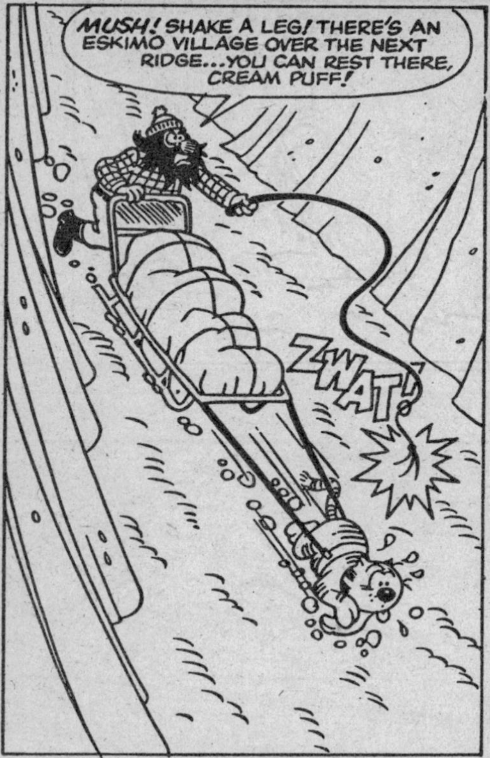
MUSH! SHAKE A LEG! THERE'S AN ESKIMO VILLAGE OVER THE NEXT RIDGE...YOU CAN REST THERE, CREAM PUFF!
ZWAT!

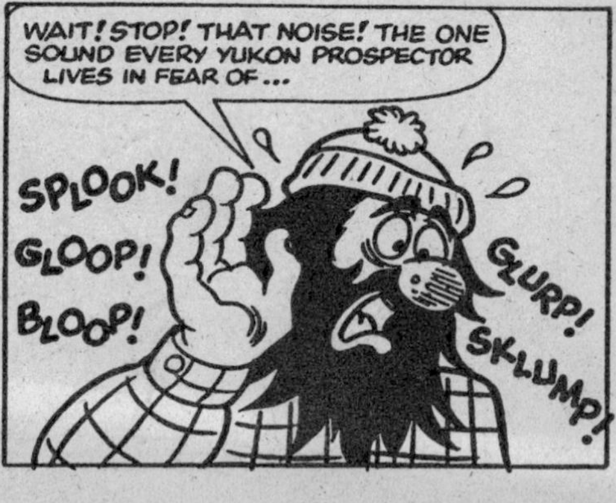
WAIT! STOP! THAT NOISE! THE ONE SOUND EVERY YUKON PROSPECTOR LIVES IN FEAR OF...
SPLOOK!
GLOOP!
BLOOP!
GLURP!
SKLUMP!

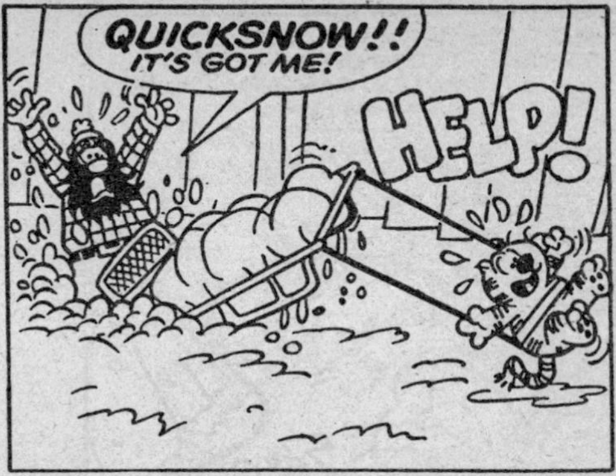
QUICKSNOW!! IT'S GOT ME!
HELP!

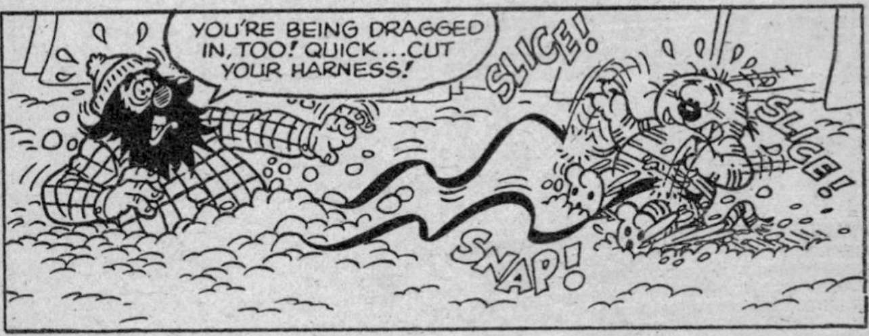
YOU'RE BEING DRAGGED IN, TOO! QUICK...CUT YOUR HARNESS!
SLICE!
SLICE!
SNAP!

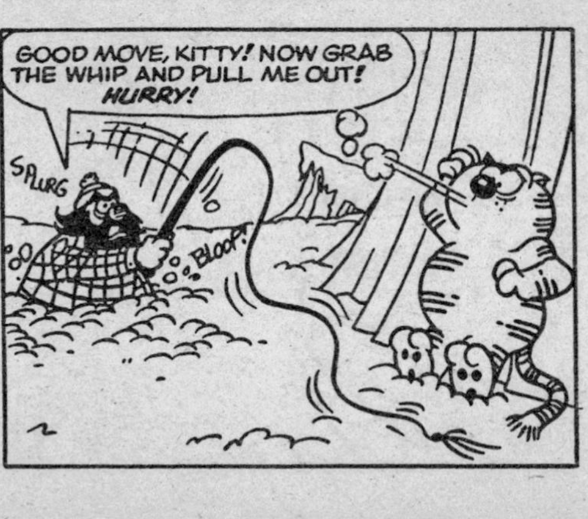
GOOD MOVE, KITTY! NOW GRAB THE WHIP AND PULL ME OUT! HURRY!
SPLURG
BLOOP!

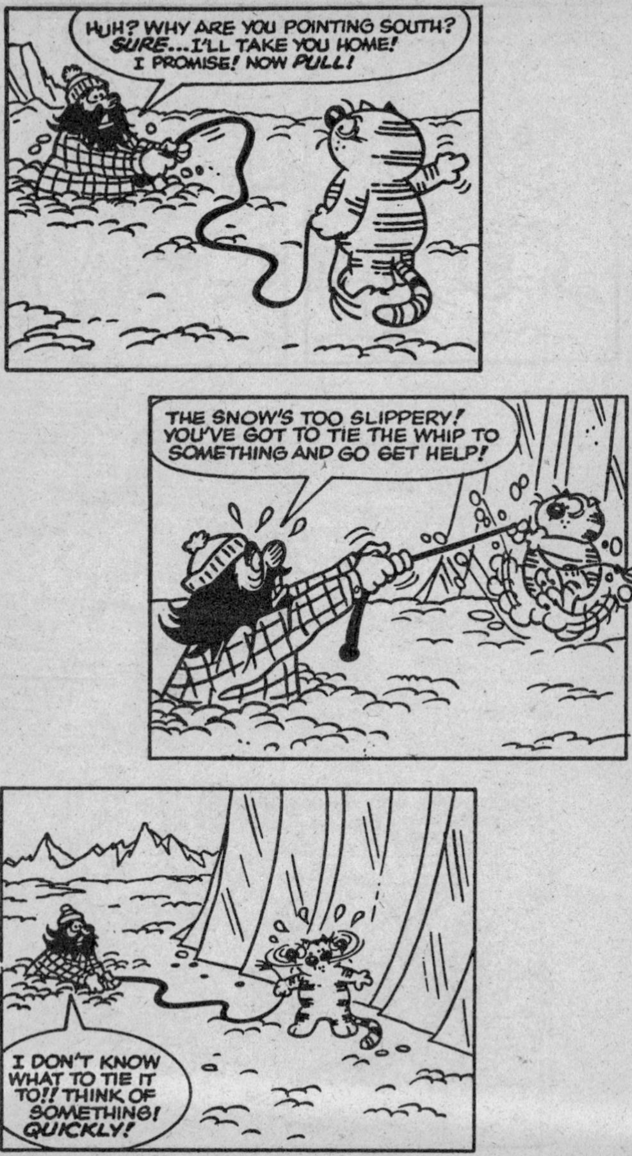
HUH? WHY ARE YOU POINTING SOUTH? SURE...I'LL TAKE YOU HOME! I PROMISE! NOW PULL!
THE SNOW'S TOO SLIPPERY! YOU'VE GOT TO TIE THE WHIP TO SOMETHING AND GO GET HELP!
I DON'T KNOW WHAT TO TIE IT TO!! THINK OF SOMETHING! QUICKLY!

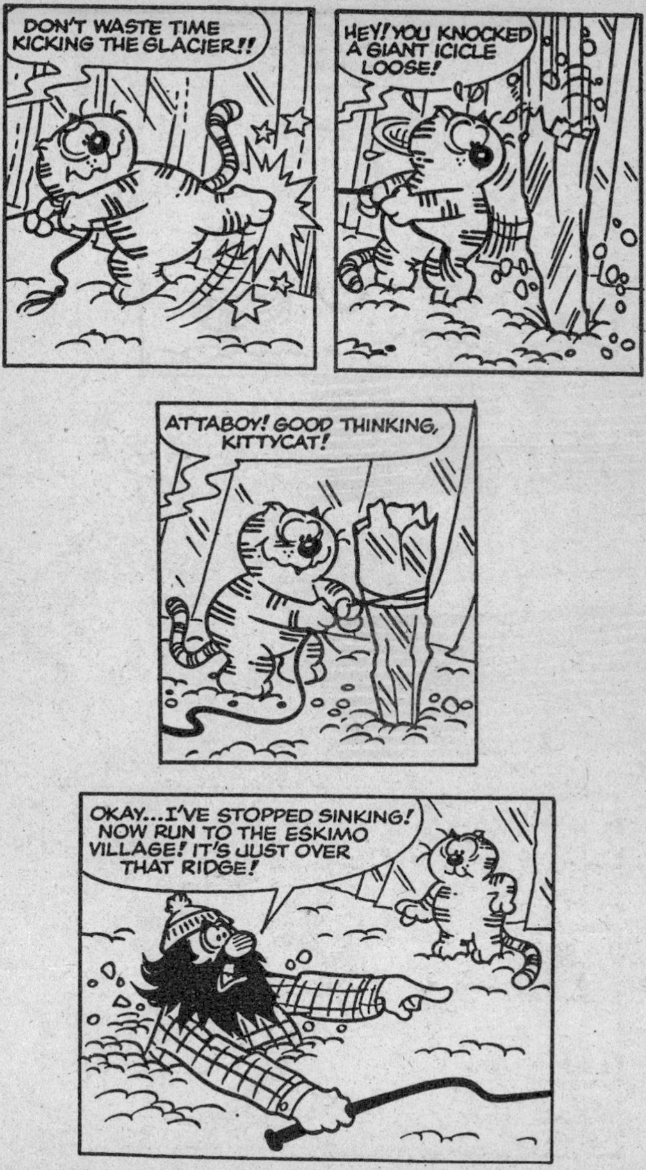
DON'T WASTE TIME KICKING THE GLACIER!!
HEY! YOU KNOCKED A GIANT ICICLE LOOSE!
ATTABOY! GOOD THINKING, KITTYCAT!
OKAY...I'VE STOPPED SINKING! NOW RUN TO THE ESKIMO VILLAGE! IT'S JUST OVER THAT RIDGE!

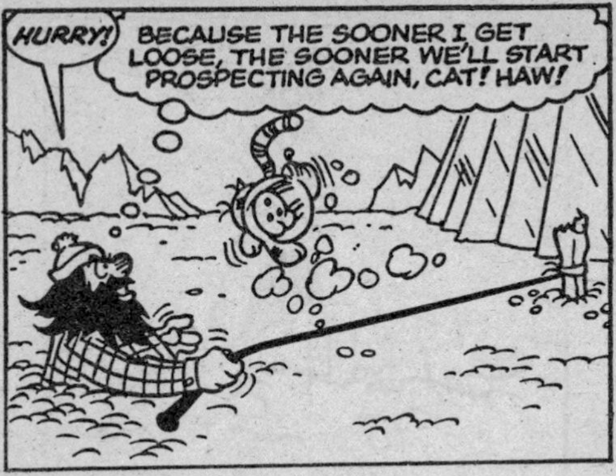
HURRY!
BECAUSE THE SOONER I GET LOOSE, THE SOONER WE'LL START PROSPECTING AGAIN, CAT! HAW!

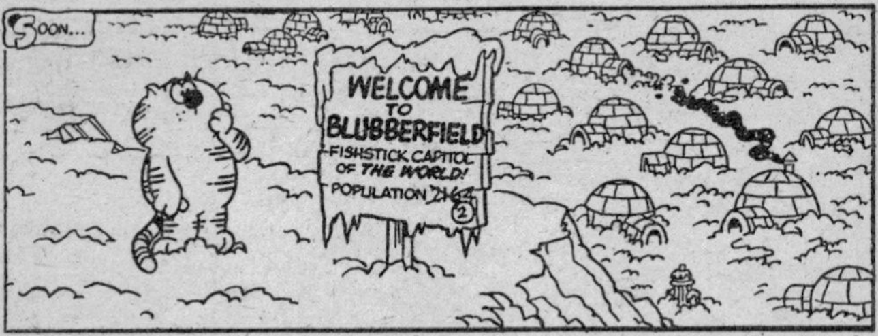
SOON...
WELCOME TO BLUBBERFIELD
FISHSTICK CAPITOL OF THE WORLD!
POPULATION
2

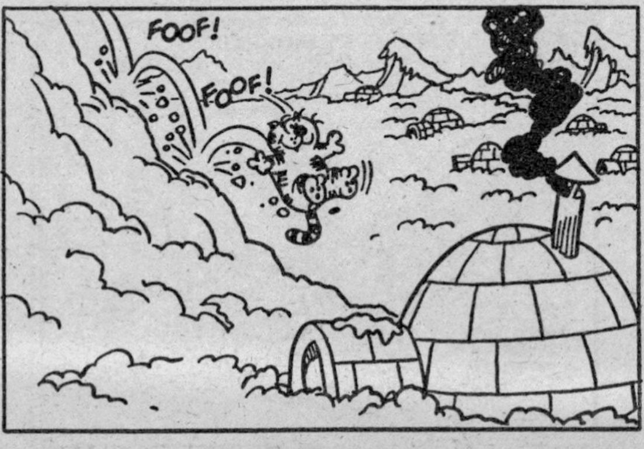
FOOF!
FOOF!

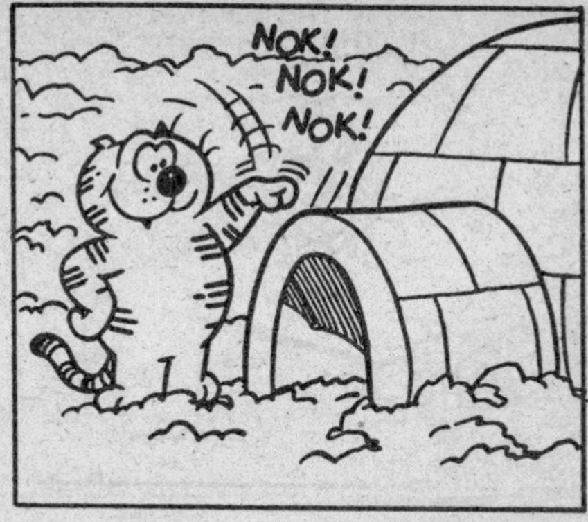
NOK!
NOK!
NOK!

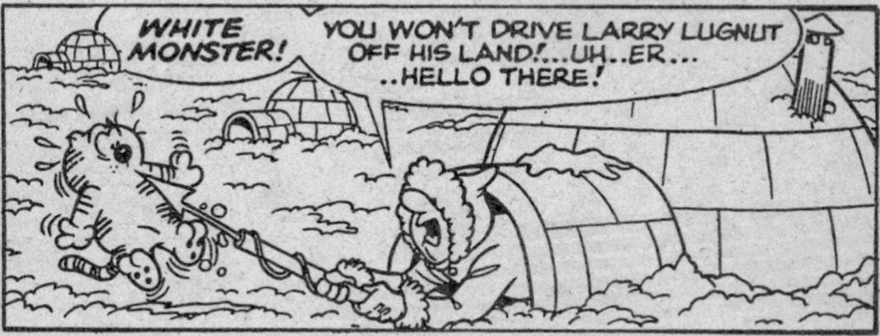
WHITE MONSTER!
YOU WON'T DRIVE LARRY LUGNUT OFF HIS LAND!...UH..ER... ..HELLO THERE!

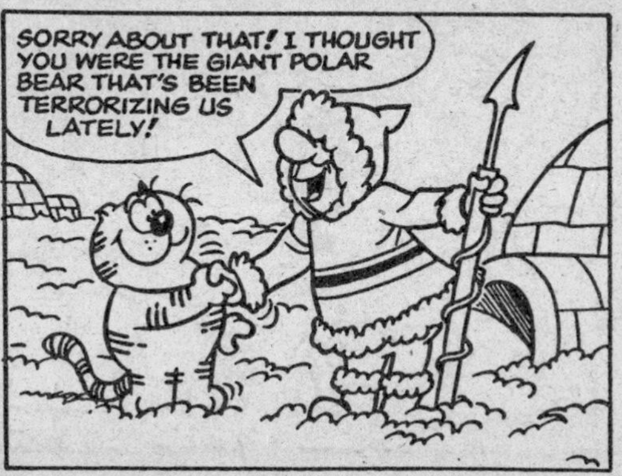
SORRY ABOUT THAT! I THOUGHT YOU WERE THE GIANT POLAR BEAR THAT'S BEEN TERRORIZING US LATELY!

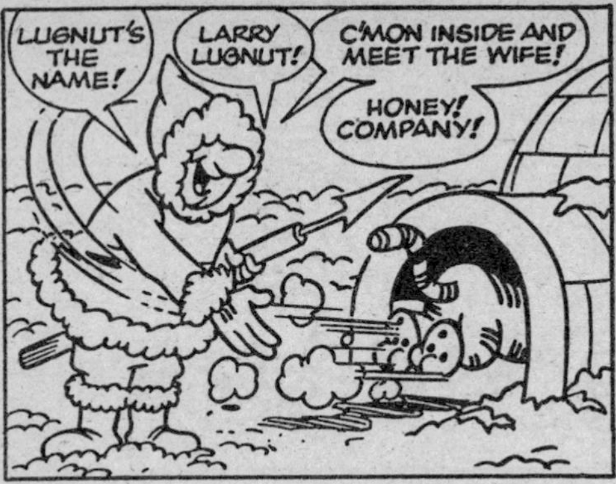
LUGNUT'S THE NAME!
LARRY LUGNUT!
C'MON INSIDE AND MEET THE WIFE!
HONEY! COMPANY!

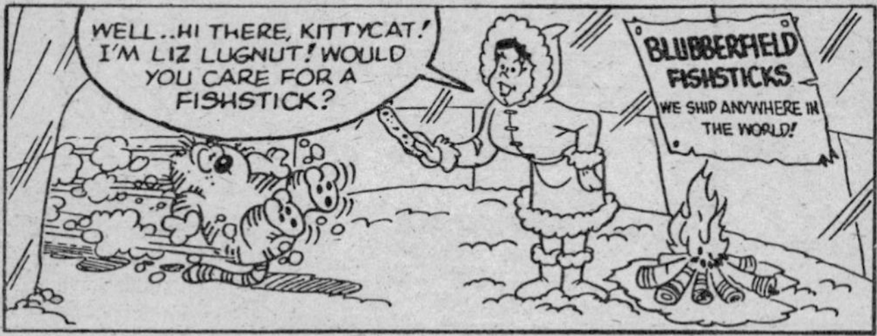
WELL..HI THERE, KITTYCAT! I'M LIZ LUGNUT! WOULD YOU CARE FOR A FISHSTICK?
BLUBBERFIELD FISHSTICKS
WE SHIP ANYWHERE IN THE WORLD!

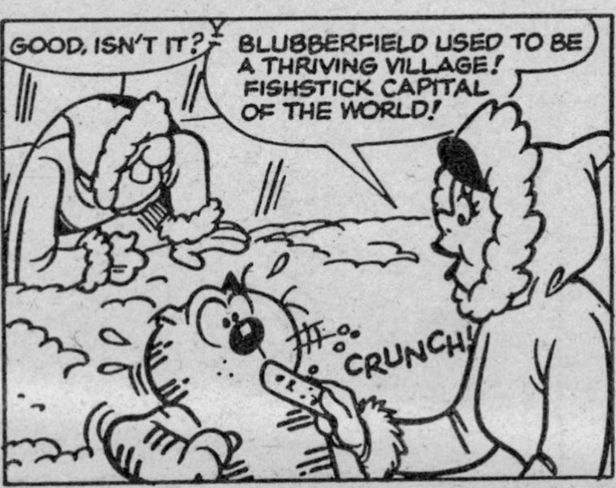
GOOD, ISN'T IT?
BLUBBERFIELD USED TO BE A THRIVING VILLAGE! FISHSTICK CAPITAL OF THE WORLD!
CRUNCH!

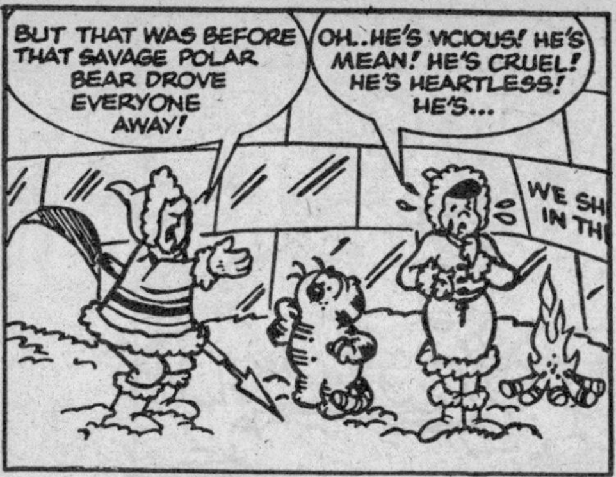
BUT THAT WAS BEFORE THAT SAVAGE POLAR BEAR DROVE EVERYONE AWAY!
OH..HE'S VICIOUS! HE'S MEAN! HE'S CRUEL! HE'S HEARTLESS! HE'S...
WE SH
IN TH

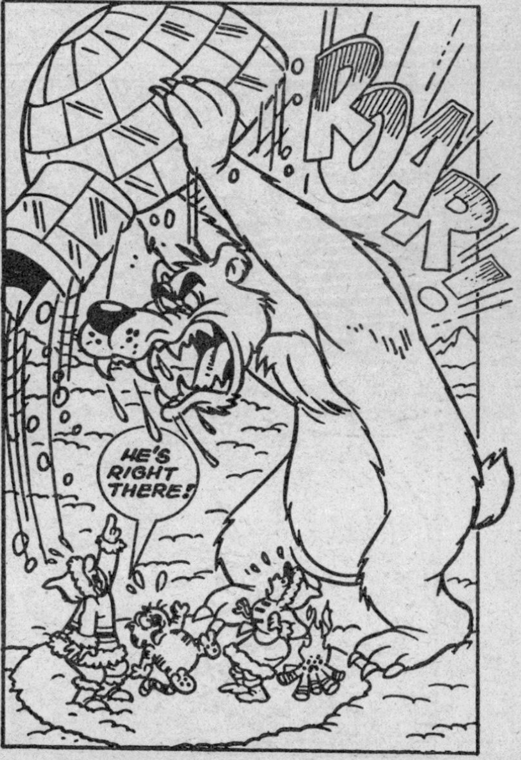
ROAR!
HE'S RIGHT THERE!

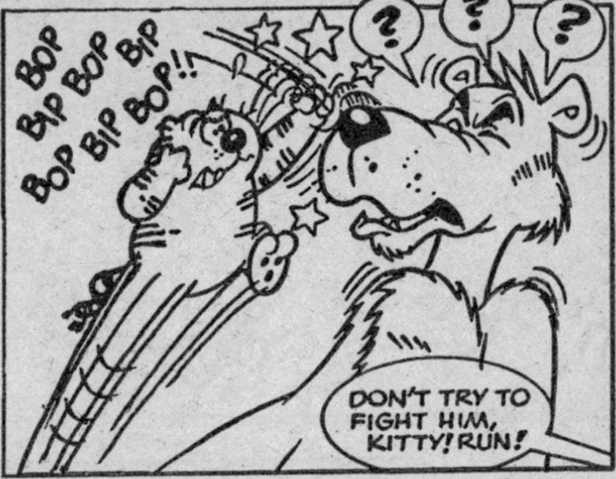
BOP BIP BOP BIP
BOP BIP BOP!!
?
?
?
DON'T TRY TO FIGHT HIM, KITTY! RUN!

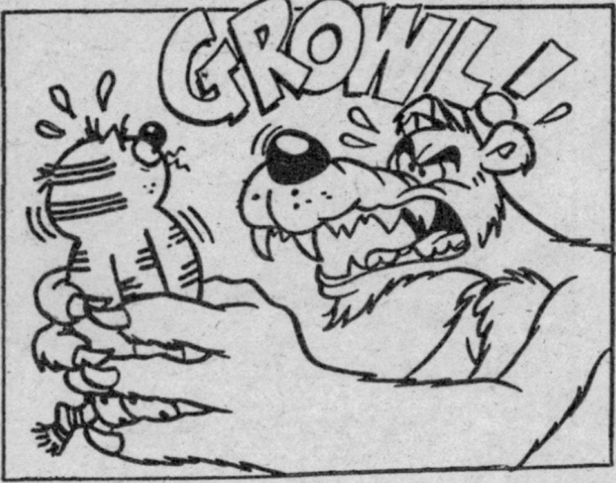
GROWL!

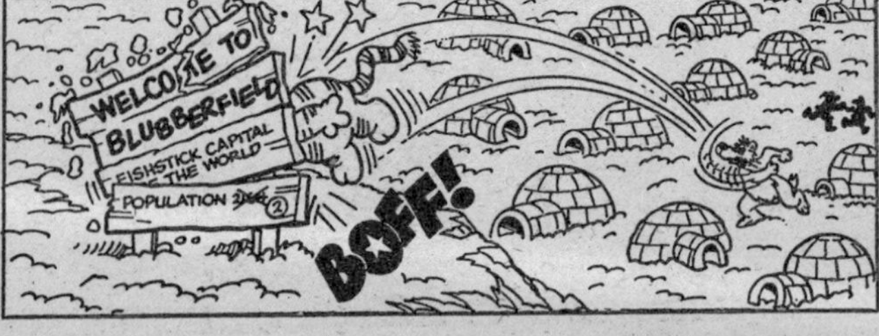
WELCOME TO
BLUBBERFIELD
FISHSTICK CAPITAL OF THE WORLD
POPULATION 2
BOFF!

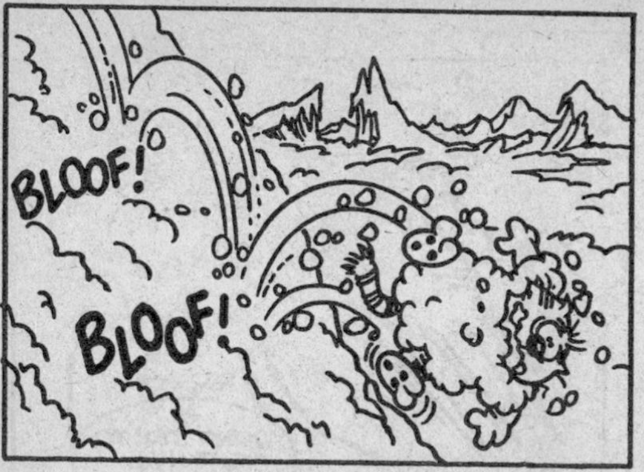
BLOOF!
BLOOF!

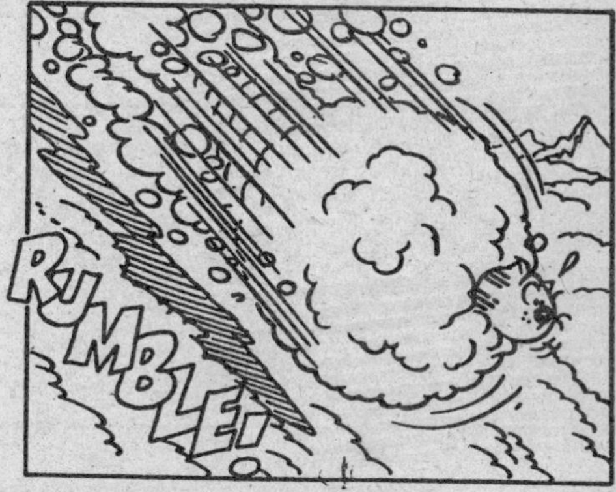
RUMBLE!

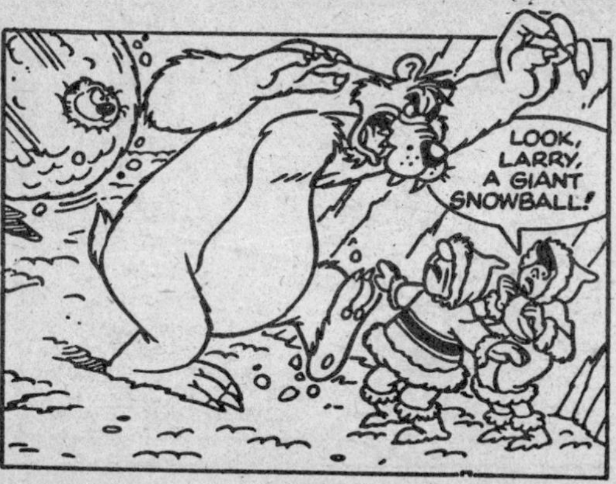
LOOK, LARRY, A GIANT SNOWBALL!

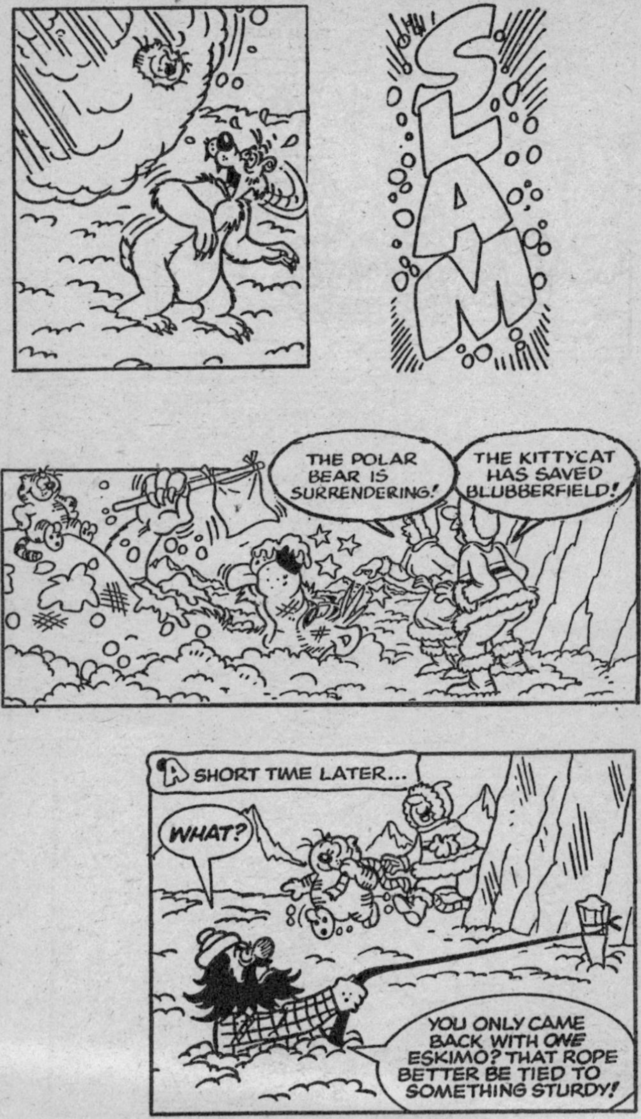
SLAM
THE POLAR BEAR IS SURRENDERING!
THE KITTYCAT HAS SAVED BLUBBERFIELD!
A SHORT TIME LATER...
WHAT?
YOU ONLY CAME BACK WITH *ONE* ESKIMO? THAT ROPE BETTER BE TIED TO SOMETHING STURDY!

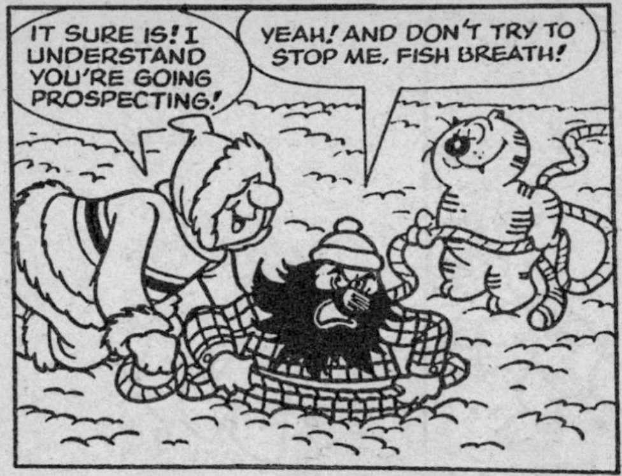
IT SURE IS! I UNDERSTAND YOU'RE GOING PROSPECTING!
YEAH! AND DON'T TRY TO STOP ME, FISH BREATH!

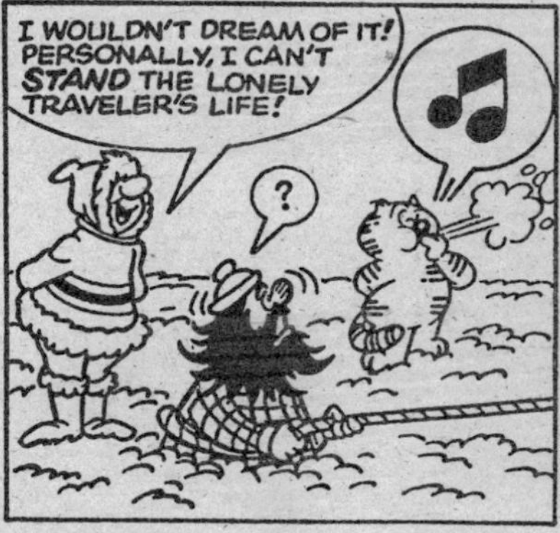
I WOULDN'T DREAM OF IT! PERSONALLY, I CAN'T STAND THE LONELY TRAVELER'S LIFE!
?

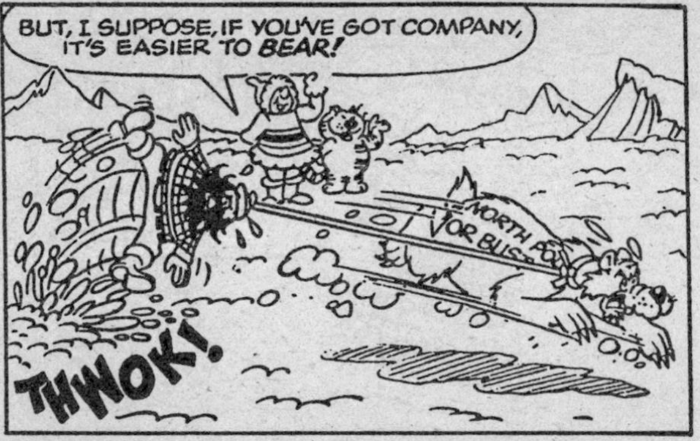
BUT, I SUPPOSE, IF YOU'VE GOT COMPANY, IT'S EASIER TO BEAR!
NORTH POLE OR BUST
THWOK!

GOSH, KITTYCAT... I SURE WISH THERE WAS A WAY TO THANK YOU ON BEHALF OF BLUBBERFIELD!

COULD WE SHIP A BOX OF FISHSTICKS TO SOME LOVED ONES? GUARANTEED NEXT DAY DELIVERY!!

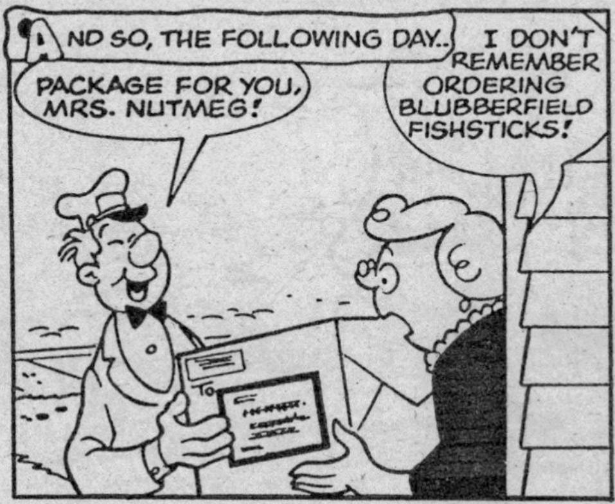
AND SO, THE FOLLOWING DAY..
PACKAGE FOR YOU, MRS. NUTMEG!
I DON'T REMEMBER ORDERING BLUBBERFIELD FISHSTICKS!

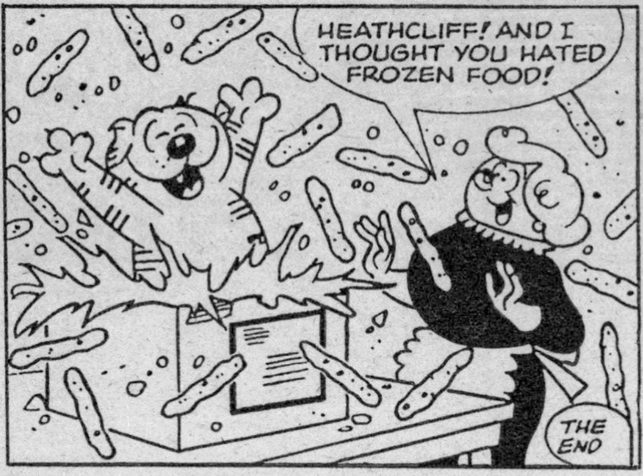
HEATHCLIFF! AND I THOUGHT YOU HATED FROZEN FOOD!
THE END

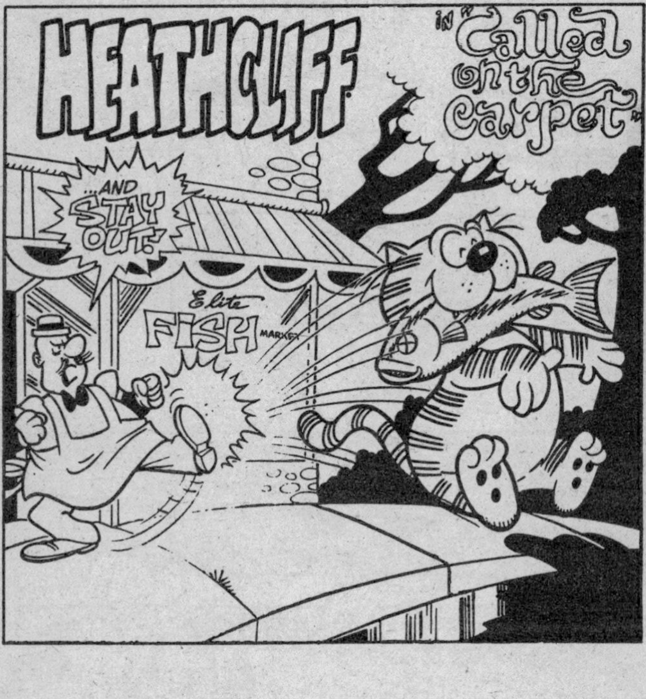
HEATHCLIFF
in "Called on the carpet"
...AND STAY OUT!
Elite FISH MARKET

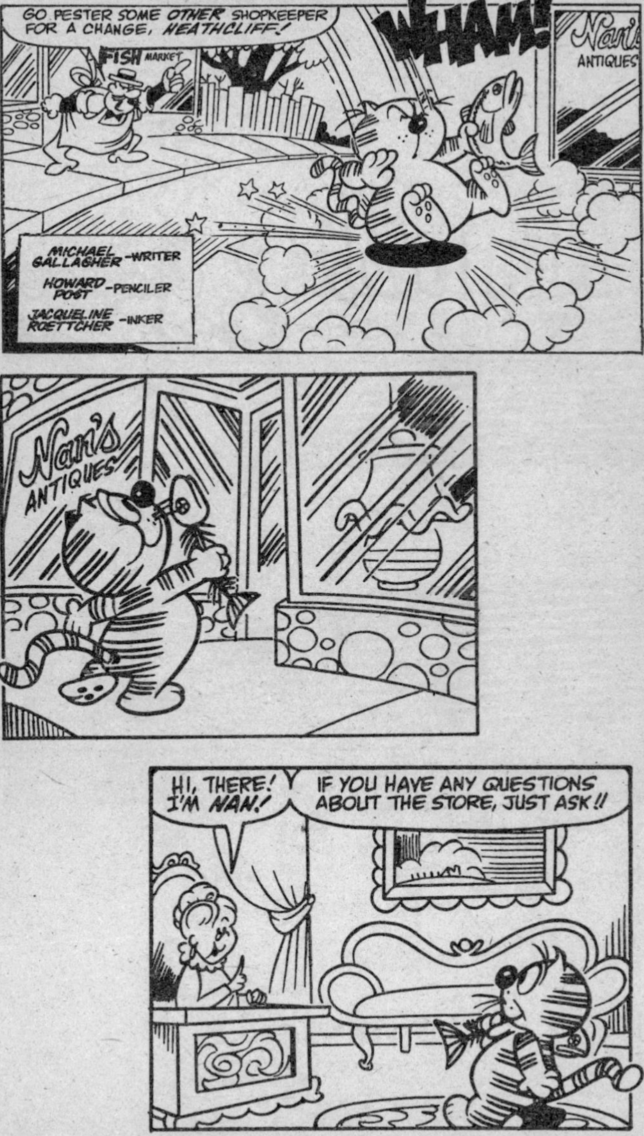
GO PESTER SOME OTHER SHOPKEEPER FOR A CHANGE, HEATHCLIFF!
FISH MARKET
WHAM!
Nan's ANTIQUES
MICHAEL GALLAGHER -WRITER
HOWARD POST -PENCILER
JACQUELINE ROETTCHER -INKER
Nan's ANTIQUES
HI, THERE! I'M NAN!
IF YOU HAVE ANY QUESTIONS ABOUT THE STORE, JUST ASK!!

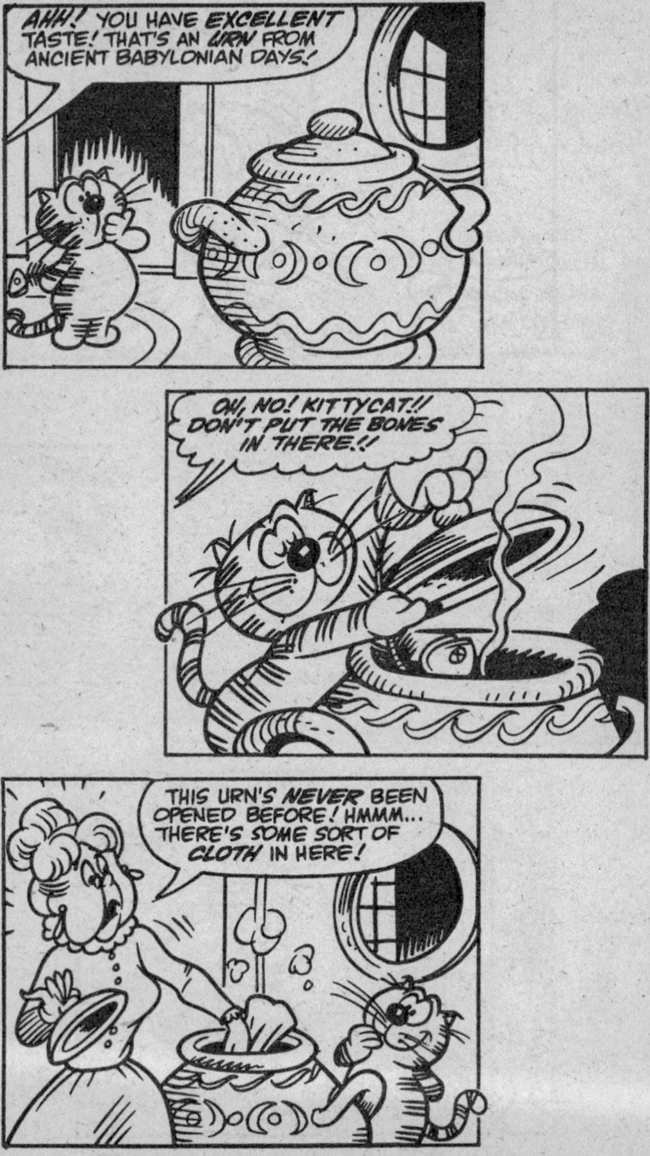
AHH! YOU HAVE EXCELLENT TASTE! THAT'S AN URN FROM ANCIENT BABYLONIAN DAYS!
OH, NO! KITTYCAT!! DON'T PUT THE BONES IN THERE!!
THIS URN'S NEVER BEEN OPENED BEFORE! HMMM... THERE'S SOME SORT OF CLOTH IN HERE!

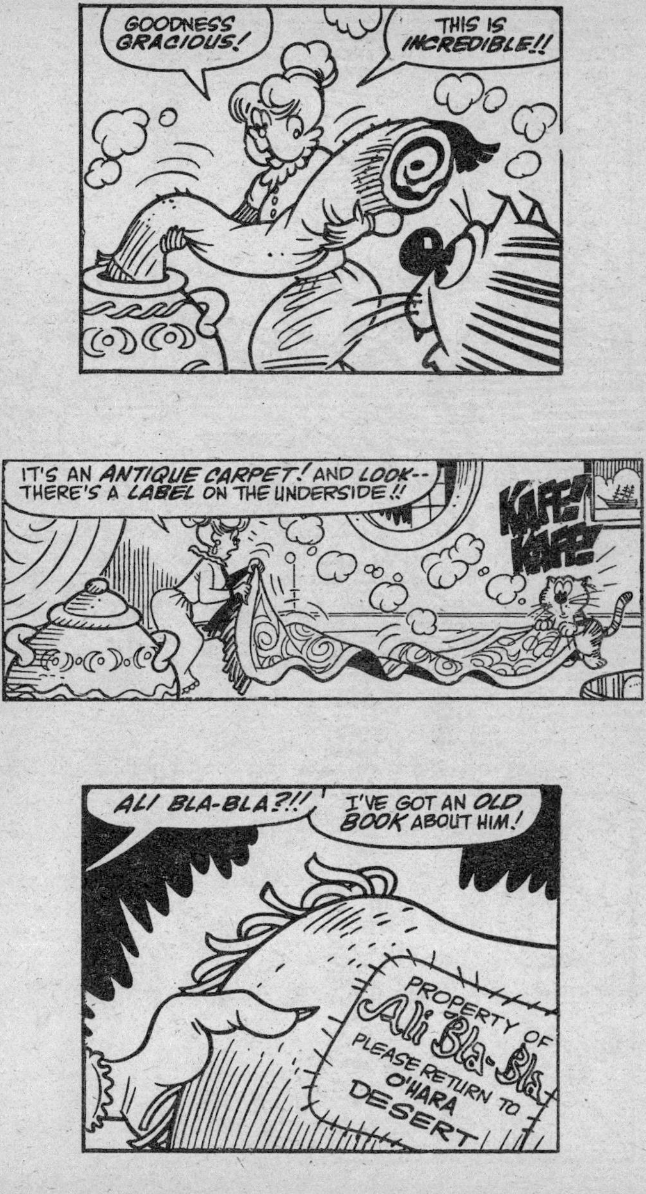
GOODNESS GRACIOUS!
THIS IS INCREDIBLE!!
IT'S AN ANTIQUE CARPET! AND LOOK-- THERE'S A LABEL ON THE UNDERSIDE!!
KAFF! KAFF!
ALI BLA-BLA?!!
I'VE GOT AN OLD BOOK ABOUT HIM!
PROPERTY OF Ali Bla-Bla PLEASE RETURN TO O'HARA DESERT

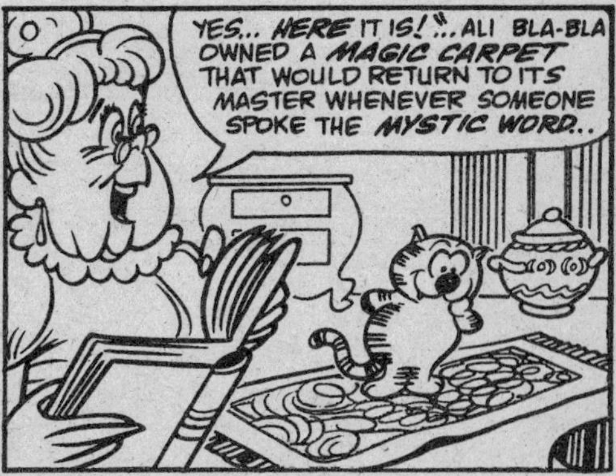
YES... HERE IT IS! "...ALI BLA-BLA OWNED A MAGIC CARPET THAT WOULD RETURN TO ITS MASTER WHENEVER SOMEONE SPOKE THE MYSTIC WORD..

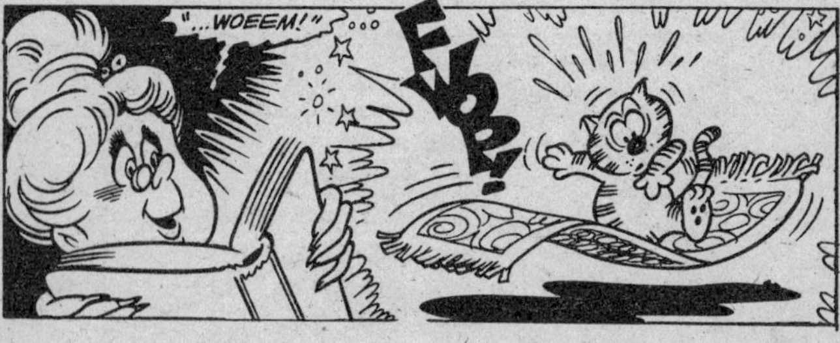
"...WOEEM!"
FWOOM!

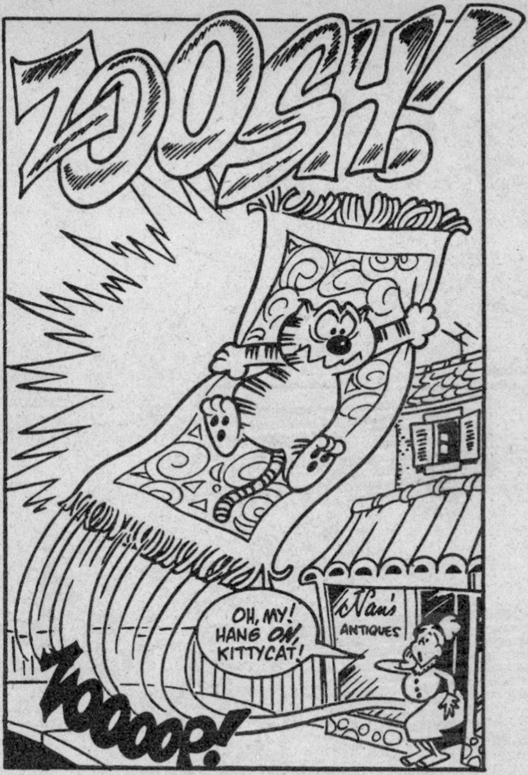
ZOOSH!
OH, MY! HANG ON, KITTYCAT!
Nan's ANTIQUES
ZOOOOP!

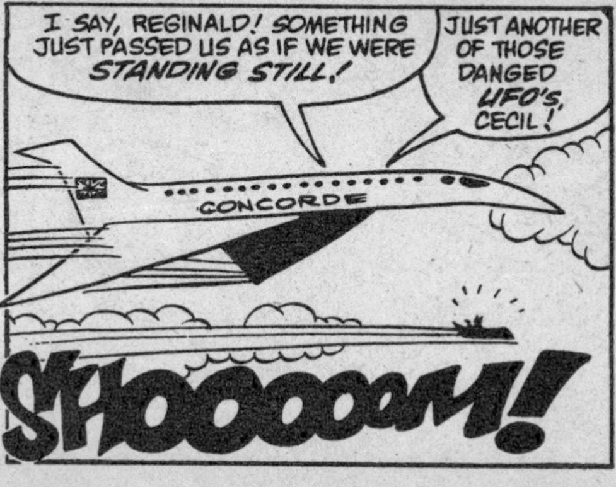
I SAY, REGINALD! SOMETHING JUST PASSED US AS IF WE WERE STANDING STILL!
JUST ANOTHER OF THOSE DANGED UFO's, CECIL!
CONCORDE
SHOOOOOM!

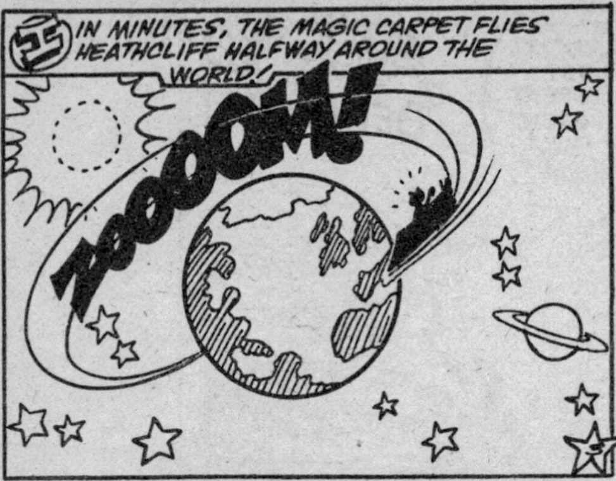
IN MINUTES, THE MAGIC CARPET FLIES HEATHCLIFF HALFWAY AROUND THE WORLD!
ZOOOOM!

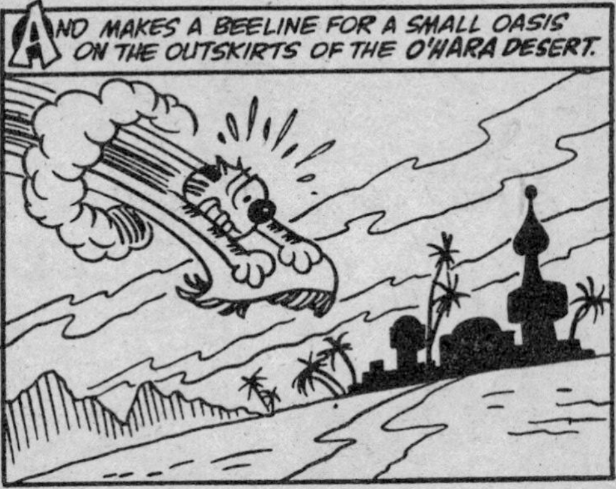
AND MAKES A BEELINE FOR A SMALL OASIS ON THE OUTSKIRTS OF THE O'HARA DESERT.

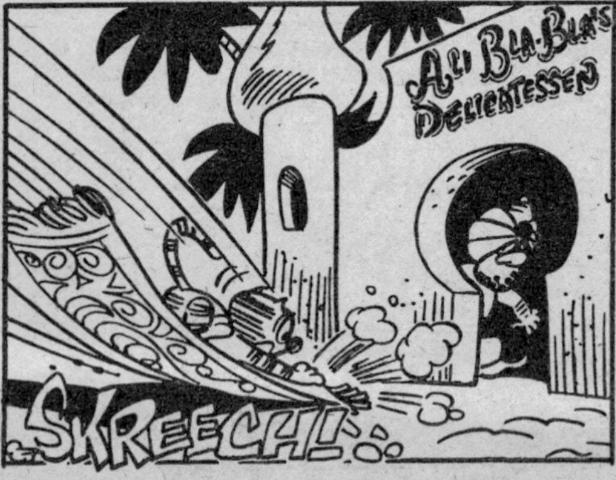
ALI BLA-BLA'S DELICATESSEN
SKREECH!

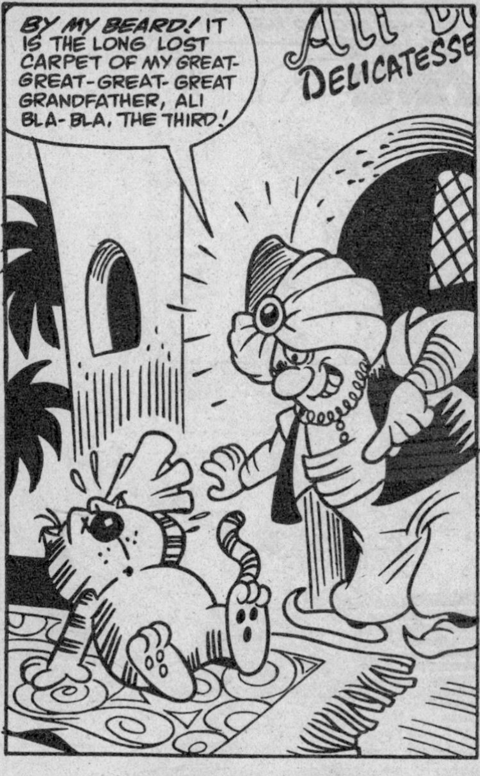
BY MY BEARD! IT IS THE LONG LOST CARPET OF MY GREAT-GREAT-GREAT-GREAT GRANDFATHER, ALI BLA-BLA, THE THIRD!
DELICATESSE

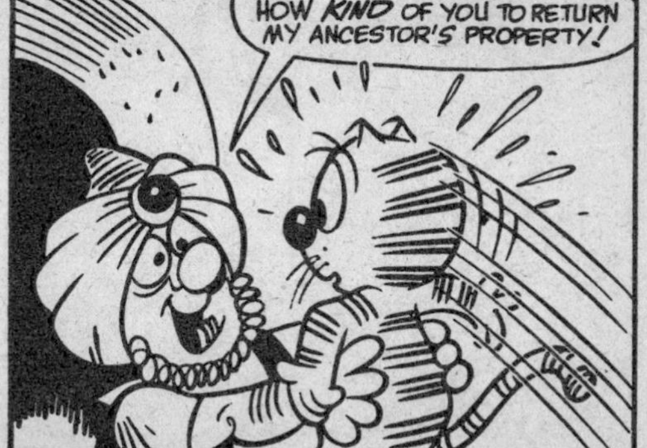
HOW KIND OF YOU TO RETURN MY ANCESTOR'S PROPERTY!

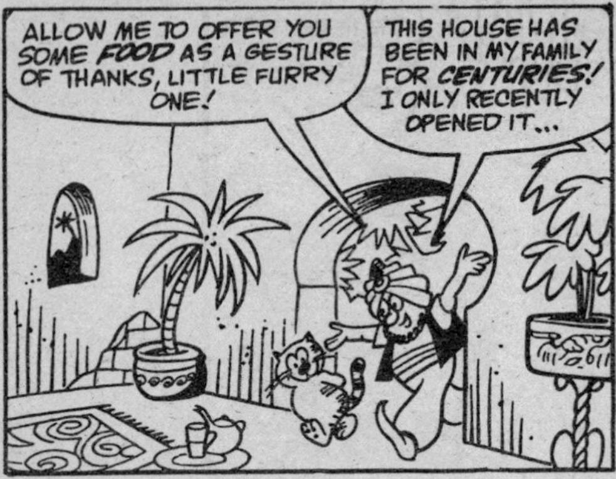
ALLOW ME TO OFFER YOU SOME FOOD AS A GESTURE OF THANKS, LITTLE FURRY ONE!
THIS HOUSE HAS BEEN IN MY FAMILY FOR CENTURIES! I ONLY RECENTLY OPENED IT...

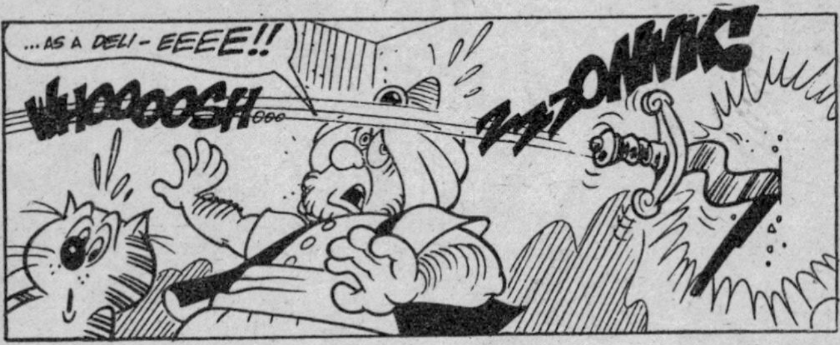
...AS A DELI-EEEEE!!
WHOOOOOSH
ZZZZONNK!

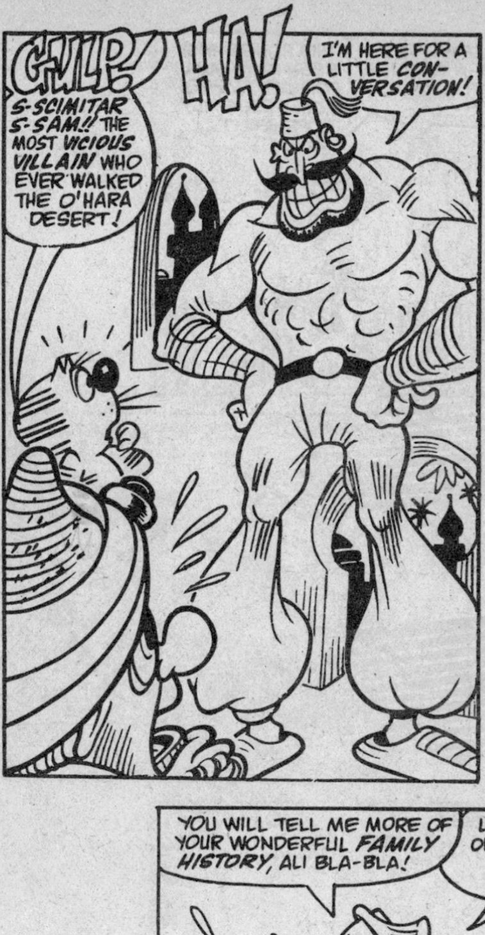
GULP!
S-SCIMITAR S-SAM!! THE MOST VICIOUS VILLAIN WHO EVER WALKED THE O'HARA DESERT!
HA!
I'M HERE FOR A LITTLE CON-VERSATION!

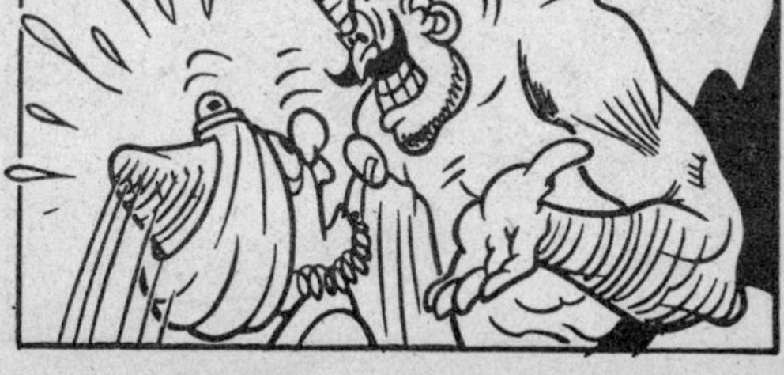
YOU WILL TELL ME MORE OF YOUR WONDERFUL FAMILY HISTORY, ALI BLA-BLA!
LIKE WHERE THE OLD TREASURE ROOM IS LOCATED!

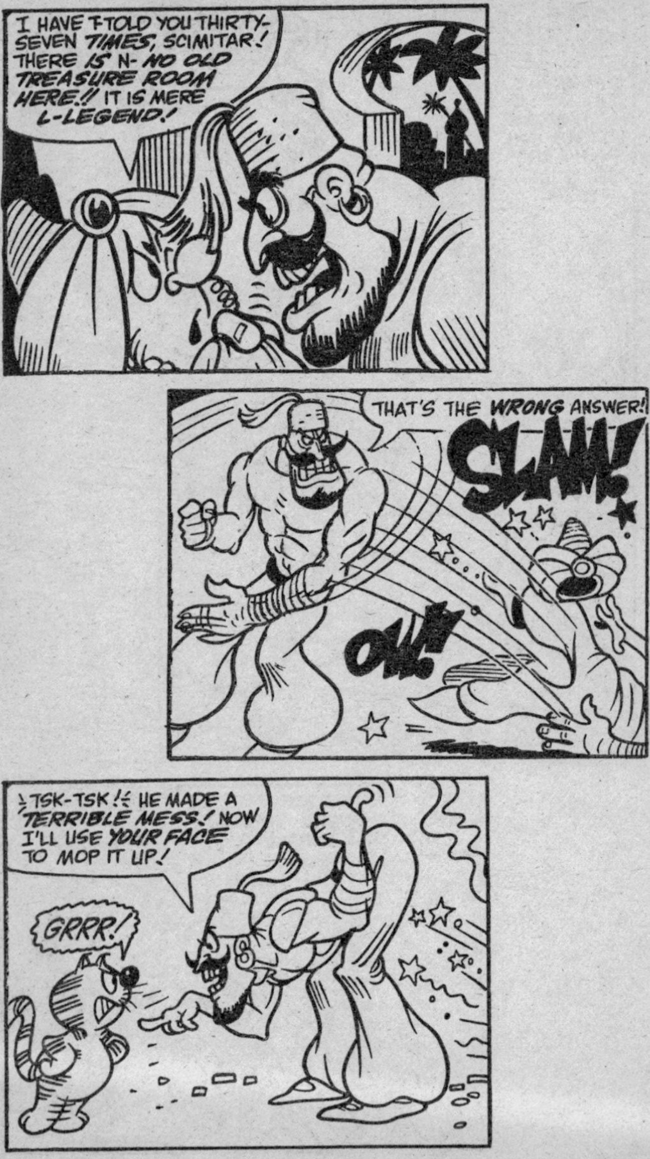
I HAVE T-TOLD YOU THIRTY-SEVEN TIMES, SCIMITAR! THERE IS N- NO OLD TREASURE ROOM HERE!! IT IS MERE L-LEGEND!
THAT'S THE WRONG ANSWER!
SLAM!
OW!
TSK-TSK! HE MADE A TERRIBLE MESS! NOW I'LL USE YOUR FACE TO MOP IT UP!
GRRR!

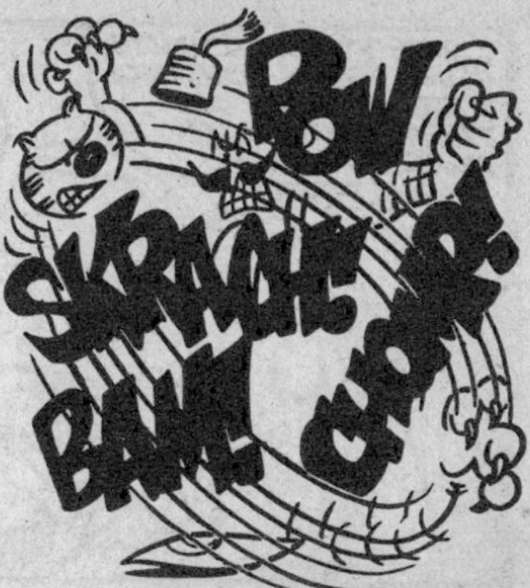
BAM!

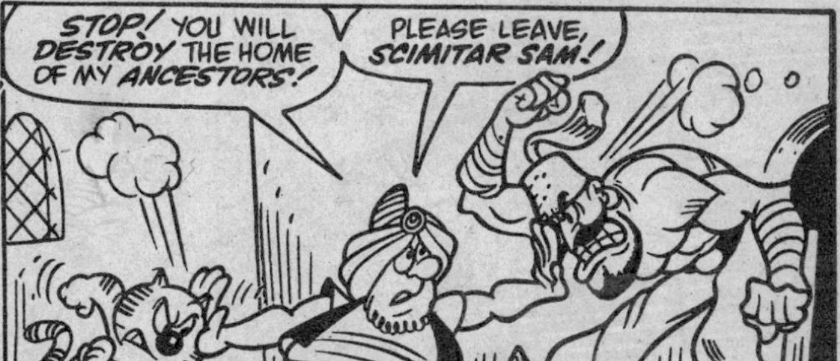
STOP! YOU WILL DESTROY THE HOME OF MY ANCESTORS!
PLEASE LEAVE, SCIMITAR SAM!

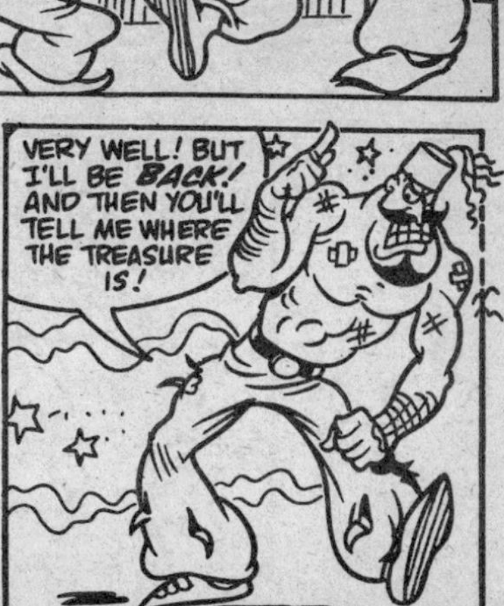
VERY WELL! BUT I'LL BE BACK! AND THEN YOU'LL TELL ME WHERE THE TREASURE IS!

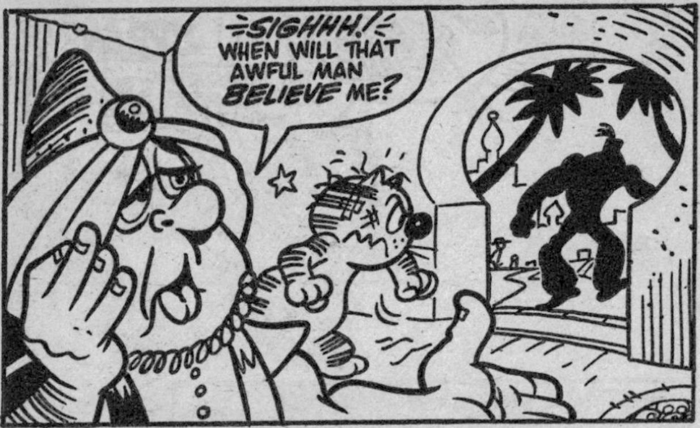
SIGHHH! WHEN WILL THAT AWFUL MAN BELIEVE ME?

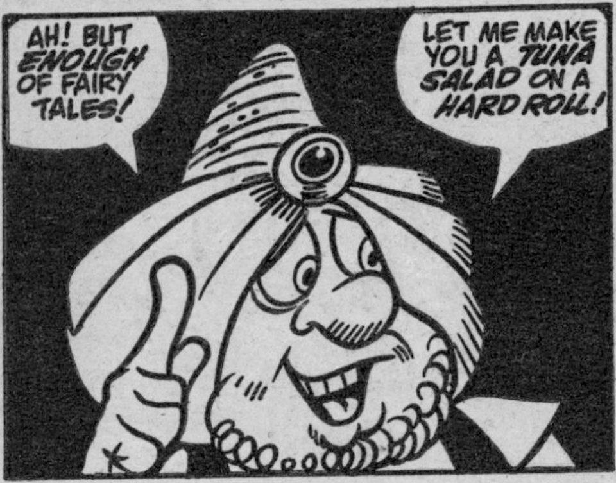
AH! BUT ENOUGH OF FAIRY TALES!
LET ME MAKE YOU A TUNA SALAD ON A HARD ROLL!

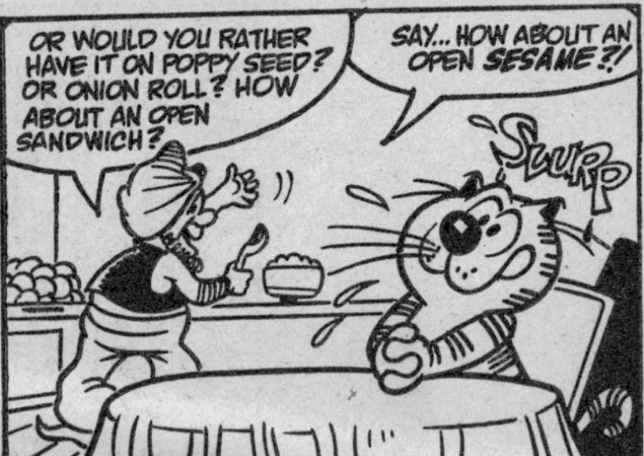
OR WOULD YOU RATHER HAVE IT ON POPPY SEED? OR ONION ROLL? HOW ABOUT AN OPEN SANDWICH?
SAY... HOW ABOUT AN OPEN SESAME?!
SLURP

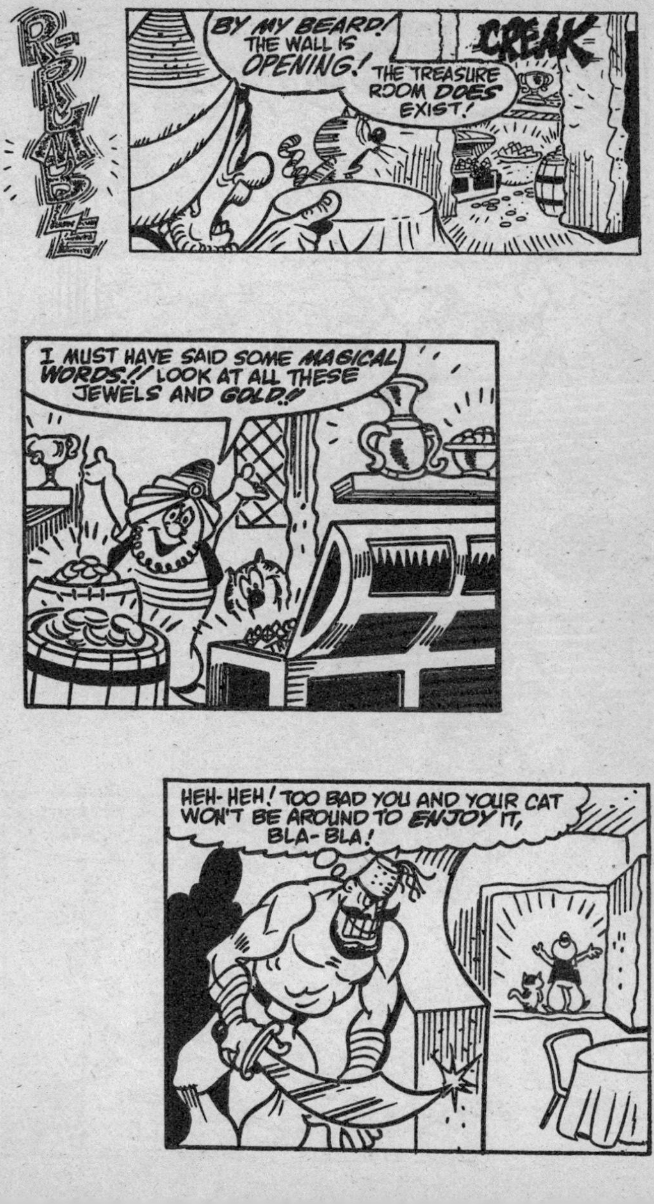
R-RUMBLE
BY MY BEARD! THE WALL IS OPENING!
CREAK
THE TREASURE ROOM DOES EXIST!
I MUST HAVE SAID SOME MAGICAL WORDS!! LOOK AT ALL THESE JEWELS AND GOLD!!
HEH-HEH! TOO BAD YOU AND YOUR CAT WON'T BE AROUND TO ENJOY IT, BLA-BLA!

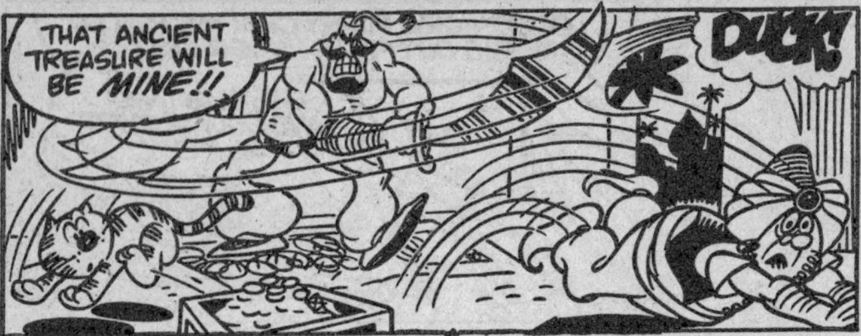
THAT ANCIENT TREASURE WILL BE MINE!!
DUCK!

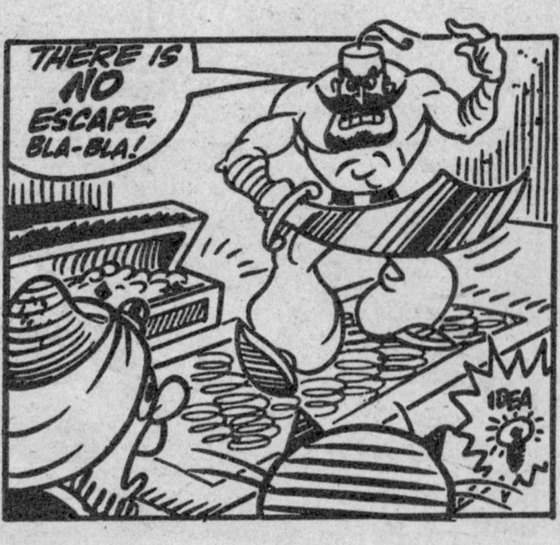
THERE IS NO ESCAPE, BLA-BLA!
IDEA

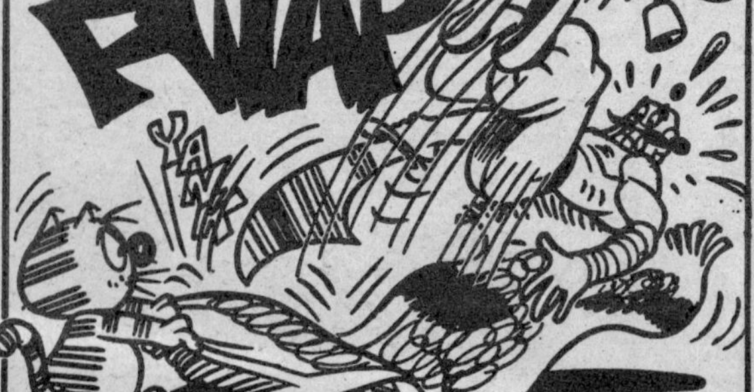
FWAP

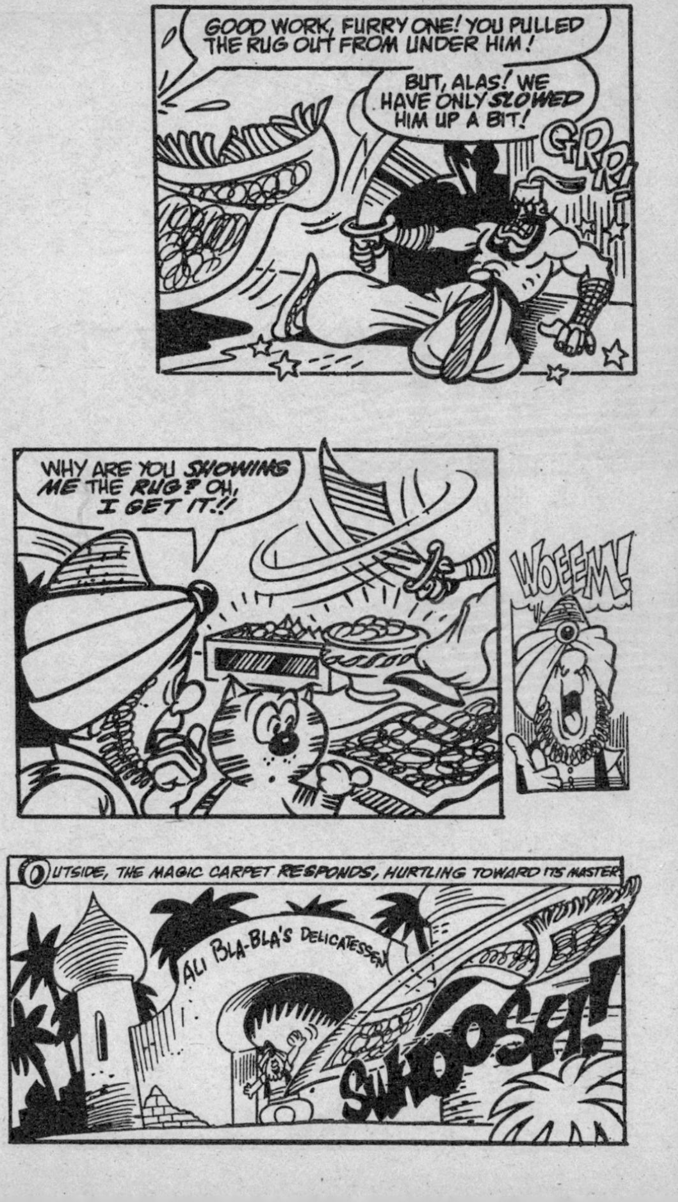
GOOD WORK, FURRY ONE! YOU PULLED THE RUG OUT FROM UNDER HIM!
BUT, ALAS! WE HAVE ONLY SLOWED HIM UP A BIT!
GRR!
WHY ARE YOU SHOWING ME THE RUG? OH, I GET IT!!
WOEEM!
OUTSIDE, THE MAGIC CARPET RESPONDS, HURTLING TOWARD ITS MASTER!
ALI BLA-BLA'S DELICATESSEN
SHOOSH!

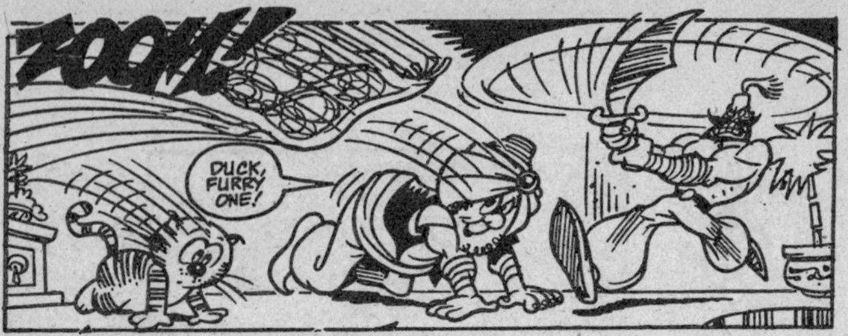
ZOOM!
DUCK, FURRY ONE!

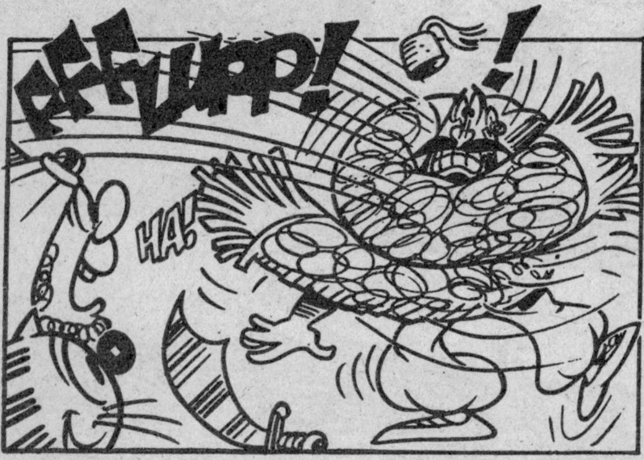
PFFLUPP!
!
HA!

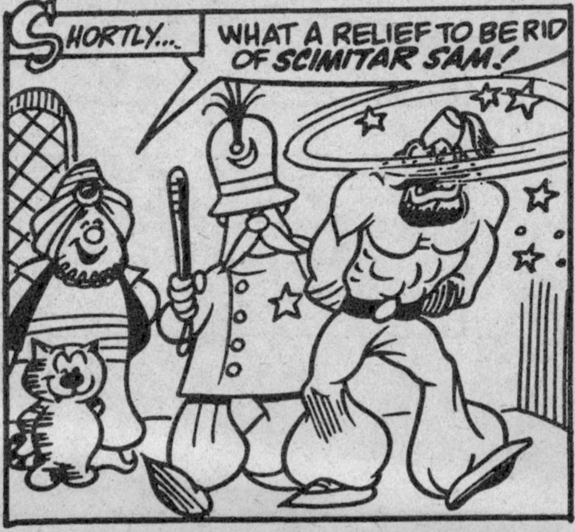
SHORTLY...
WHAT A RELIEF TO BE RID OF SCIMITAR SAM!

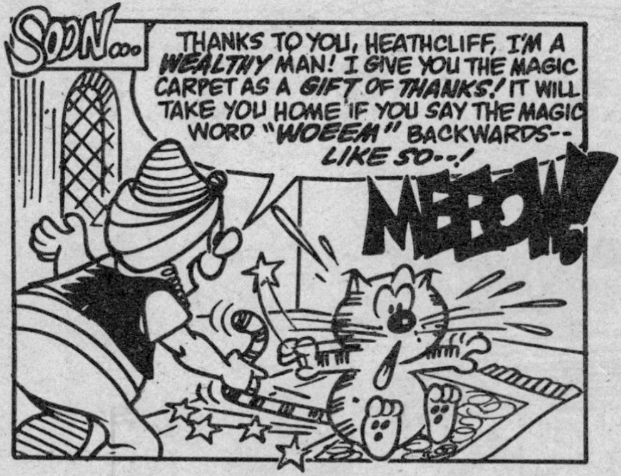
SOON...
THANKS TO YOU, HEATHCLIFF, I'M A WEALTHY MAN! I GIVE YOU THE MAGIC CARPET AS A GIFT OF THANKS! IT WILL TAKE YOU HOME IF YOU SAY THE MAGIC WORD "WOEEM" BACKWARDS-- LIKE SO--!
MEEOW!

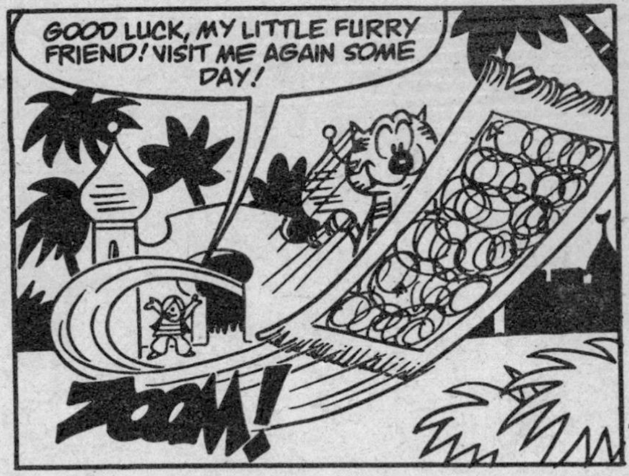
GOOD LUCK, MY LITTLE FURRY FRIEND! VISIT ME AGAIN SOME DAY!
ZOOM!

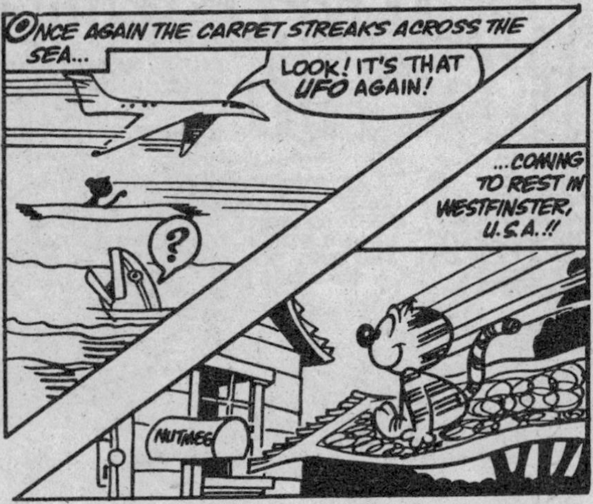
ONCE AGAIN THE CARPET STREAKS ACROSS THE SEA...
LOOK! IT'S THAT UFO AGAIN!
?
...COMING TO REST IN WESTFINSTER, U.S.A.!!
NUTMEG

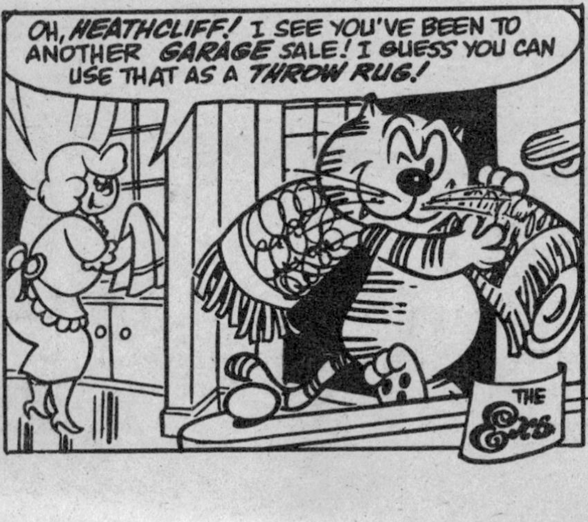
OH, HEATHCLIFF! I SEE YOU'VE BEEN TO ANOTHER GARAGE SALE! I GUESS YOU CAN USE THAT AS A THROW RUG!
THE

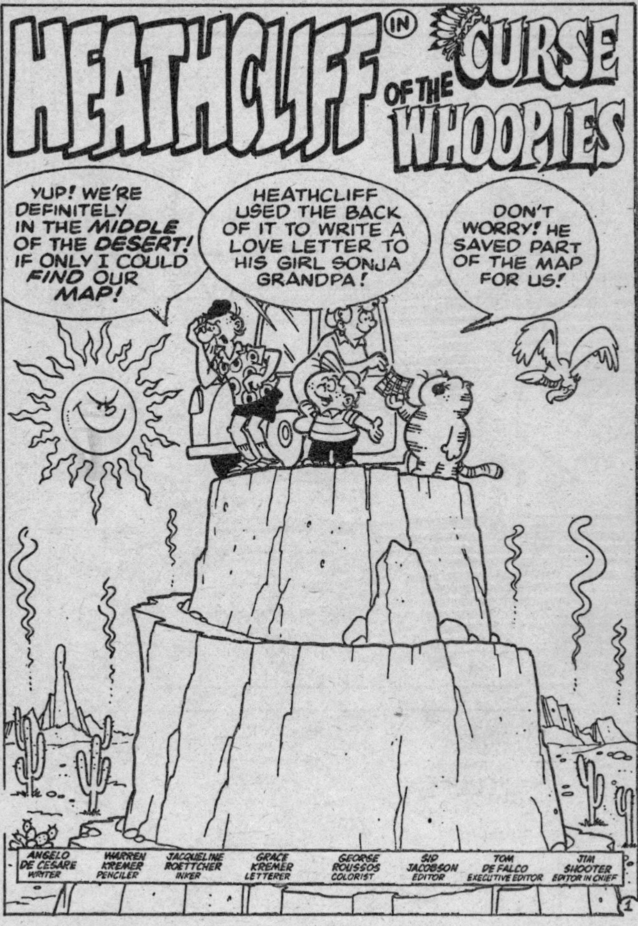

HEATHCLIFF® IN CURSE OF THE WHOOPIES
YUP! WE'RE DEFINITELY IN THE MIDDLE OF THE DESERT! IF ONLY I COULD FIND OUR MAP!
HEATHCLIFF USED THE BACK OF IT TO WRITE A LOVE LETTER TO HIS GIRL SONJA GRANDPA!
DON'T WORRY! HE SAVED PART OF THE MAP FOR US!
ANGELO DE CESARE WRITER
WARREN KREMER PENCILER
JACQUELINE ROETTCHER INKER
GRACE KREMER LETTERER
GEORGE ROUSSOS COLORIST
SID JACOBSON EDITOR
TOM DE FALCO EXECUTIVE EDITOR
JIM SHOOTER EDITOR IN CHIEF

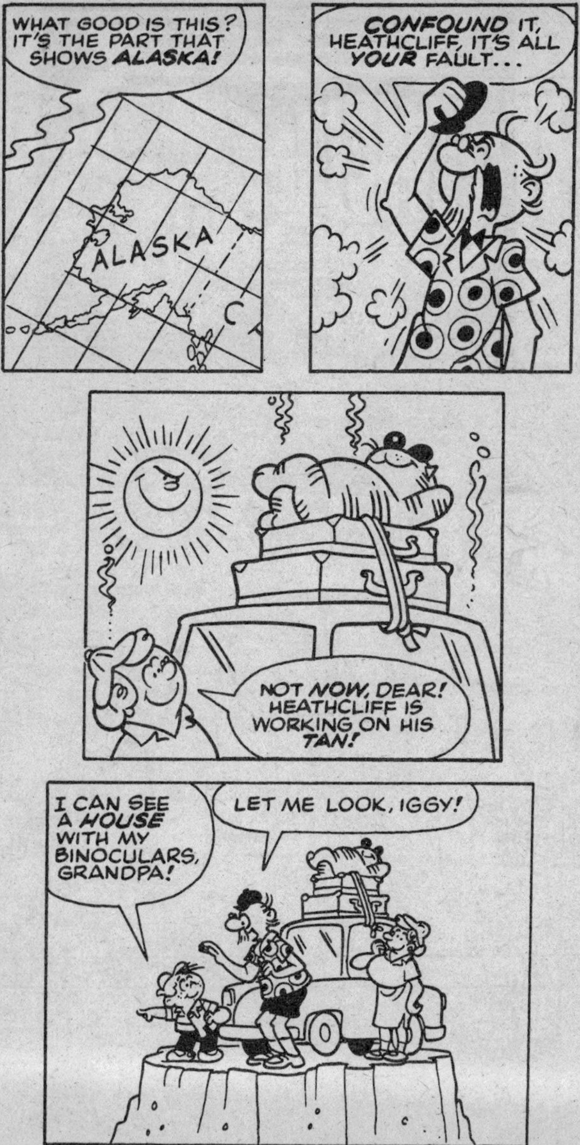
WHAT GOOD IS THIS? IT'S THE PART THAT SHOWS ALASKA!
ALASKA
CONFOUND IT, HEATHCLIFF, IT'S ALL YOUR FAULT...
NOT NOW, DEAR! HEATHCLIFF IS WORKING ON HIS TAN!
I CAN SEE A HOUSE WITH MY BINOCULARS, GRANDPA!
LET ME LOOK, IGGY!

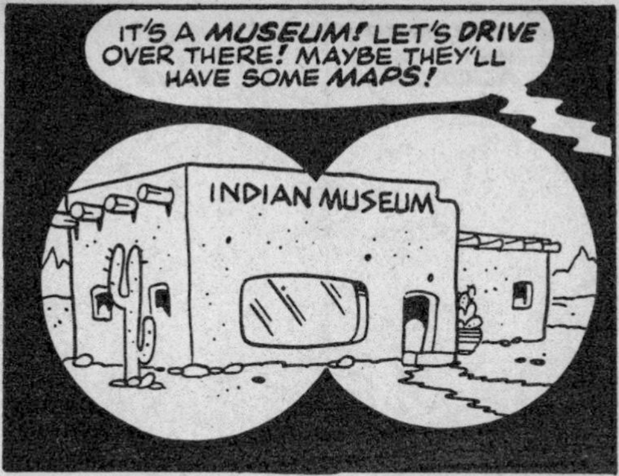
IT'S A MUSEUM! LET'S DRIVE OVER THERE! MAYBE THEY'LL HAVE SOME MAPS!
INDIAN MUSEUM

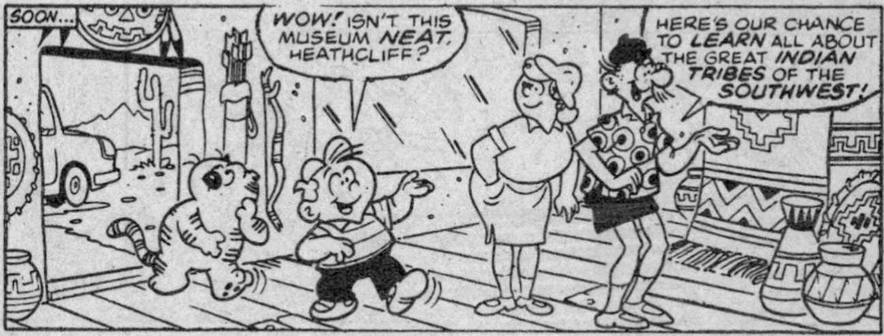
SOON...
WOW! ISN'T THIS MUSEUM NEAT, HEATHCLIFF?
HERE'S OUR CHANCE TO LEARN ALL ABOUT THE GREAT INDIAN TRIBES OF THE SOUTHWEST!

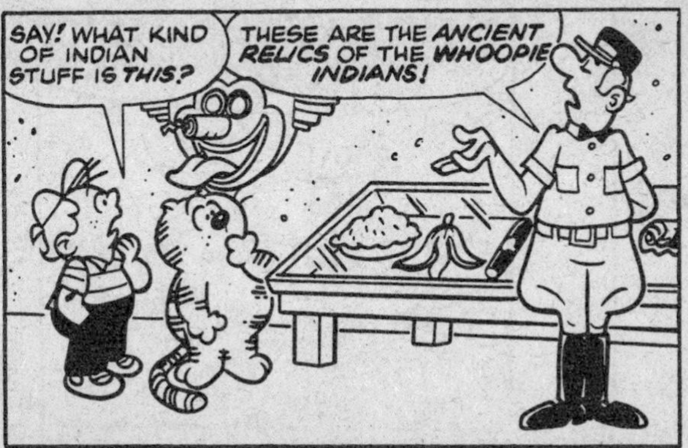
SAY! WHAT KIND OF INDIAN STUFF IS THIS?
THESE ARE THE ANCIENT RELICS OF THE WHOOPIE INDIANS!

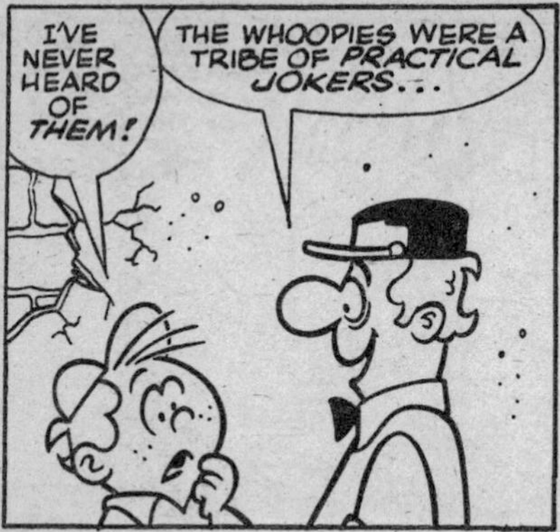
I'VE NEVER HEARD OF THEM!
THE WHOOPIES WERE A TRIBE OF PRACTICAL JOKERS...

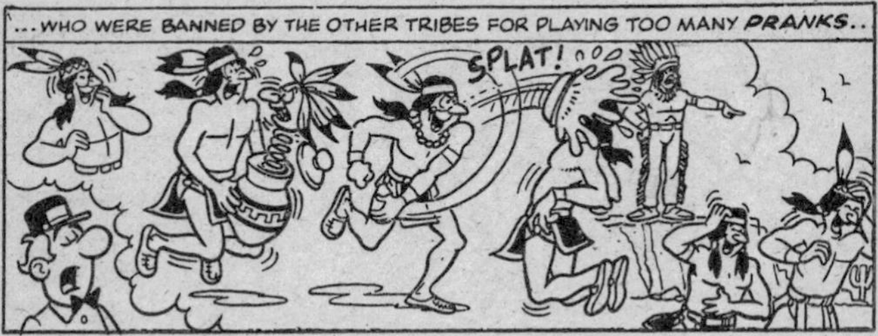
...WHO WERE BANNED BY THE OTHER TRIBES FOR PLAYING TOO MANY PRANKS..
SPLAT!

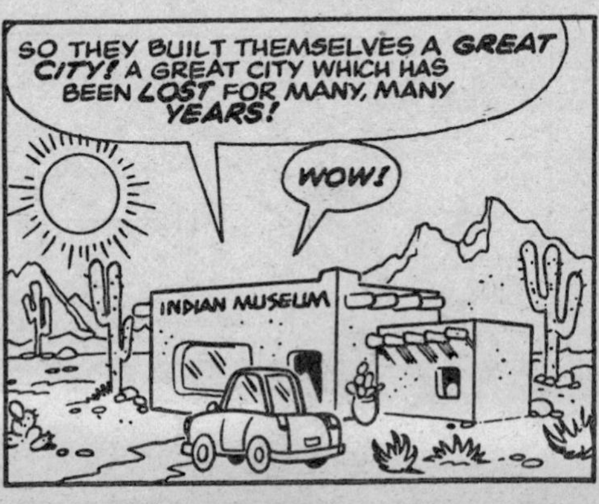
SO THEY BUILT THEMSELVES A GREAT CITY! A GREAT CITY WHICH HAS BEEN LOST FOR MANY, MANY YEARS!
WOW!
INDIAN MUSEUM

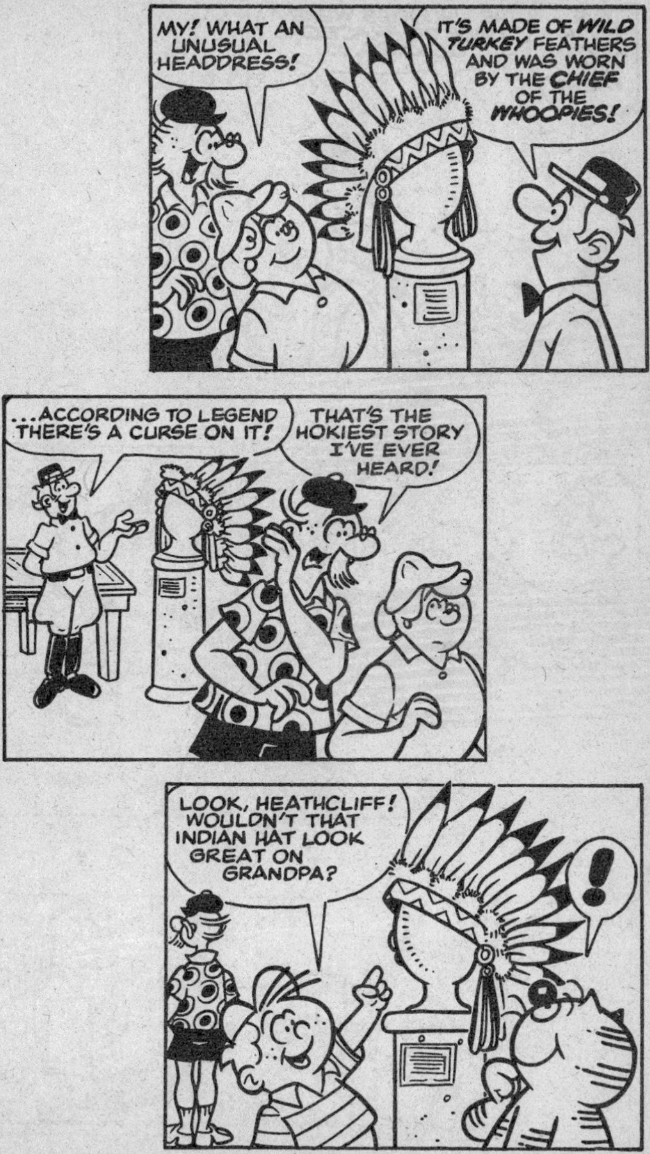
MY! WHAT AN UNUSUAL HEADDRESS!
IT'S MADE OF WILD TURKEY FEATHERS AND WAS WORN BY THE CHIEF OF THE WHOOPIES!
...ACCORDING TO LEGEND THERE'S A CURSE ON IT!
THAT'S THE HOKIEST STORY I'VE EVER HEARD!
LOOK, HEATHCLIFF! WOULDN'T THAT INDIAN HAT LOOK GREAT ON GRANDPA?
!

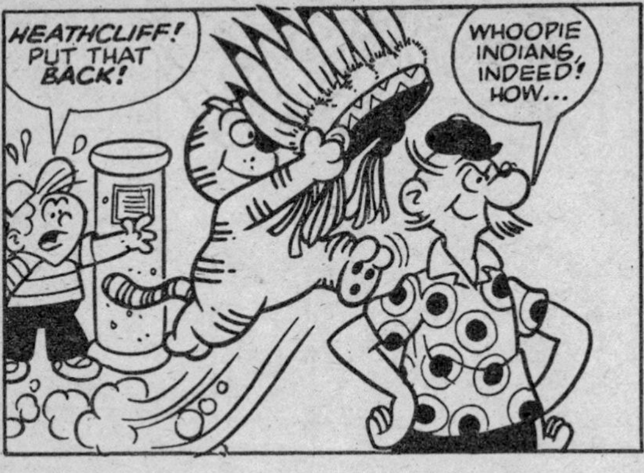
HEATHCLIFF! PUT THAT BACK!
WHOOPIE INDIANS, INDEED! HOW...

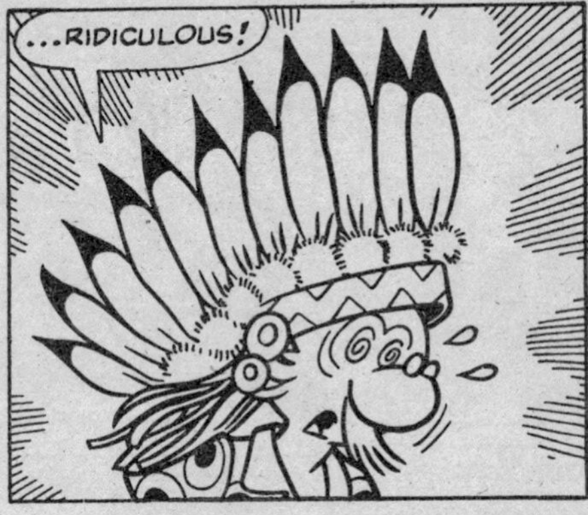
...RIDICULOUS!

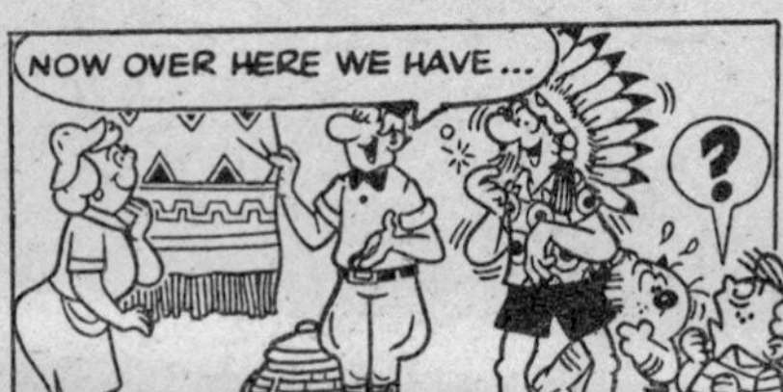
NOW OVER HERE WE HAVE...
?

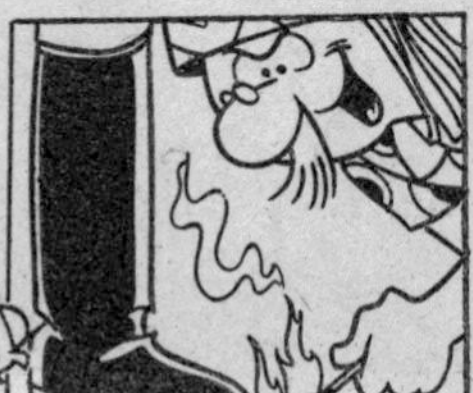
PSSSS

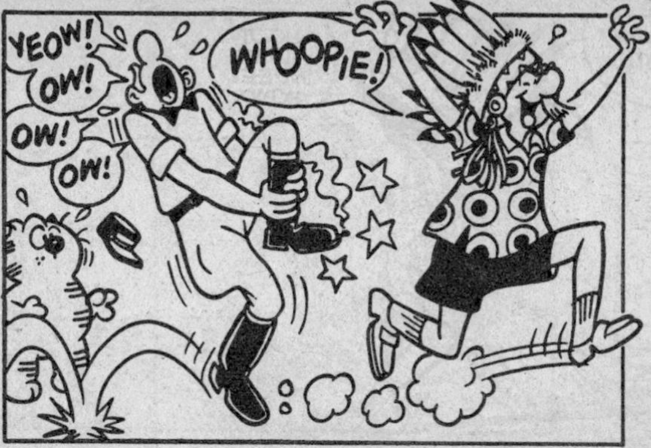
YEOW! OW!
OW!
OW!
WHOOPIE!

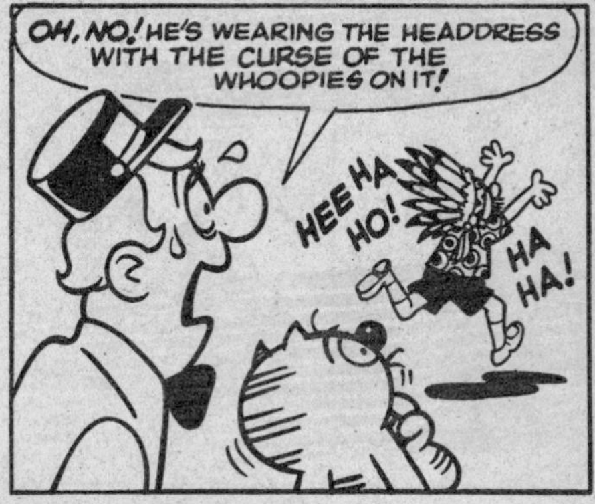
OH, NO! HE'S WEARING THE HEADDRESS WITH THE CURSE OF THE WHOOPIES ON IT!
HEE HA HO!
HA HA!

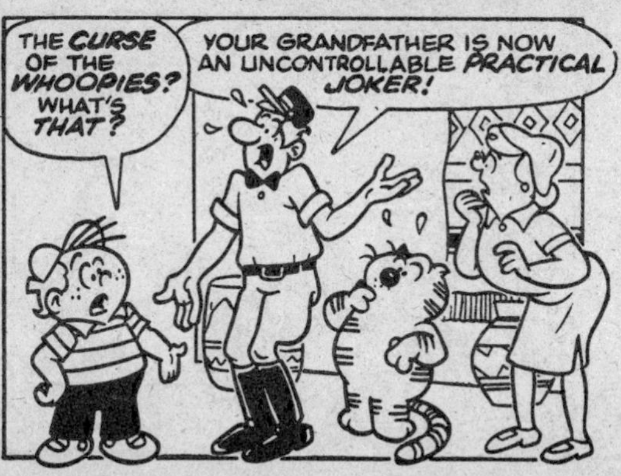
THE CURSE OF THE WHOOPIES? WHAT'S THAT?
YOUR GRANDFATHER IS NOW AN UNCONTROLLABLE PRACTICAL JOKER!

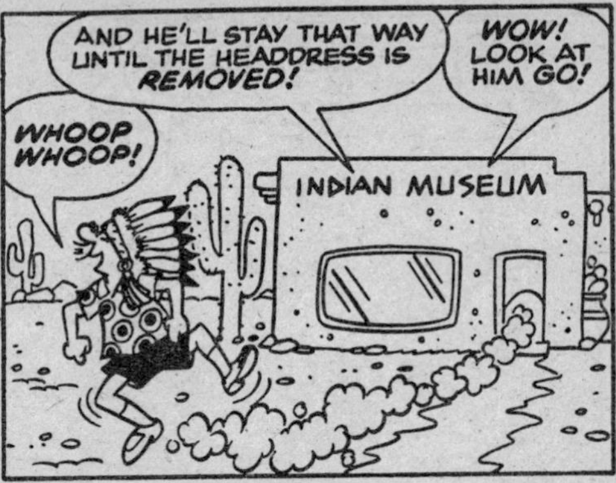
AND HE'LL STAY THAT WAY UNTIL THE HEADDRESS IS *REMOVED!*
WOW! LOOK AT HIM GO!
WHOOP WHOOP!
INDIAN MUSEUM

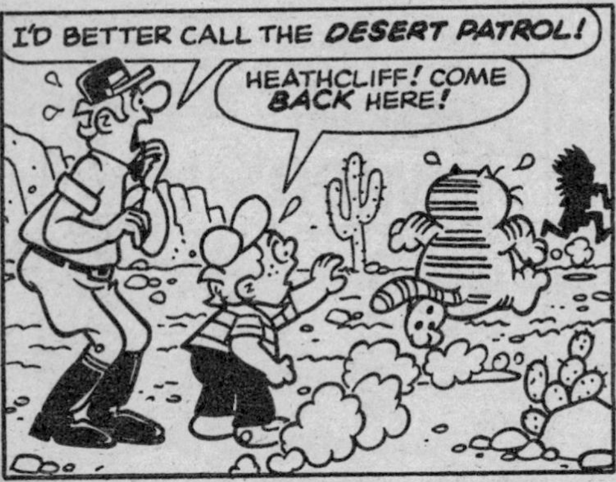
I'D BETTER CALL THE *DESERT PATROL!*
HEATHCLIFF! COME *BACK* HERE!

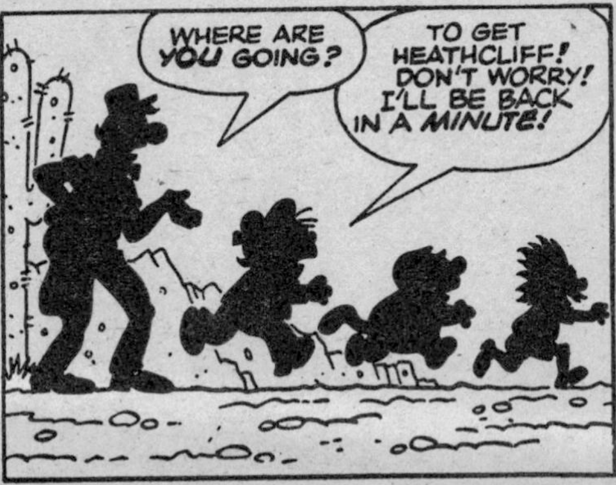
WHERE ARE *YOU* GOING?
TO GET HEATHCLIFF! DON'T WORRY! I'LL BE BACK IN A *MINUTE!*

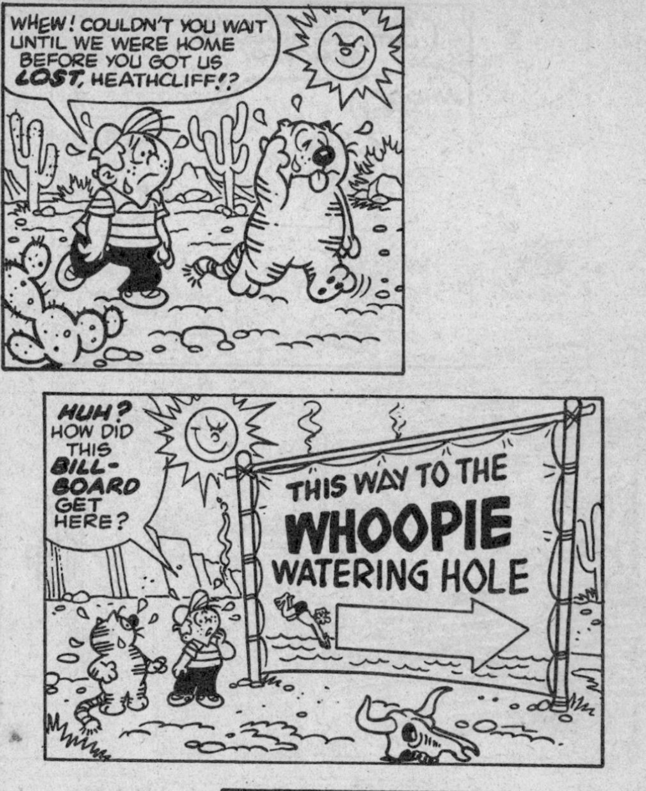
WHEW! COULDN'T YOU WAIT UNTIL WE WERE HOME BEFORE YOU GOT US LOST, HEATHCLIFF!?
HUH? HOW DID THIS BILL-BOARD GET HERE?
THIS WAY TO THE WHOOPIE WATERING HOLE
WHO CARES HOW IT GOT THERE! LET'S GO COOL OFF!

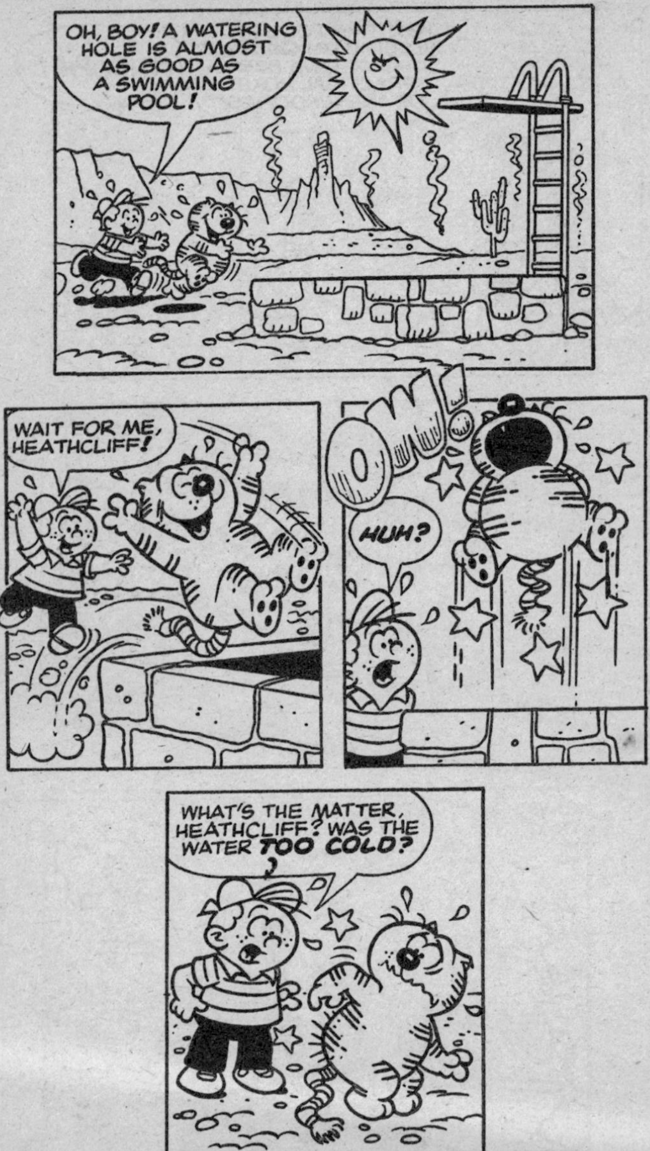
OH, BOY! A WATERING HOLE IS ALMOST AS GOOD AS A SWIMMING POOL!
WAIT FOR ME, HEATHCLIFF!
OW!
HUH?
WHAT'S THE MATTER, HEATHCLIFF? WAS THE WATER TOO COLD?

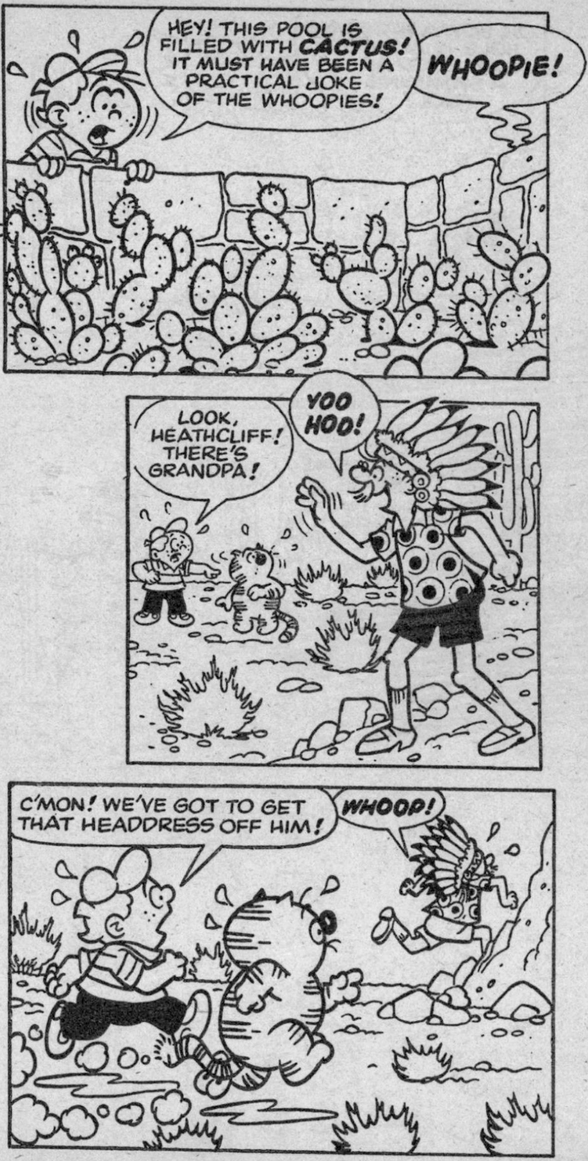
HEY! THIS POOL IS FILLED WITH CACTUS! IT MUST HAVE BEEN A PRACTICAL JOKE OF THE WHOOPIES!
WHOOPIE!
LOOK, HEATHCLIFF! THERE'S GRANDPA!
YOO HOO!
C'MON! WE'VE GOT TO GET THAT HEADDRESS OFF HIM!
WHOOP!

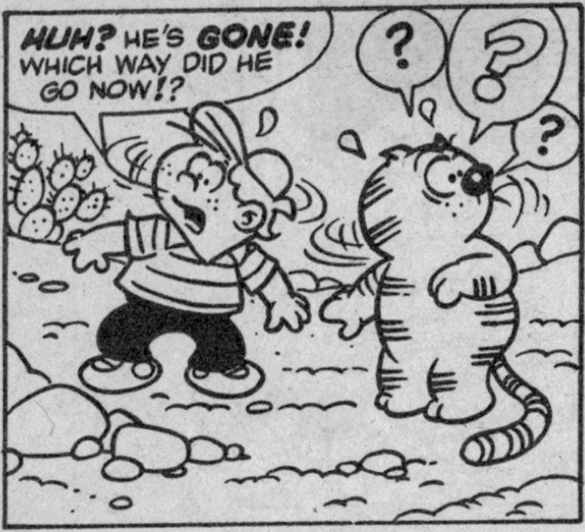
HUH? HE'S GONE! WHICH WAY DID HE GO NOW!?
?
?
?

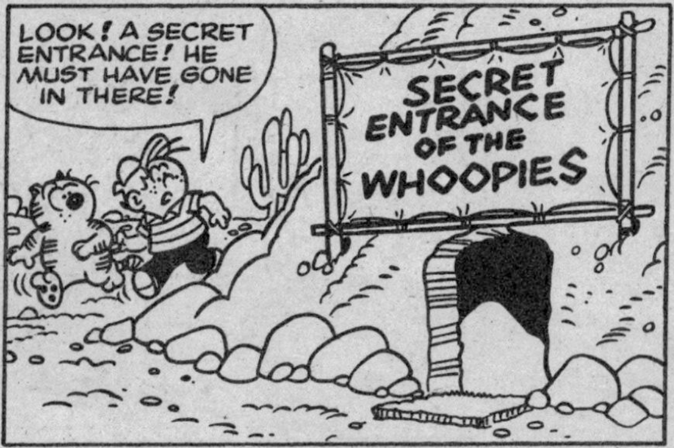
LOOK! A SECRET ENTRANCE! HE MUST HAVE GONE IN THERE!
SECRET ENTRANCE OF THE WHOOPIES

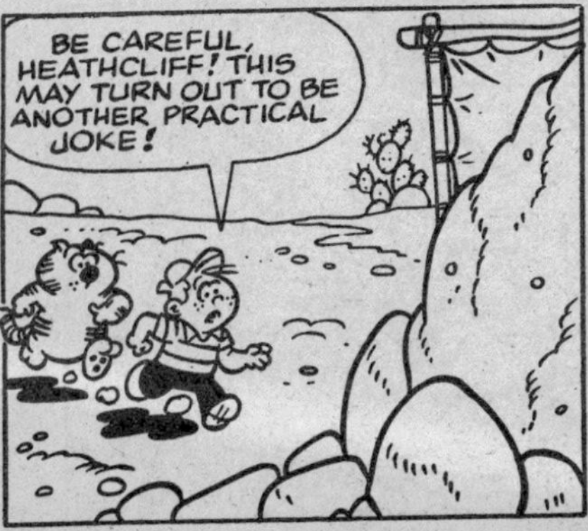
BE CAREFUL, HEATHCLIFF! THIS MAY TURN OUT TO BE ANOTHER PRACTICAL JOKE!

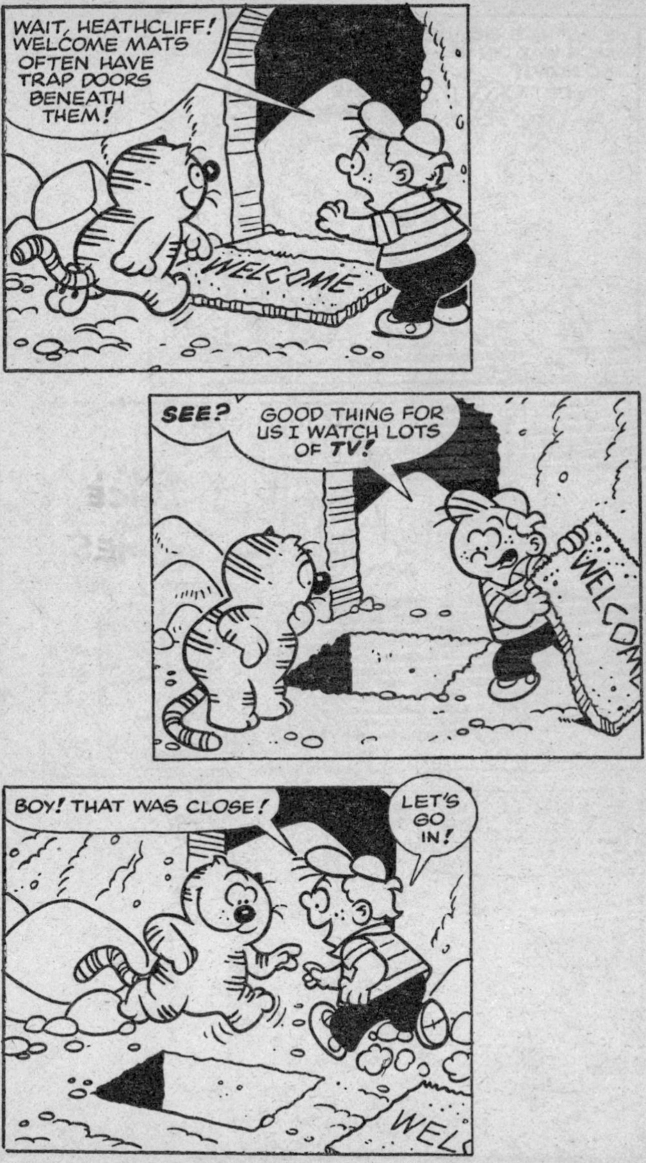
WAIT, HEATHCLIFF! WELCOME MATS OFTEN HAVE TRAP DOORS BENEATH THEM!
WELCOME
SEE?
GOOD THING FOR US I WATCH LOTS OF TV!
BOY! THAT WAS CLOSE!
LET'S GO IN!

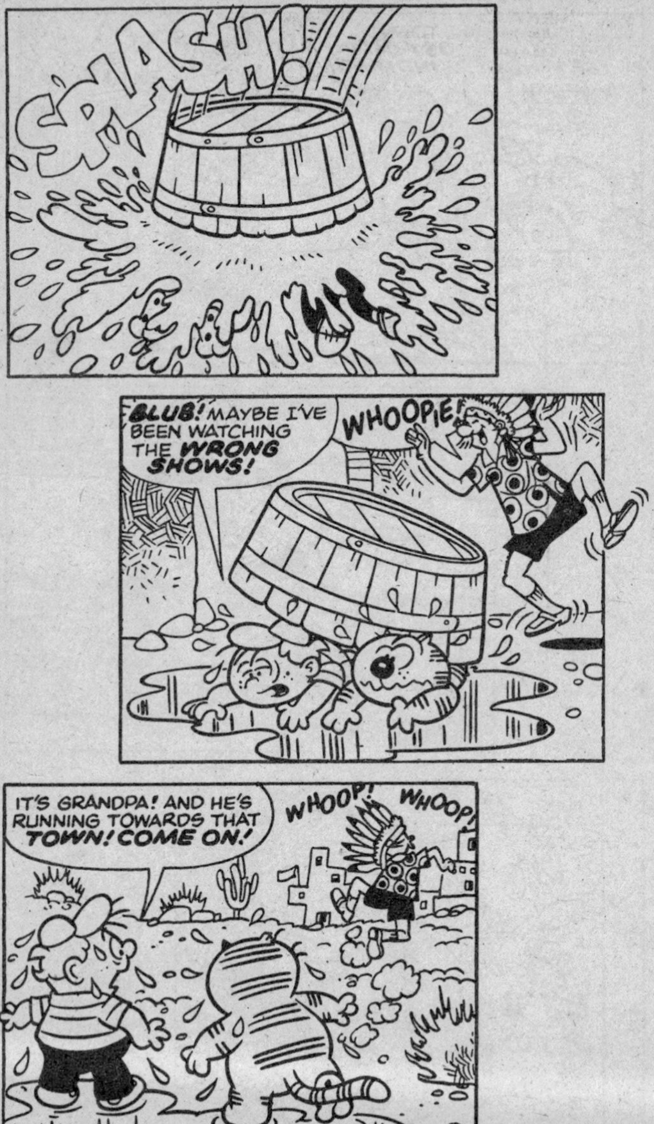
SPLASH!
BLUB! MAYBE I'VE BEEN WATCHING THE WRONG SHOWS!
WHOOPIE!
IT'S GRANDPA! AND HE'S RUNNING TOWARDS THAT TOWN! COME ON!
WHOOP!
WHOOP!

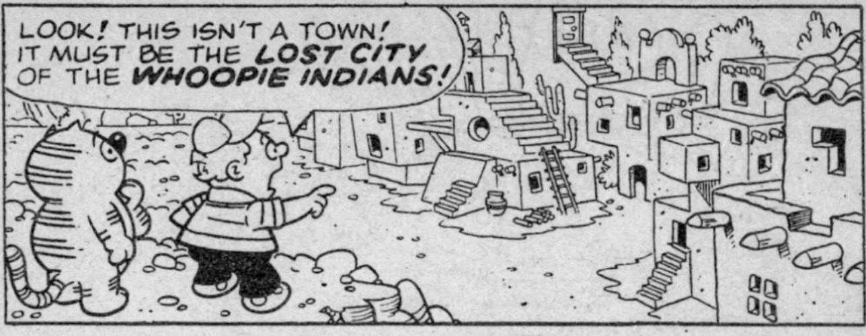
LOOK! THIS ISN'T A TOWN! IT MUST BE THE LOST CITY OF THE WHOOPIE INDIANS!

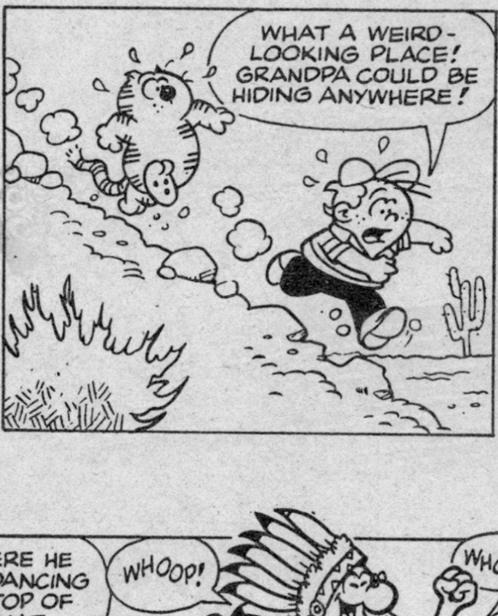
WHAT A WEIRD-LOOKING PLACE! GRANDPA COULD BE HIDING ANYWHERE!

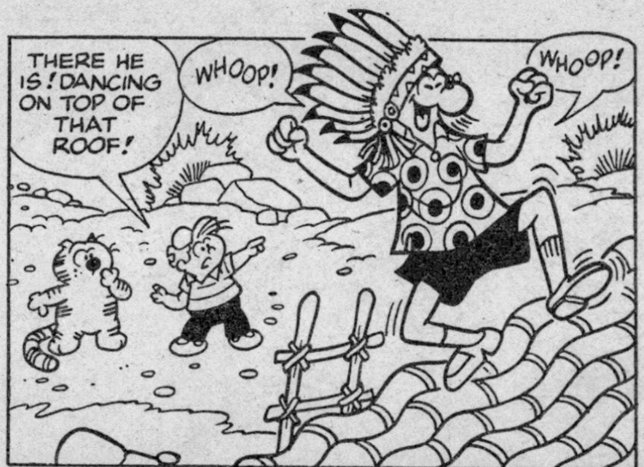
THERE HE IS! DANCING ON TOP OF THAT ROOF!
WHOOP!
WHOOP!

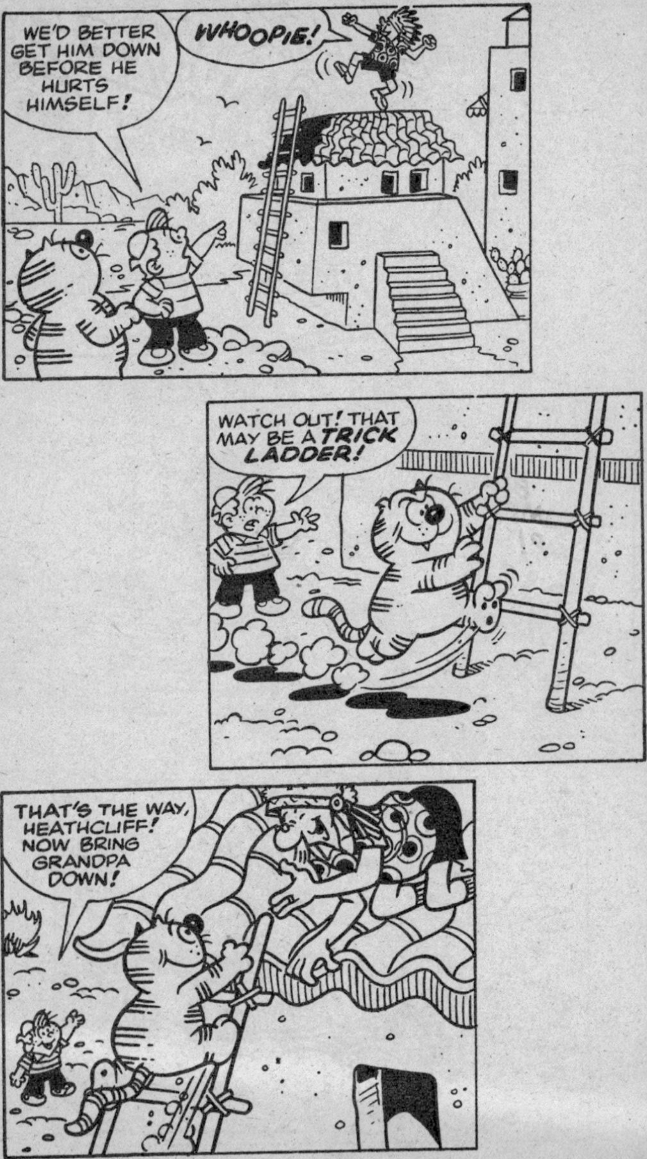
WE'D BETTER GET HIM DOWN BEFORE HE HURTS HIMSELF!
WHOOPIE!
WATCH OUT! THAT MAY BE A TRICK LADDER!
THAT'S THE WAY, HEATHCLIFF! NOW BRING GRANDPA DOWN!

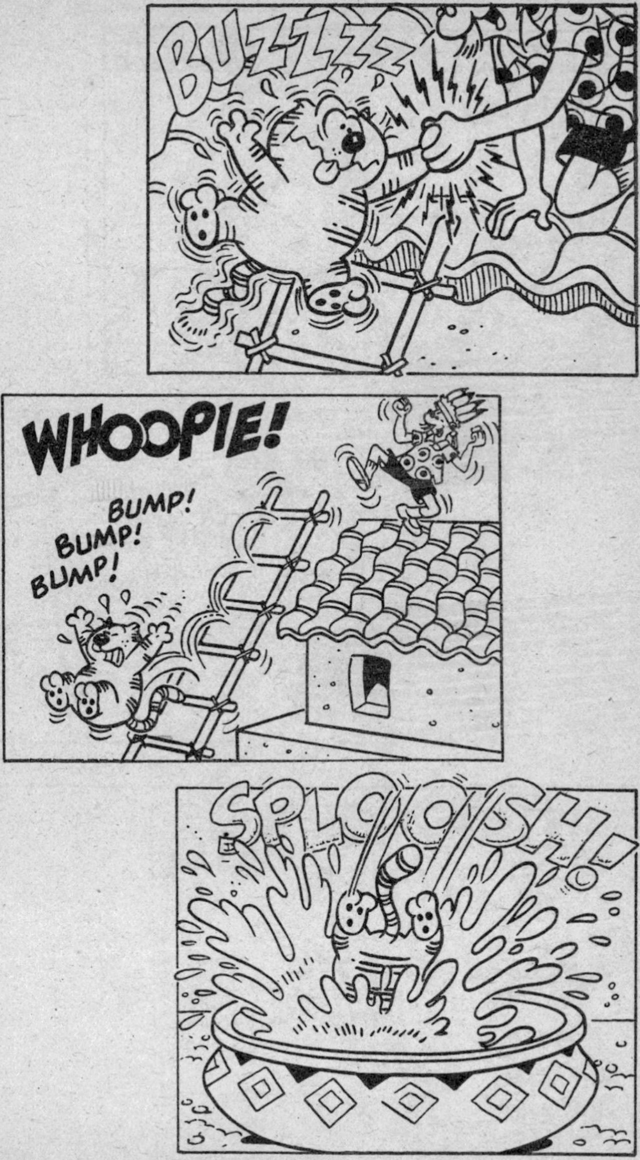
BUZZZZ
WHOOPIE!
BUMP!
BUMP!
BUMP!
SPLOOSH!

BOY! TWO BATHS IN ONE DAY! I GUESS YOU DIDN'T EXPECT HIM TO HAVE A HAND BUZZER!
YOU SHOULDN'T LET GRANDPA FOOL YOU LIKE THAT, HEATHCLIFF!
HE WENT DOWN THE OTHER SIDE! LET'S TRY TO HEAD HIM OFF!

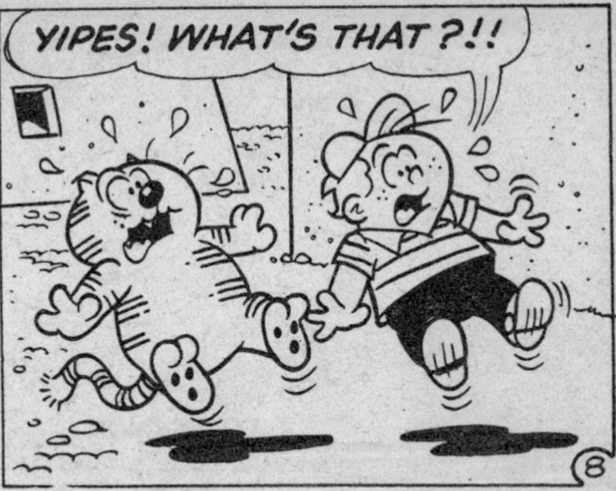
YIPES! WHAT'S THAT?!!
8

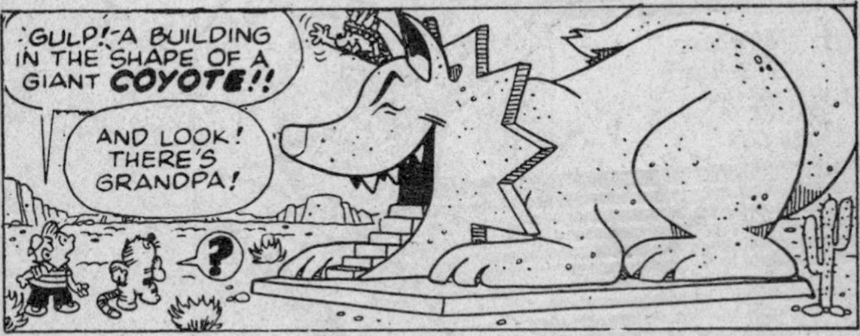
-GULP!- A BUILDING IN THE SHAPE OF A GIANT COYOTE!!
AND LOOK! THERE'S GRANDPA!
?

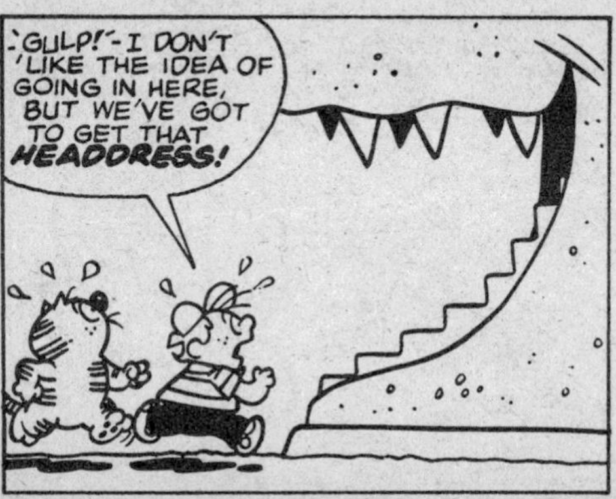
-GULP!- I DON'T LIKE THE IDEA OF GOING IN HERE, BUT WE'VE GOT TO GET THAT HEADDRESS!

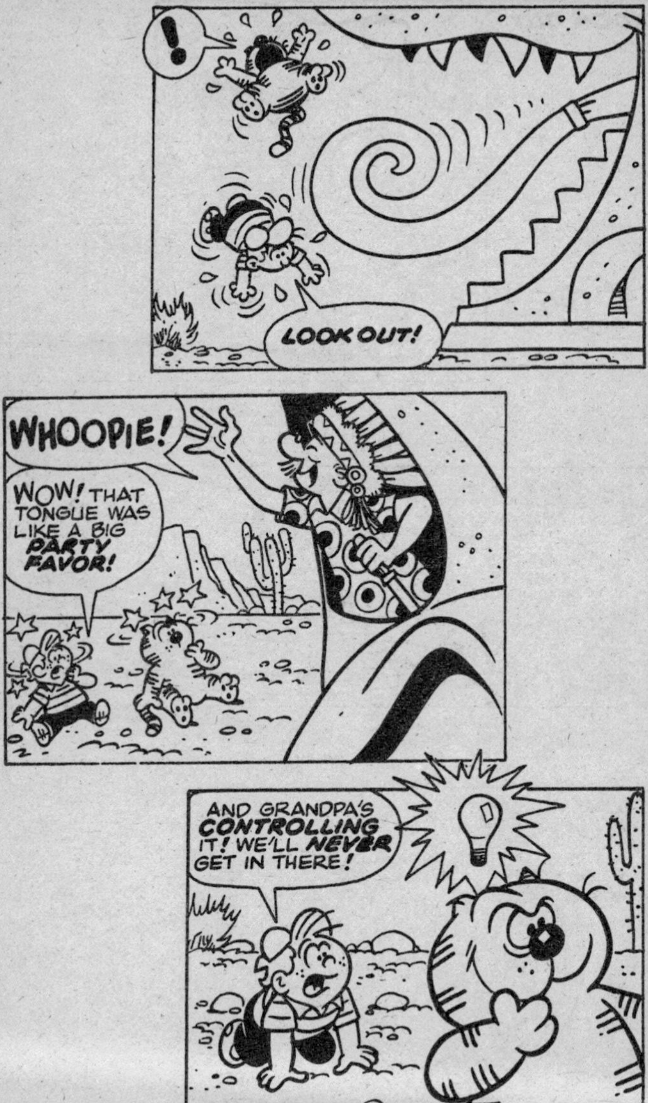
!
LOOK OUT!
WHOOPIE!
WOW! THAT TONGUE WAS LIKE A BIG PARTY FAVOR!
AND GRANDPA'S CONTROLLING IT! WE'LL NEVER GET IN THERE!

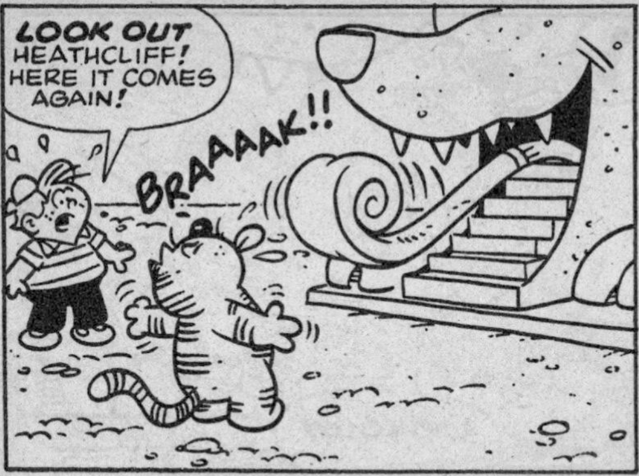
LOOK OUT HEATHCLIFF! HERE IT COMES AGAIN!
BRAAAAK!!

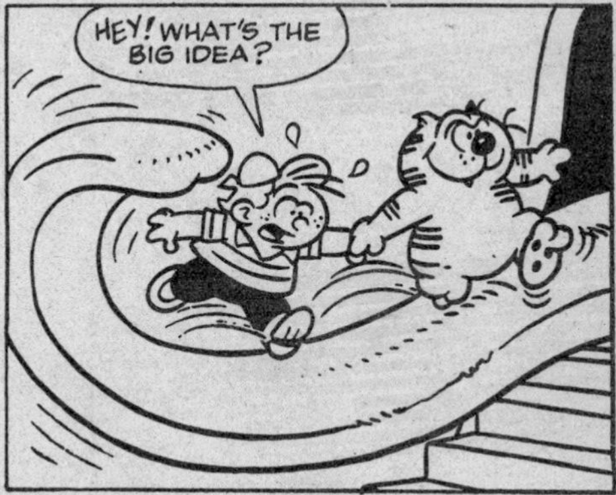
HEY! WHAT'S THE BIG IDEA?

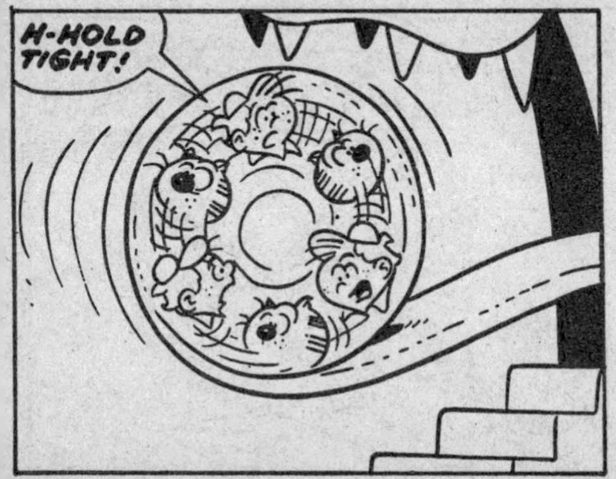
H-HOLD TIGHT!

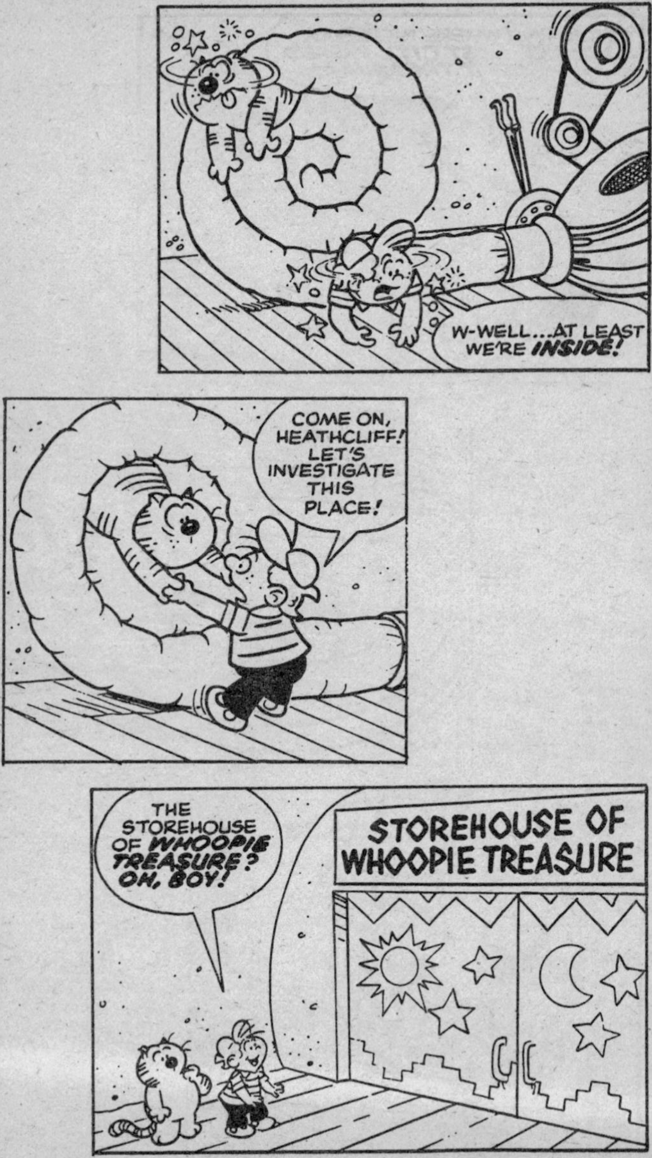
W-WELL...AT LEAST WE'RE *INSIDE!*
COME ON, HEATHCLIFF! LET'S INVESTIGATE THIS PLACE!
THE STOREHOUSE OF *WHOOPIE TREASURE? OH, BOY!*
STOREHOUSE OF WHOOPIE TREASURE

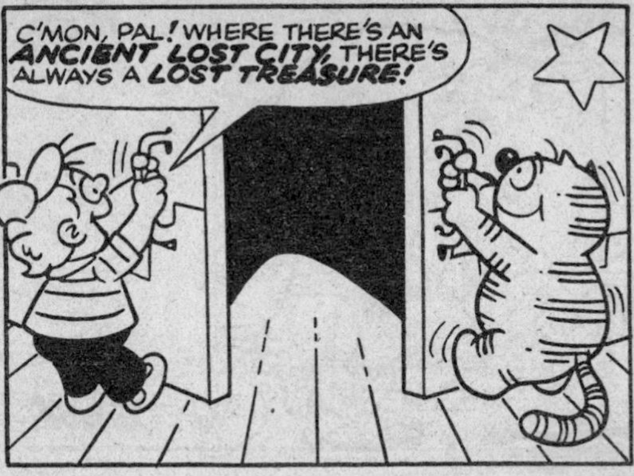
C'MON, PAL! WHERE THERE'S AN ANCIENT LOST CITY, THERE'S ALWAYS A LOST TREASURE!

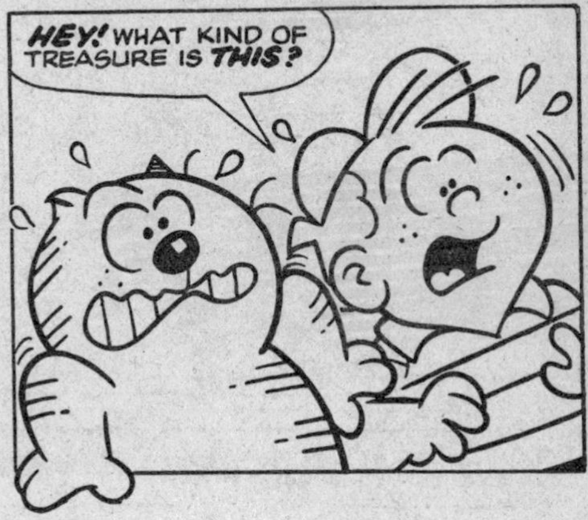
HEY! WHAT KIND OF TREASURE IS THIS?

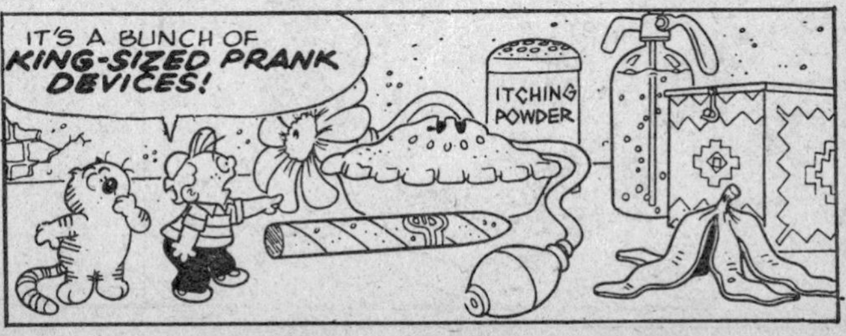
IT'S A BUNCH OF KING-SIZED PRANK DEVICES!
ITCHING POWDER

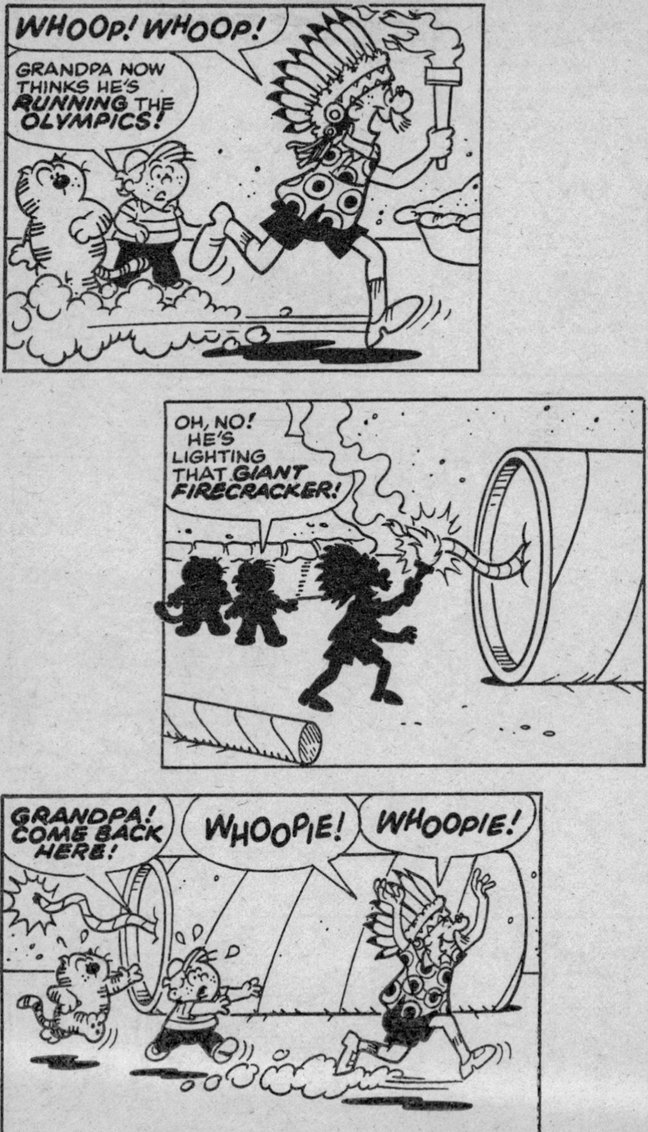
WHOOP! WHOOP!
GRANDPA NOW THINKS HE'S RUNNING THE OLYMPICS!
OH, NO! HE'S LIGHTING THAT GIANT FIRECRACKER!
GRANDPA! COME BACK HERE!
WHOOPIE!
WHOOPIE!

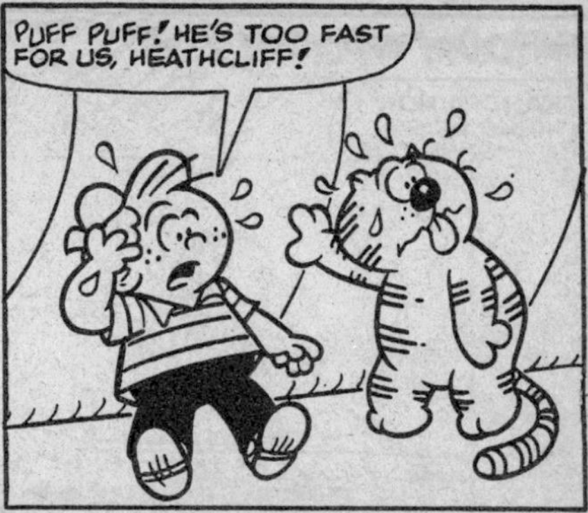
PUFF PUFF! HE'S TOO FAST FOR US, HEATHCLIFF!

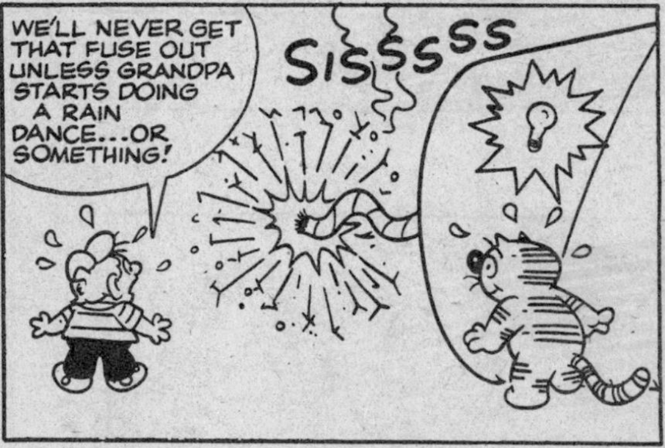
WE'LL NEVER GET THAT FUSE OUT UNLESS GRANDPA STARTS DOING A RAIN DANCE...OR SOMETHING!
SISSSSSS

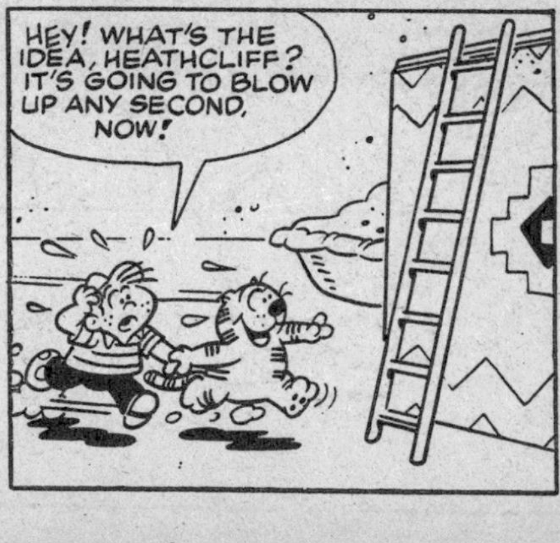
HEY! WHAT'S THE IDEA, HEATHCLIFF? IT'S GOING TO BLOW UP ANY SECOND, NOW!

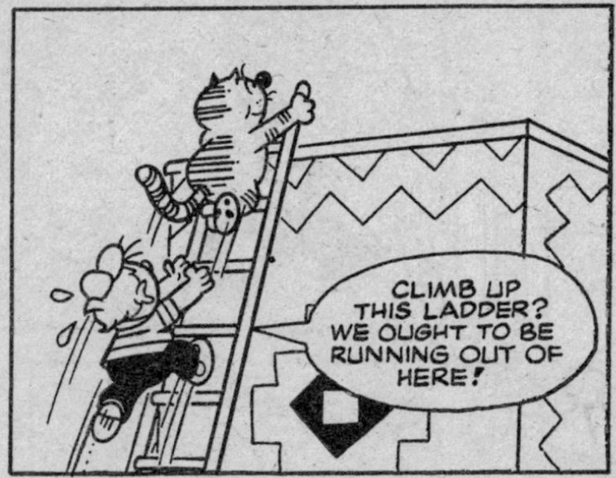
CLIMB UP THIS LADDER? WE OUGHT TO BE RUNNING OUT OF HERE!

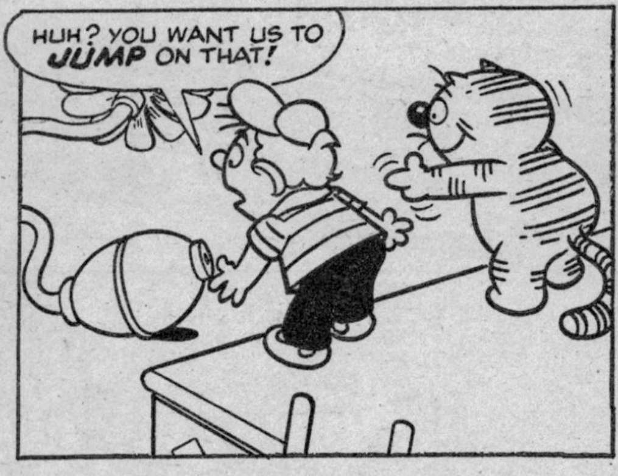
HUH? YOU WANT US TO JUMP ON THAT!

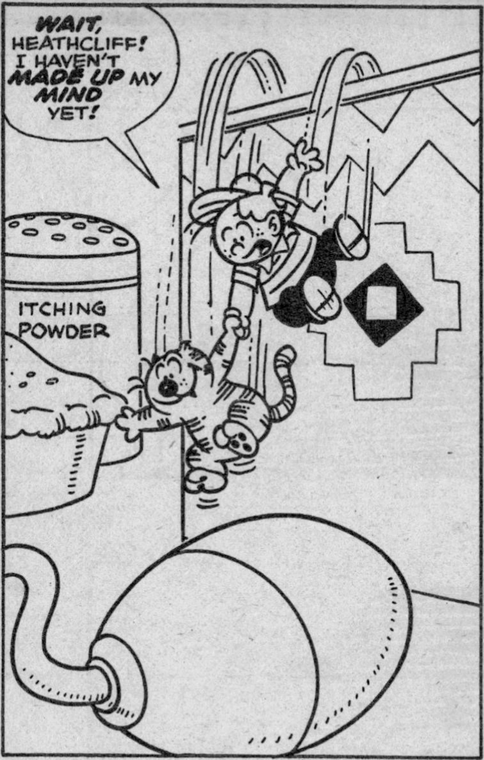
WAIT, HEATHCLIFF! I HAVEN'T MADE UP MY MIND YET!
ITCHING POWDER

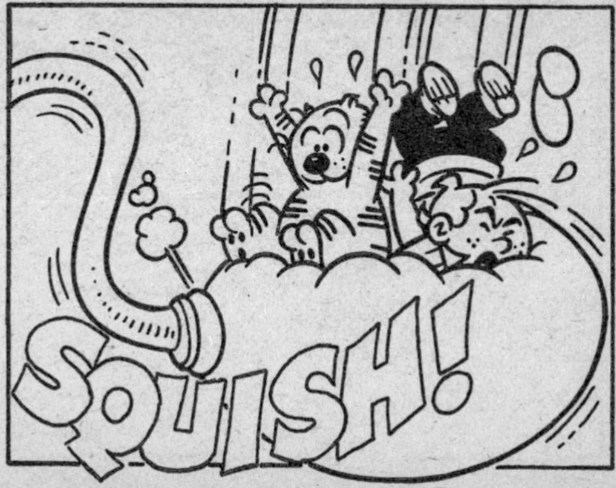
SQUISH!

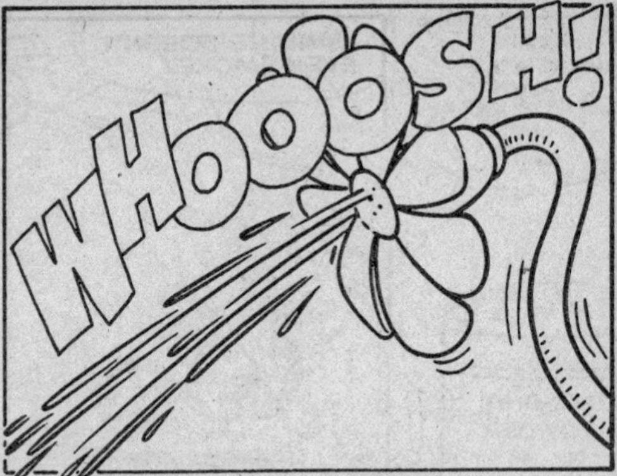
WHOOOSH!

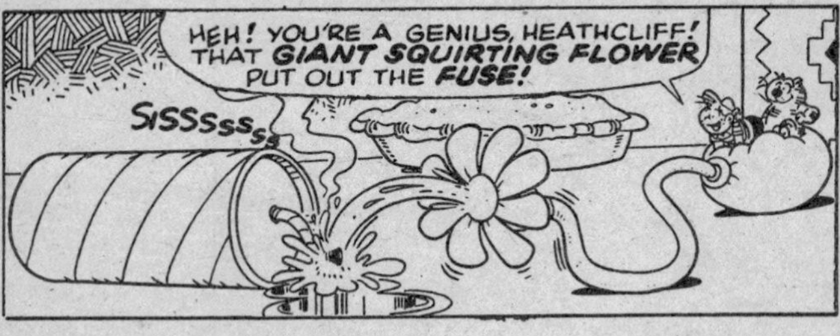
HEH! YOU'RE A GENIUS, HEATHCLIFF! THAT GIANT SQUIRTING FLOWER PUT OUT THE FUSE!
SISSSSSSSS

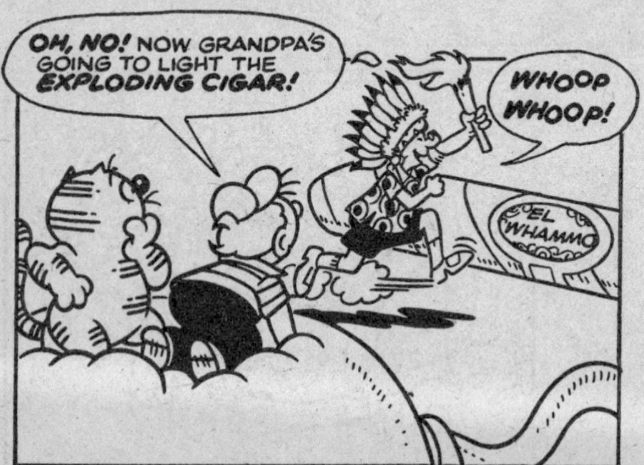
OH, NO! NOW GRANDPA'S GOING TO LIGHT THE EXPLODING CIGAR!
WHOOP WHOOP!
EL WHAMMO

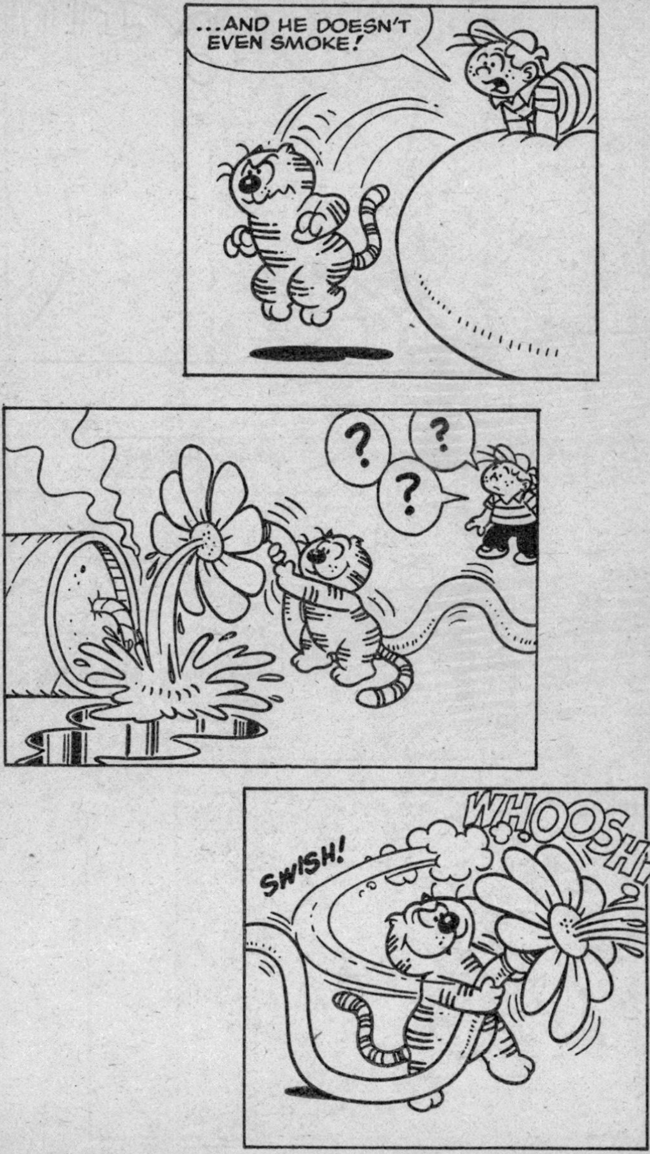
...AND HE DOESN'T EVEN SMOKE!
?
?
?
SWISH!
WHOOSH!

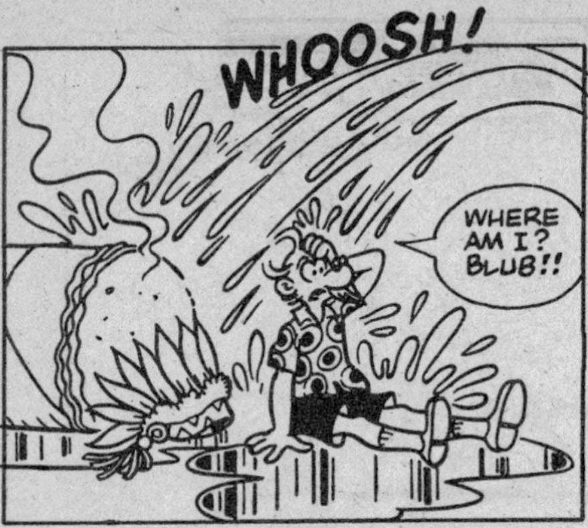
WHOOSH!
WHERE AM I? BLUB!!

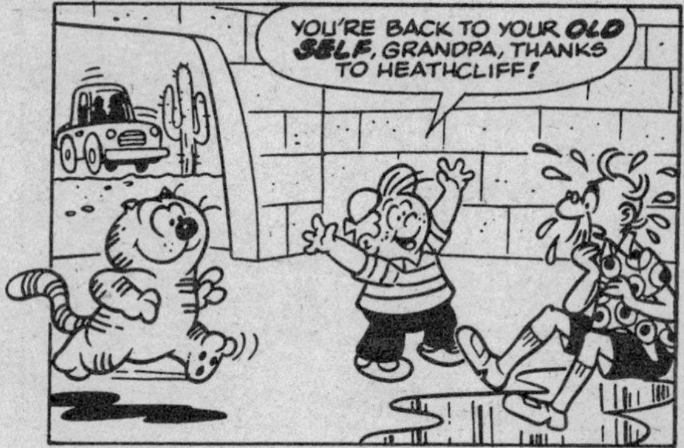
YOU'RE BACK TO YOUR OLD SELF, GRANDPA, THANKS TO HEATHCLIFF!

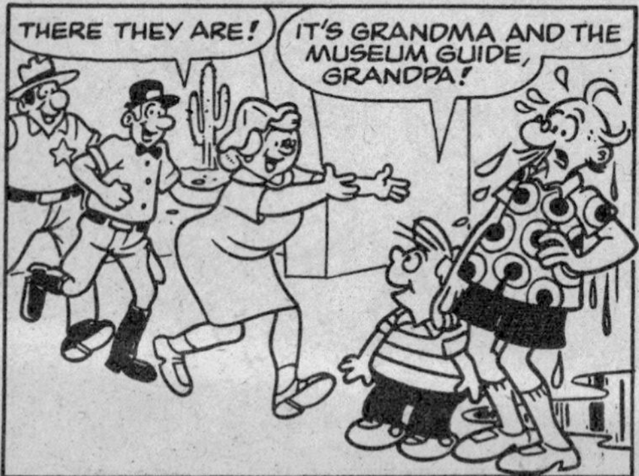
THERE THEY ARE!
IT'S GRANDMA AND THE MUSEUM GUIDE, GRANDPA!

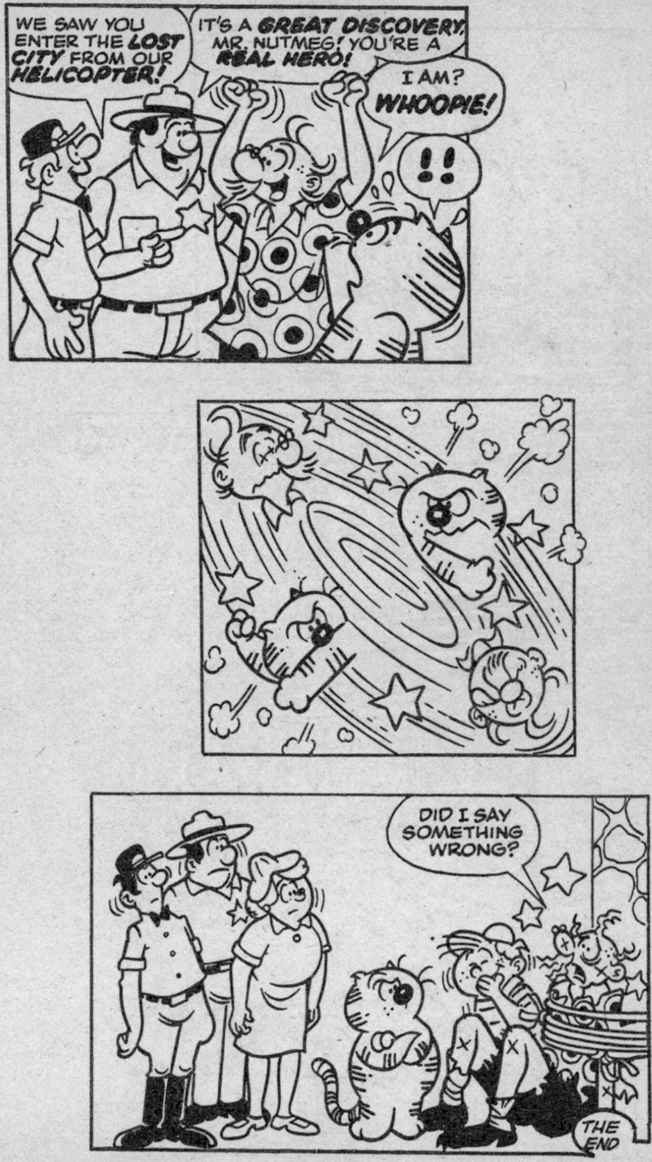
WE SAW YOU ENTER THE LOST CITY FROM OUR HELICOPTER!
IT'S A GREAT DISCOVERY, MR. NUTMEG! YOU'RE A REAL HERO!
I AM? WHOOPIE!
!!
DID I SAY SOMETHING WRONG?
THE END

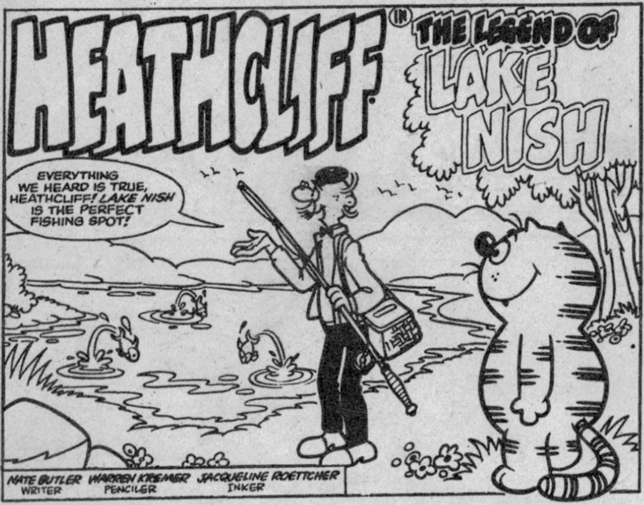
HEATHCLIFF
IN
THE LEGEND OF LAKE NISH
EVERYTHING WE HEARD IS TRUE, HEATHCLIFF! LAKE NISH IS THE PERFECT FISHING SPOT!
NATE BUTLER WRITER
WARREN KREMER PENCILER
JACQUELINE ROETTCHER INKER

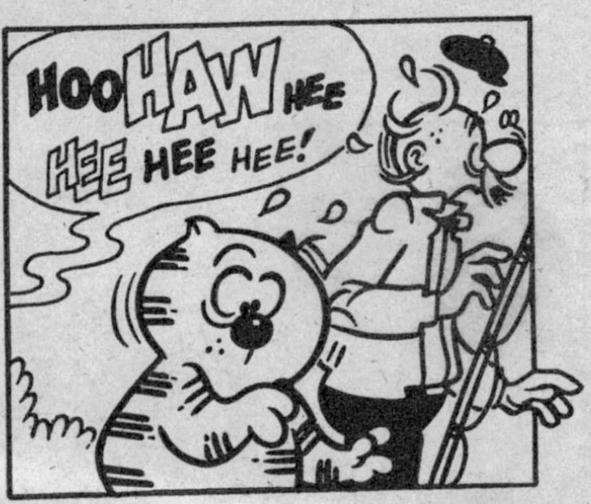
HOO HAW HEE HEE HEE HEE!

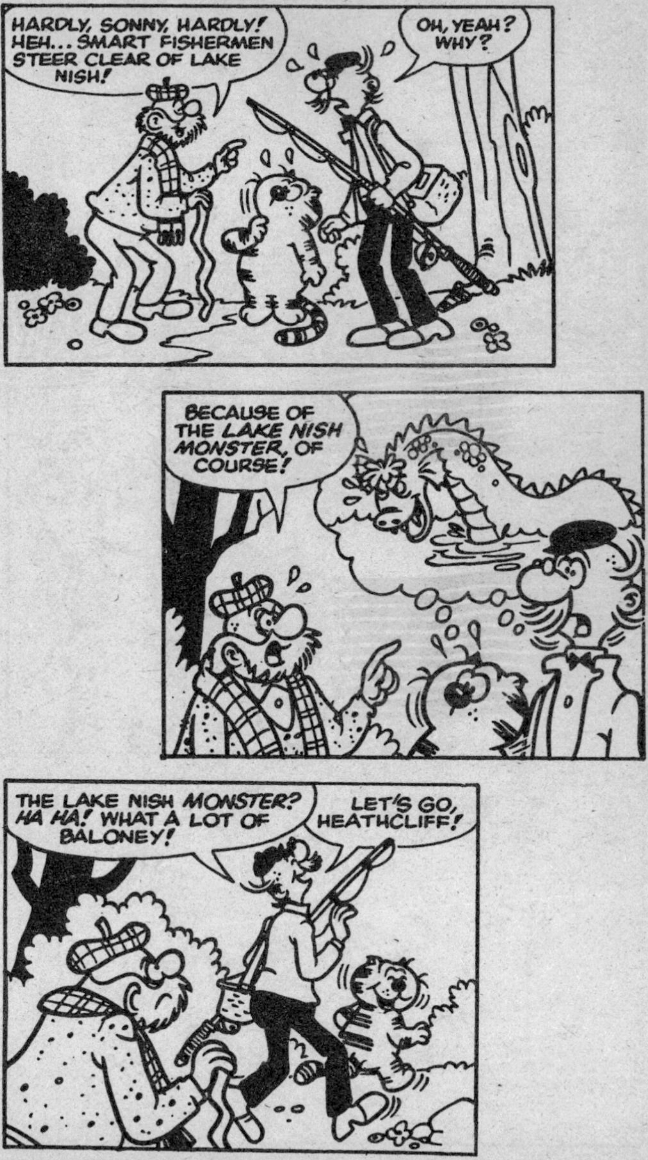
HARDLY, SONNY, HARDLY! HEH... SMART FISHERMEN STEER CLEAR OF LAKE NISH!
OH, YEAH? WHY?
BECAUSE OF THE LAKE NISH MONSTER, OF COURSE!
THE LAKE NISH MONSTER? HA HA! WHAT A LOT OF BALONEY!
LET'S GO, HEATHCLIFF!

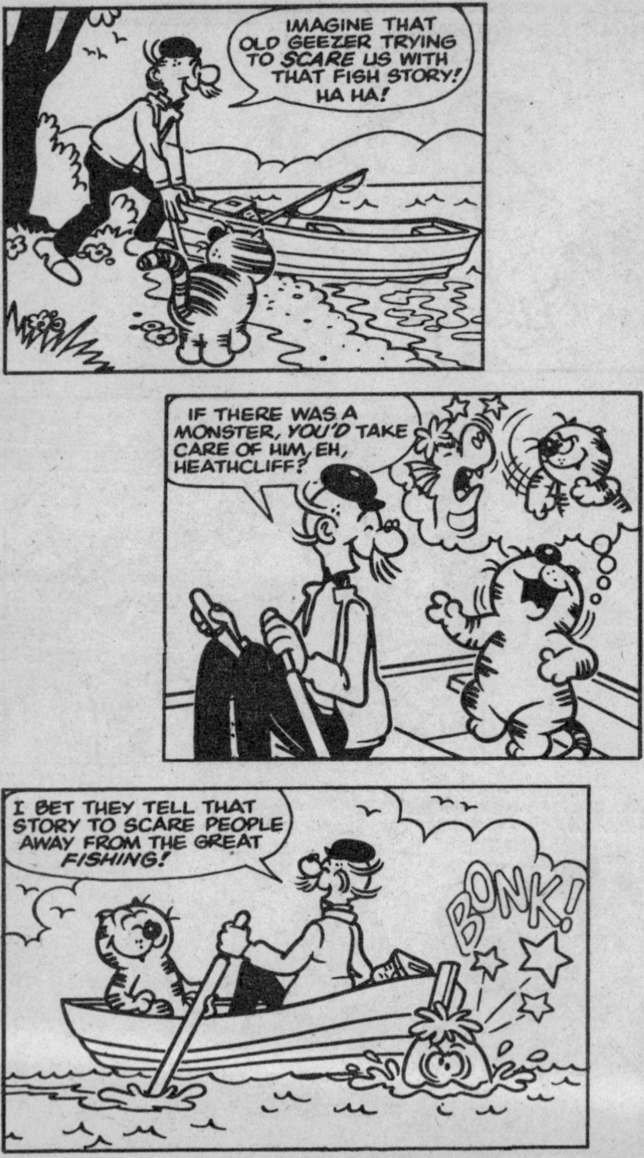
IMAGINE THAT OLD GEEZER TRYING TO *SCARE* US WITH THAT FISH STORY! HA HA!
IF THERE WAS A MONSTER, *YOU'D* TAKE CARE OF HIM, EH, HEATHCLIFF?
I BET THEY TELL THAT STORY TO SCARE PEOPLE AWAY FROM THE GREAT *FISHING!*
BONK!

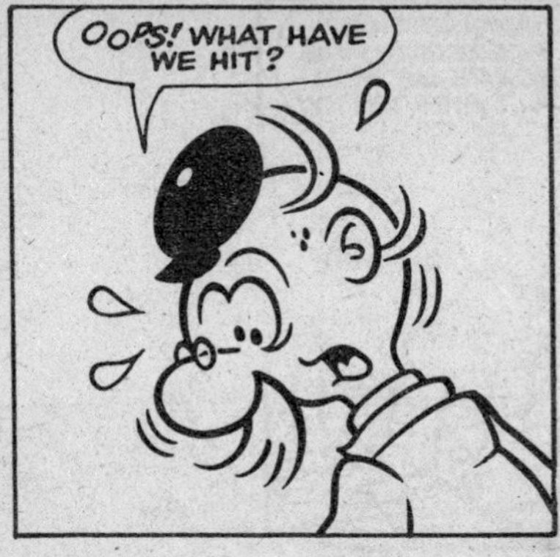
OOPS! WHAT HAVE WE HIT?

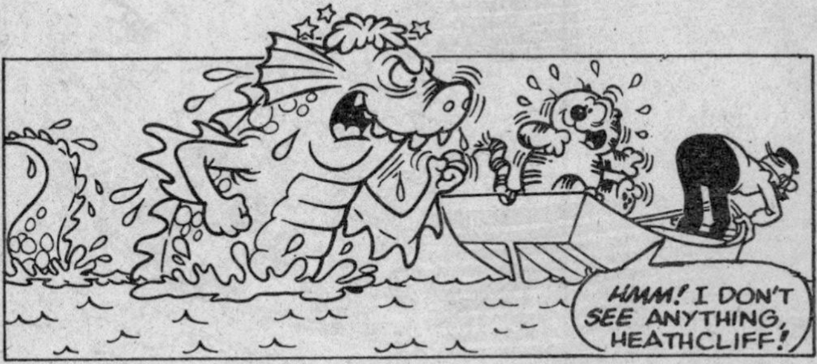
HMM! I DON'T SEE ANYTHING, HEATHCLIFF!

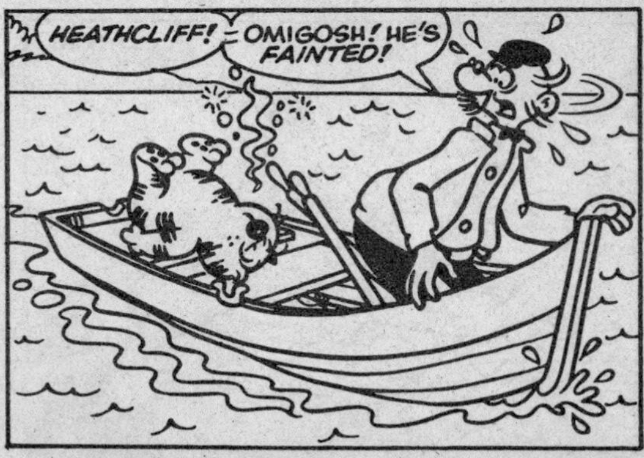
HEATHCLIFF!
OMIGOSH! HE'S FAINTED!

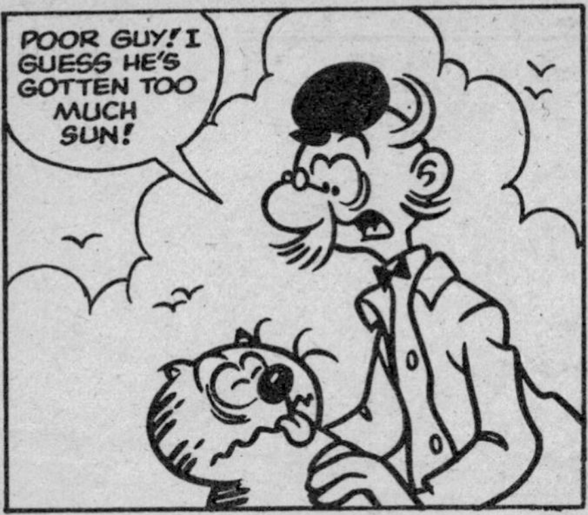
POOR GUY! I GUESS HE'S GOTTEN TOO MUCH SUN!

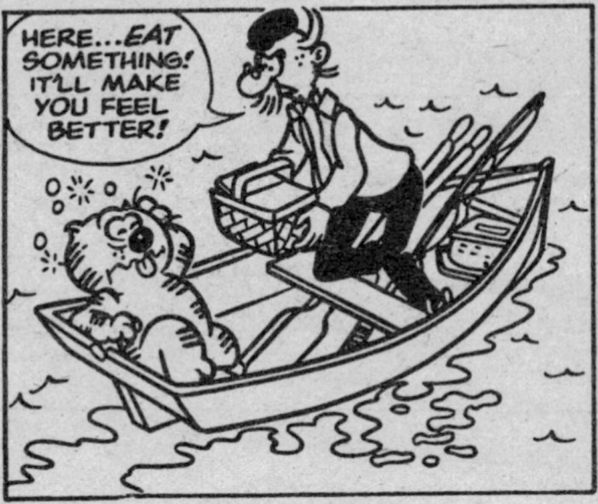
HERE...EAT SOMETHING! IT'LL MAKE YOU FEEL BETTER!

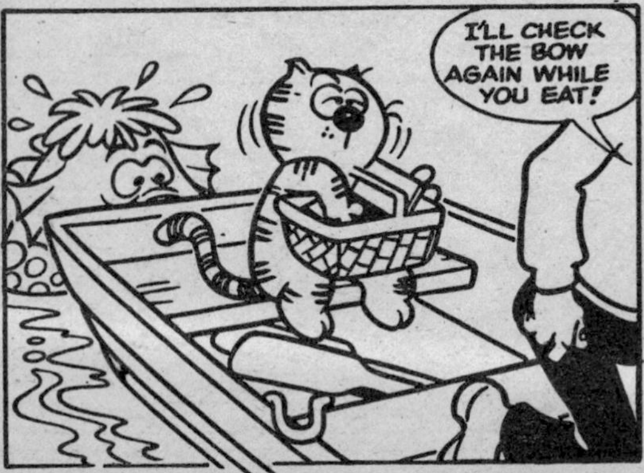
I'LL CHECK THE BOW AGAIN WHILE YOU EAT!

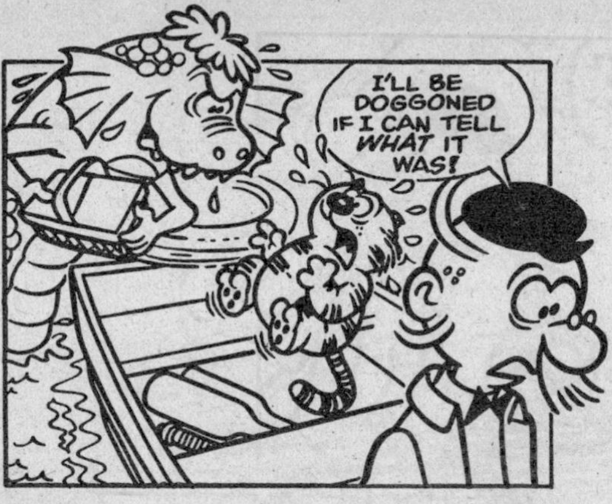
I'LL BE DOGGONED IF I CAN TELL *WHAT* IT WAS!

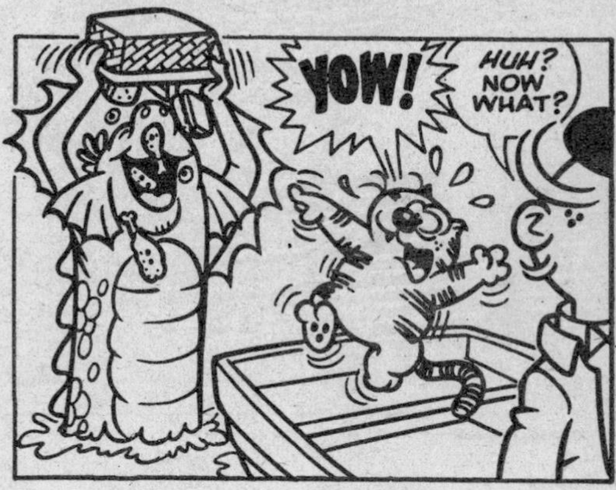
YOW!
HUH? NOW WHAT?

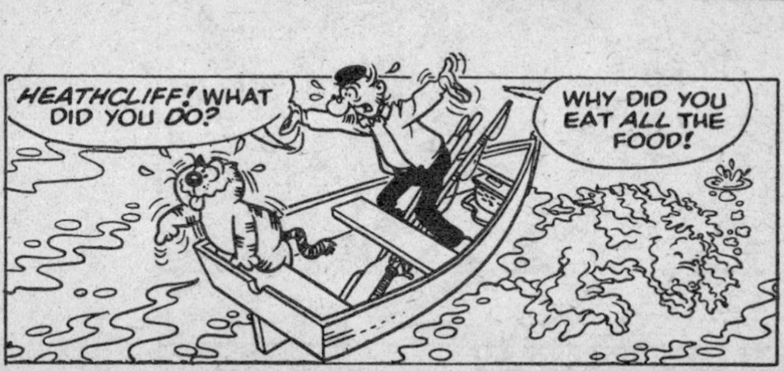
HEATHCLIFF! WHAT DID YOU *DO?*
WHY DID YOU EAT *ALL* THE FOOD!

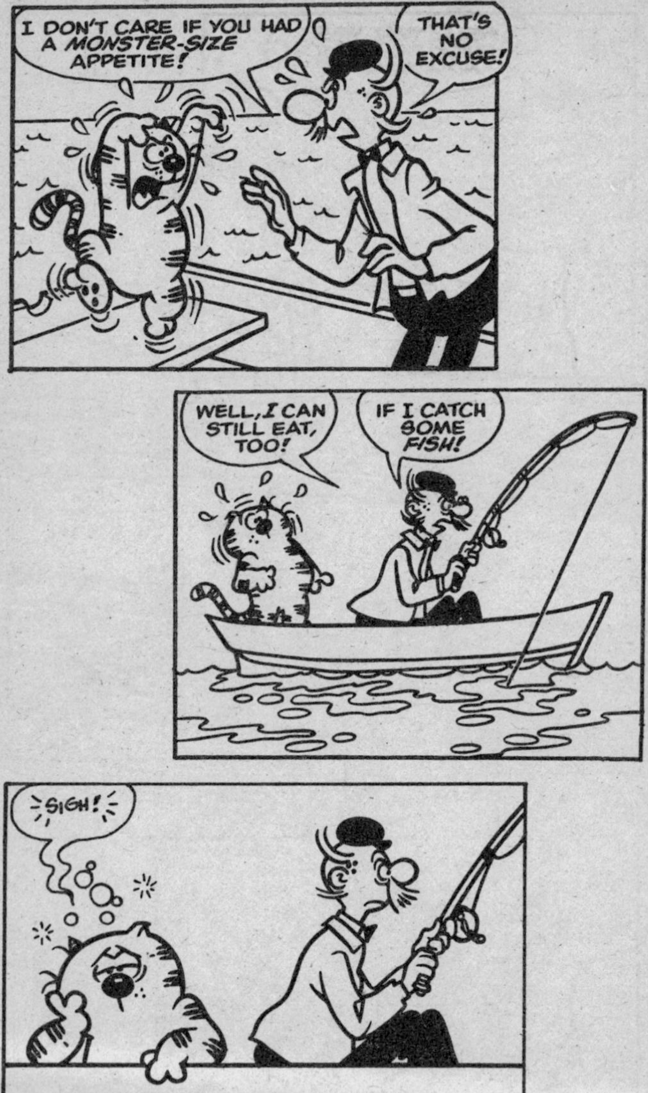
I DON'T CARE IF YOU HAD A *MONSTER-SIZE* APPETITE!
THAT'S NO EXCUSE!
WELL, *I* CAN STILL EAT, TOO!
IF I CATCH SOME *FISH*!
SIGH!

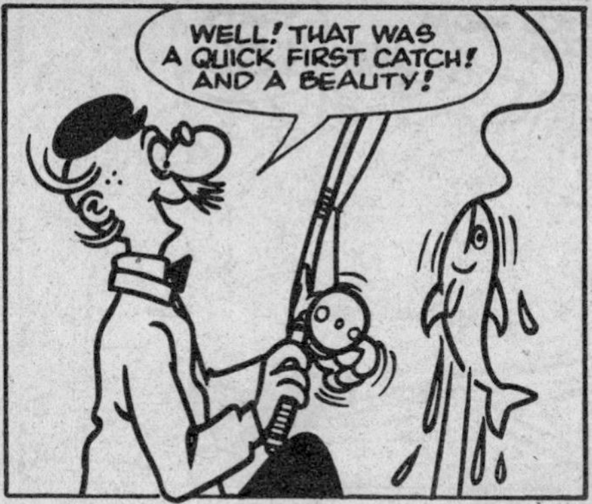
WELL! THAT WAS A QUICK FIRST CATCH! AND A BEAUTY!

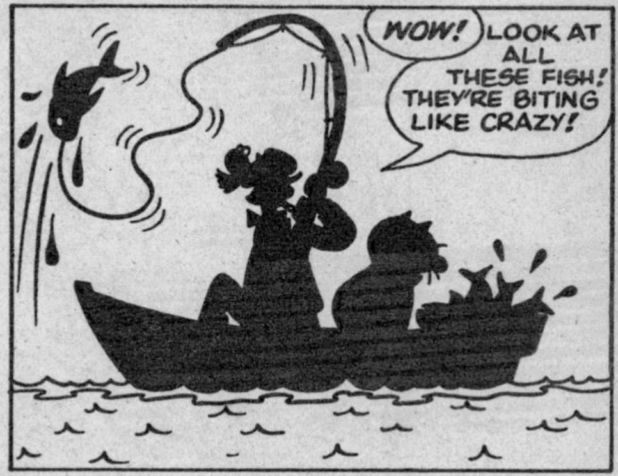
WOW! LOOK AT ALL THESE FISH! THEY'RE BITING LIKE CRAZY!

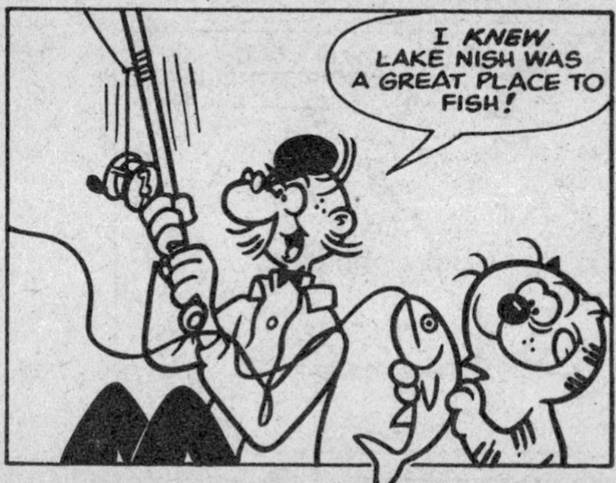
I KNEW LAKE NISH WAS A GREAT PLACE TO FISH!

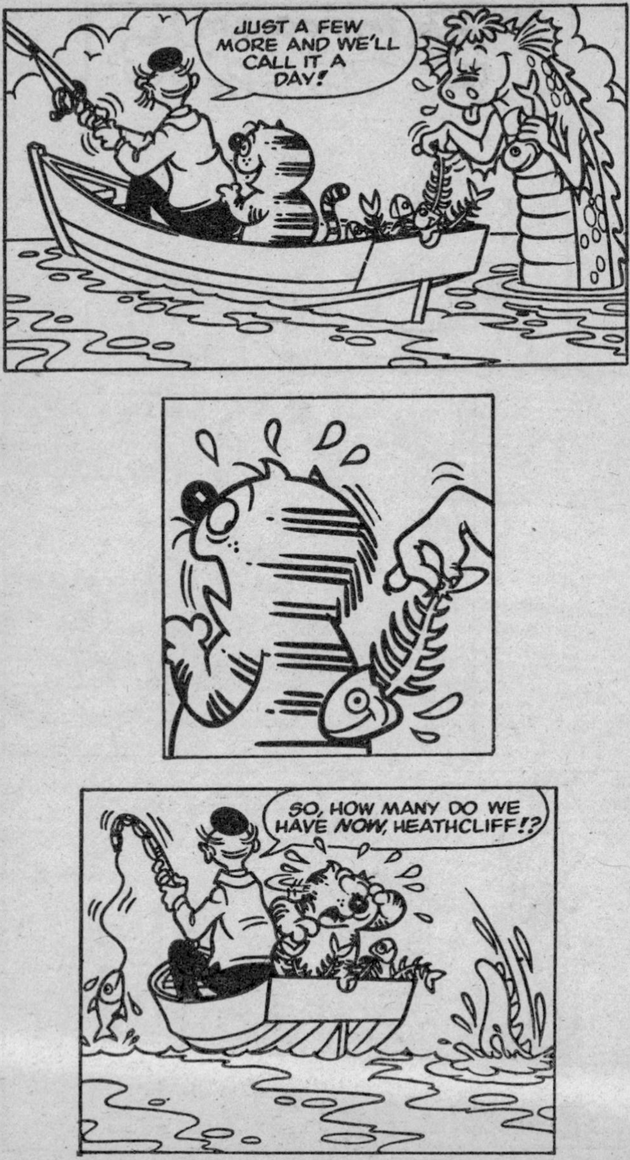
JUST A FEW MORE AND WE'LL CALL IT A DAY!
SO, HOW MANY DO WE HAVE *NOW*, HEATHCLIFF!?

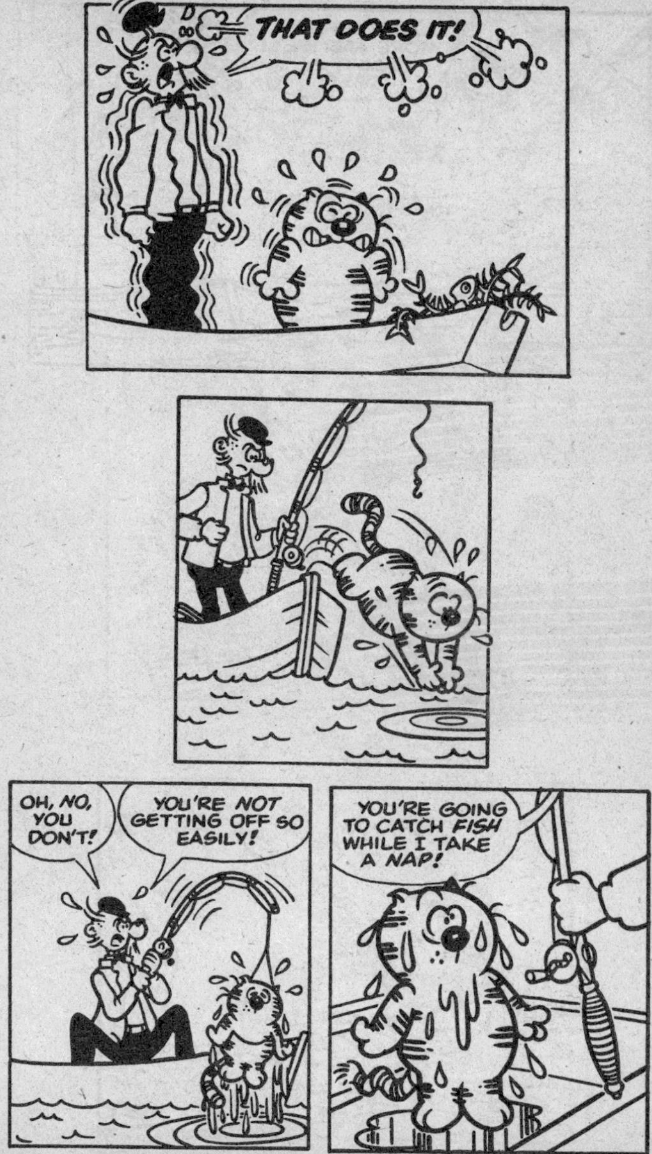
THAT DOES IT!
OH, NO, YOU DON'T!
YOU'RE NOT GETTING OFF SO EASILY!
YOU'RE GOING TO CATCH FISH WHILE I TAKE A NAP!

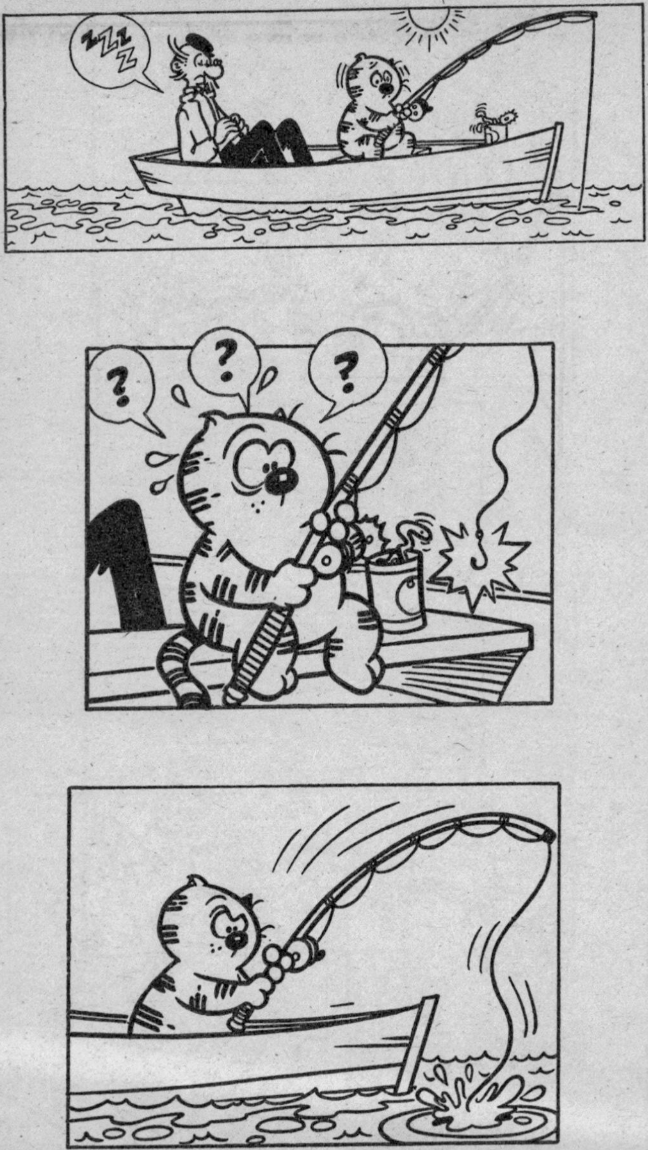
ZZZZ
?
?
?

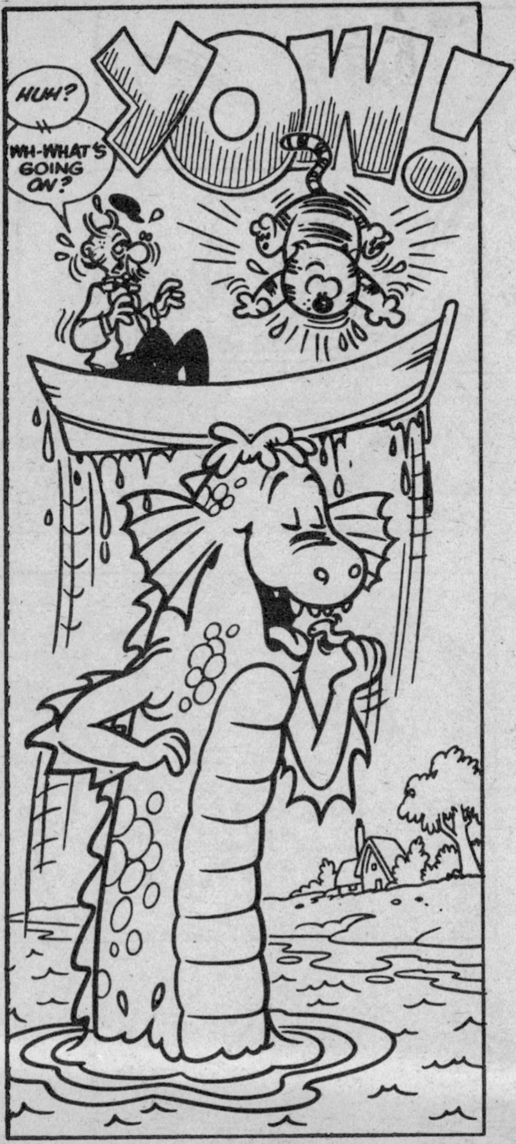
HUH?
WH-WHAT'S GOING ON?
YOW!

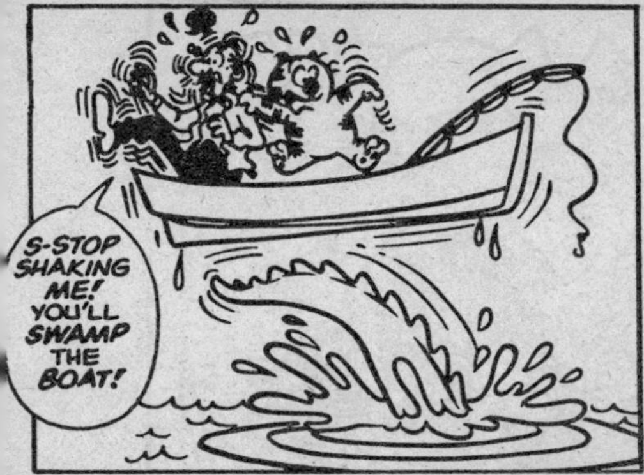
S-STOP SHAKING ME! YOU'LL SWAMP THE BOAT!

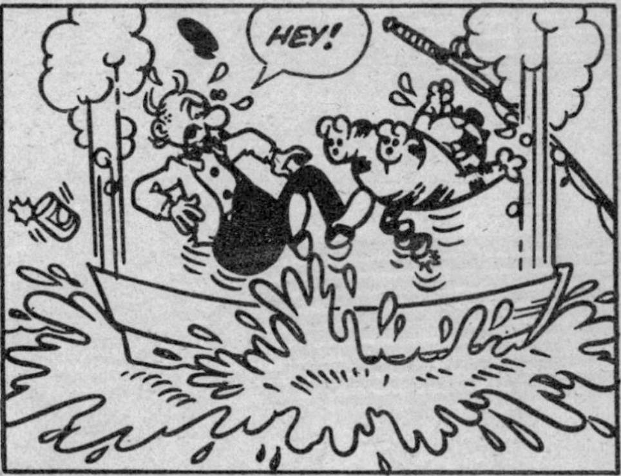
HEY!

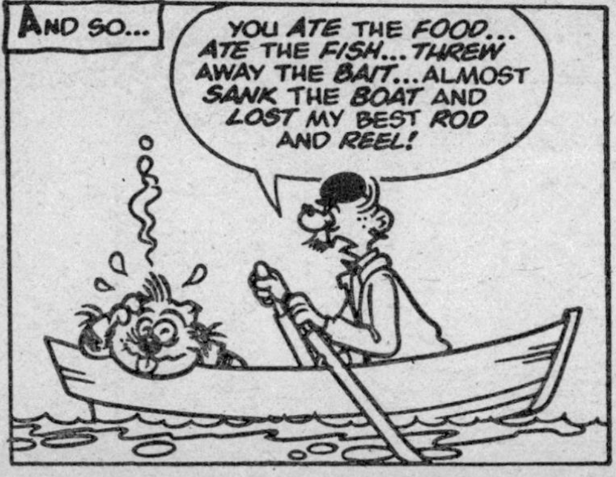
AND SO...
YOU ATE THE FOOD... ATE THE FISH... THREW AWAY THE BAIT... ALMOST SANK THE BOAT AND LOST MY BEST ROD AND REEL!

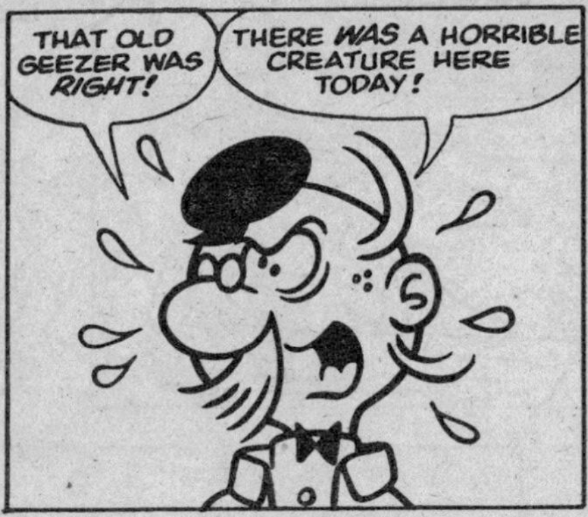
THAT OLD GEEZER WAS RIGHT!
THERE WAS A HORRIBLE CREATURE HERE TODAY!

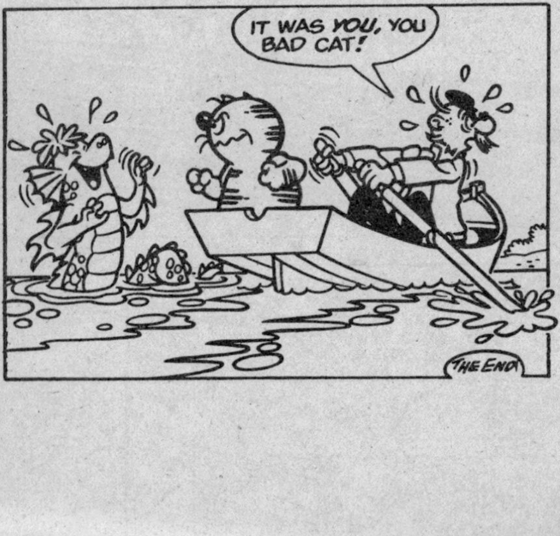
IT WAS YOU, YOU BAD CAT!
THE END

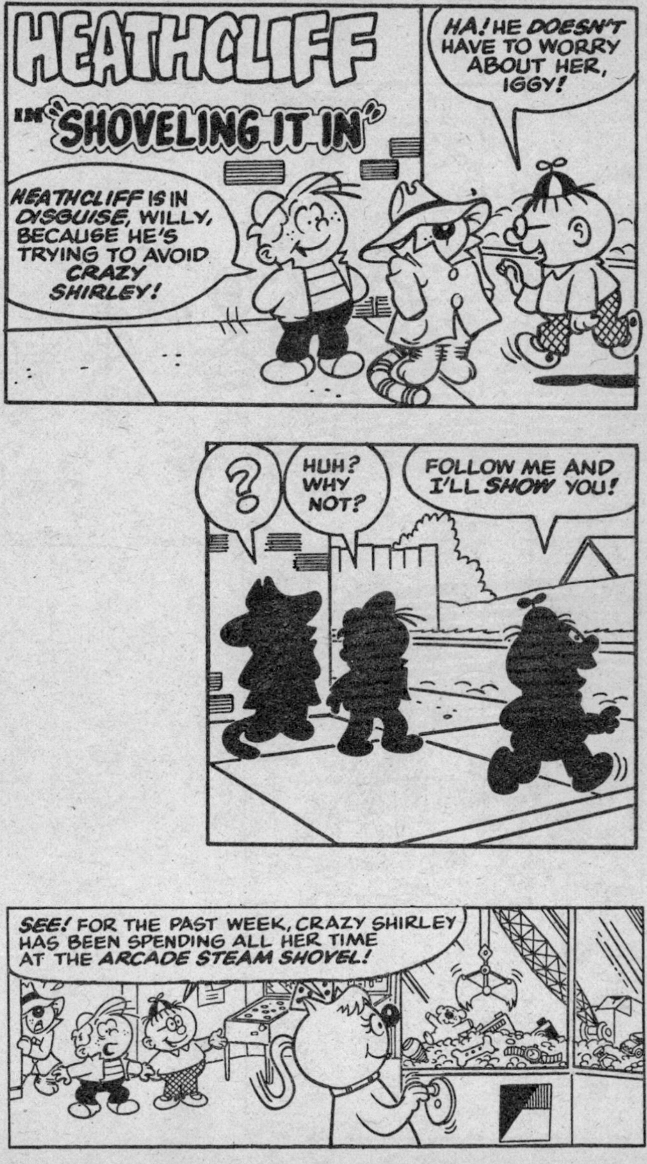
HEATHCLIFF
IN "SHOVELING IT IN"
HEATHCLIFF IS IN DISGUISE, WILLY, BECAUSE HE'S TRYING TO AVOID CRAZY SHIRLEY!
HA! HE DOESN'T HAVE TO WORRY ABOUT HER, IGGY!
?
HUH? WHY NOT?
FOLLOW ME AND I'LL SHOW YOU!
SEE! FOR THE PAST WEEK, CRAZY SHIRLEY HAS BEEN SPENDING ALL HER TIME AT THE ARCADE STEAM SHOVEL!

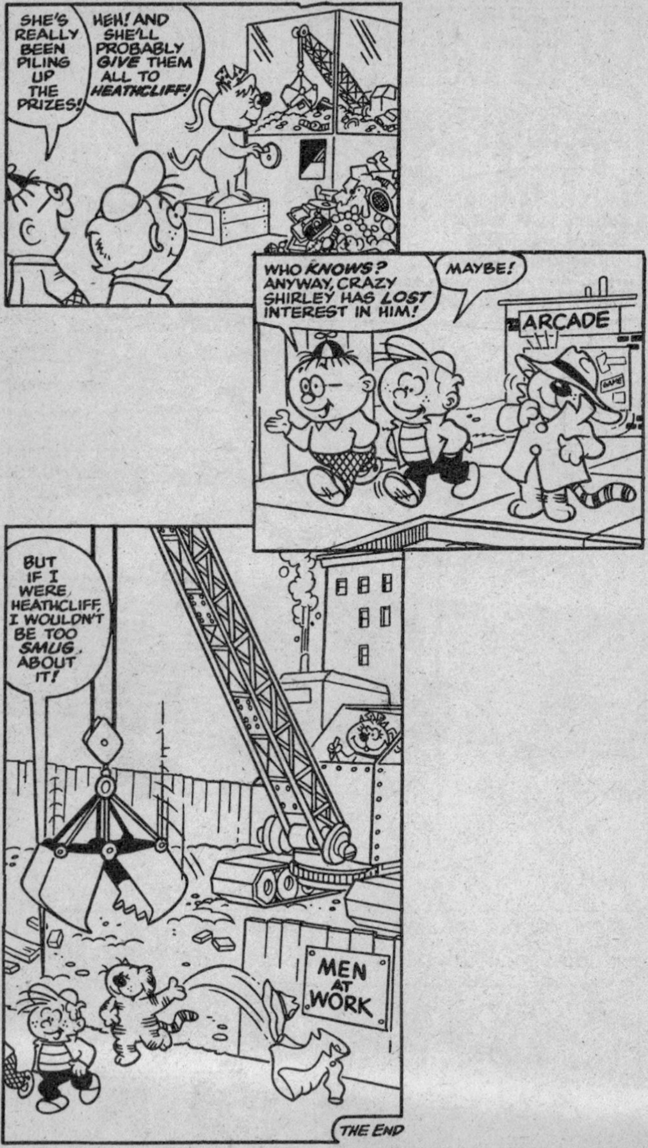
SHE'S REALLY BEEN PILING UP THE PRIZES!
HEH! AND SHE'LL PROBABLY GIVE THEM ALL TO HEATHCLIFF!
WHO KNOWS? ANYWAY, CRAZY SHIRLEY HAS LOST INTEREST IN HIM!
MAYBE!
ARCADE
BUT IF I WERE HEATHCLIFF, I WOULDN'T BE TOO SMUG ABOUT IT!
MEN AT WORK
THE END

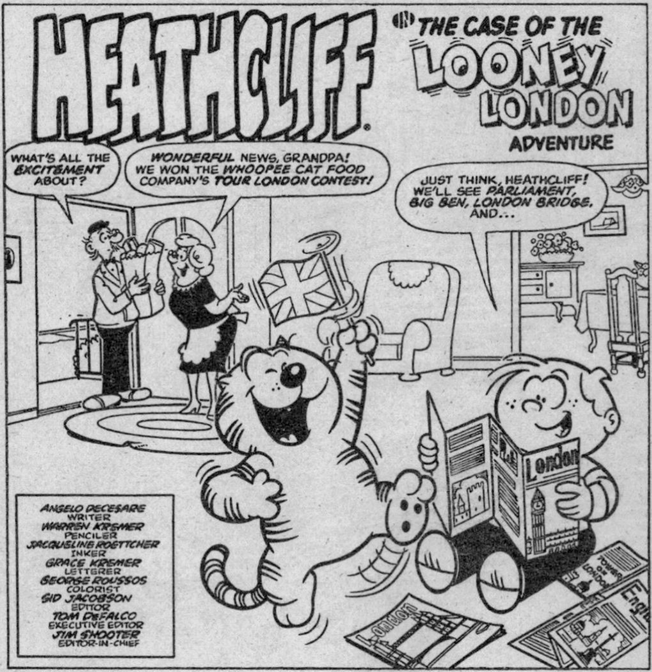
HEATHCLIFF
IN THE CASE OF THE LOONEY LONDON ADVENTURE
WHAT'S ALL THE EXCITEMENT ABOUT?
WONDERFUL NEWS, GRANDPA! WE WON THE WHOOPEE CAT FOOD COMPANY'S TOUR LONDON CONTEST!
JUST THINK, HEATHCLIFF! WE'LL SEE PARLIAMENT, BIG BEN, LONDON BRIDGE, AND...
London
ANGELO DECESARE WRITER
WARREN KREMER PENCILER
JACQUELINE ROETTCHER INKER
GRACE KREMER LETTERER
GEORGE ROUSSOS COLORIST
SID JACOBSON EDITOR
TOM DeFALCO EXECUTIVE EDITOR
JIM SHOOTER EDITOR-IN-CHIEF

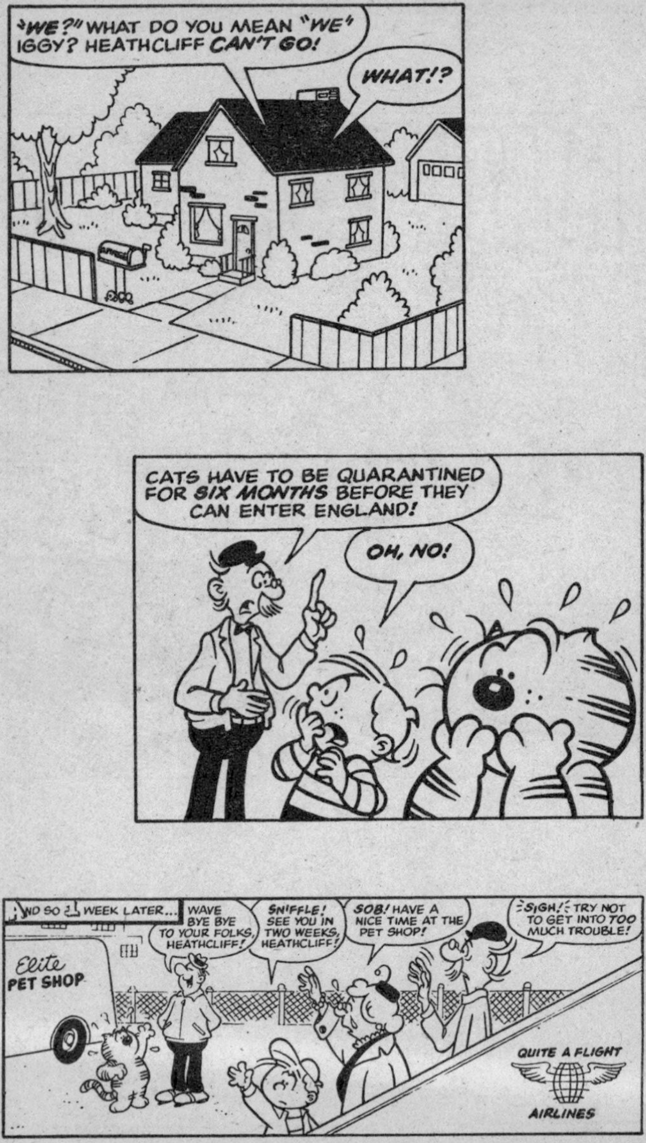
"WE?" WHAT DO YOU MEAN "WE" IGGY? HEATHCLIFF CAN'T GO!
WHAT!?
CATS HAVE TO BE QUARANTINED FOR SIX MONTHS BEFORE THEY CAN ENTER ENGLAND!
OH, NO!
AND SO 1 WEEK LATER...
WAVE BYE BYE TO YOUR FOLKS, HEATHCLIFF!
SNIFFLE! SEE YOU IN TWO WEEKS, HEATHCLIFF!
SOB! HAVE A NICE TIME AT THE PET SHOP!
SIGH! TRY NOT TO GET INTO TOO MUCH TROUBLE!
Elite PET SHOP
QUITE A FLIGHT AIRLINES

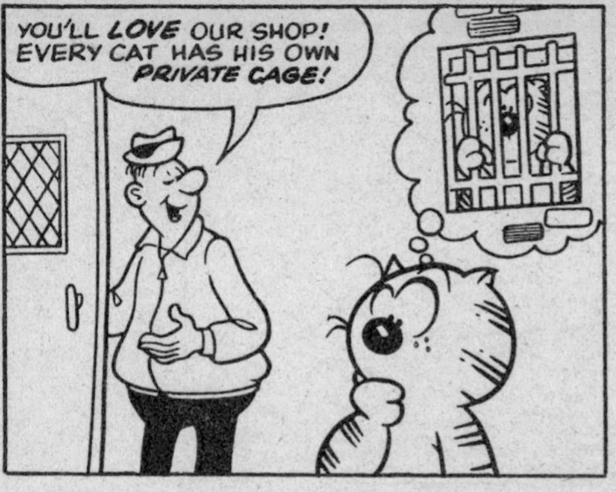
YOU'LL LOVE OUR SHOP! EVERY CAT HAS HIS OWN PRIVATE CAGE!

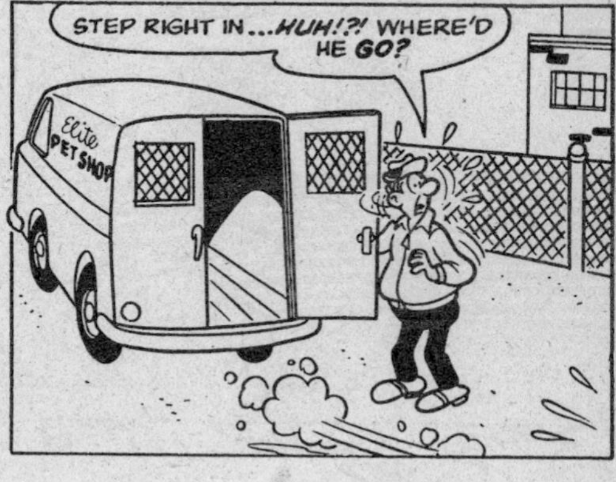
STEP RIGHT IN...HUH!?! WHERE'D HE GO?
Elite PET SHOP

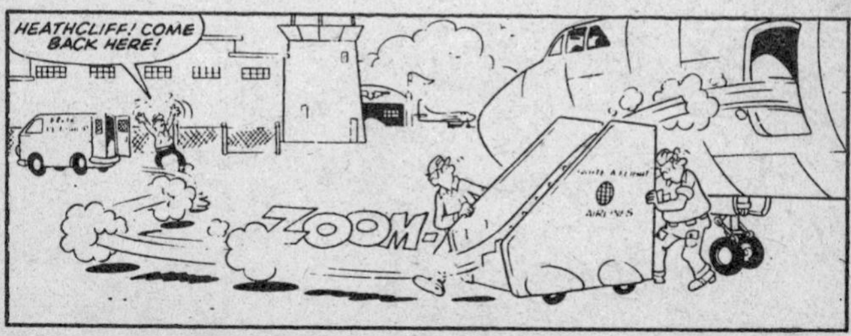
HEATHCLIFF! COME BACK HERE!
ZOOM-

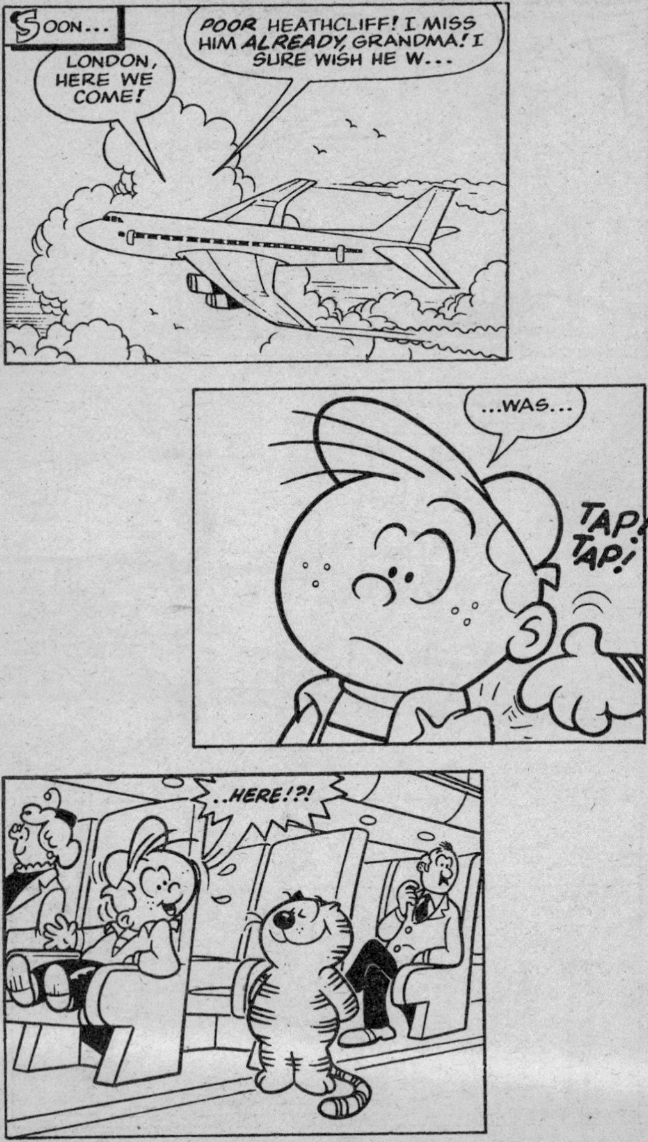
SOON...
LONDON, HERE WE COME!
POOR HEATHCLIFF! I MISS HIM ALREADY, GRANDMA! I SURE WISH HE W...
...WAS...
TAP! TAP!
..HERE!?!

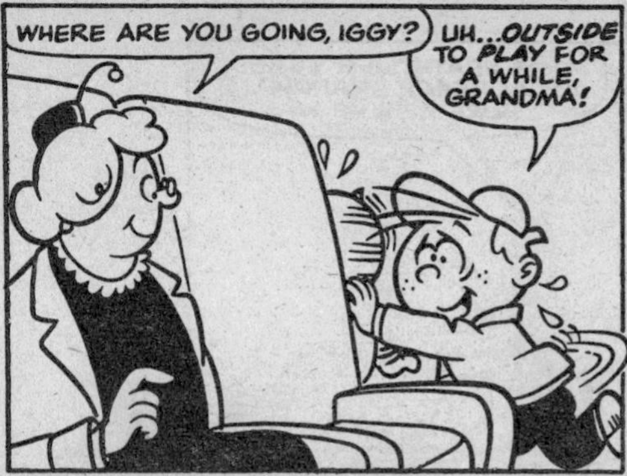
WHERE ARE YOU GOING, IGGY?
UH...OUTSIDE TO PLAY FOR A WHILE, GRANDMA!

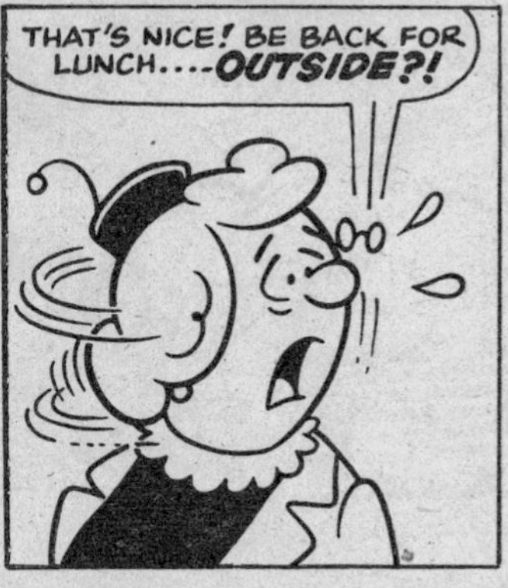
THAT'S NICE! BE BACK FOR LUNCH....OUTSIDE?!

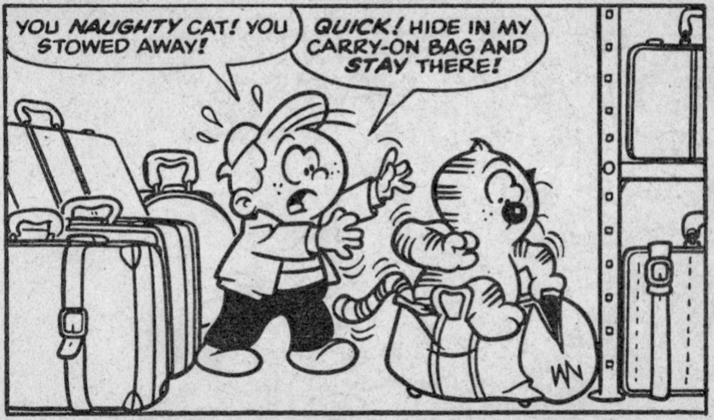
YOU NAUGHTY CAT! YOU STOWED AWAY!
QUICK! HIDE IN MY CARRY-ON BAG AND STAY THERE!

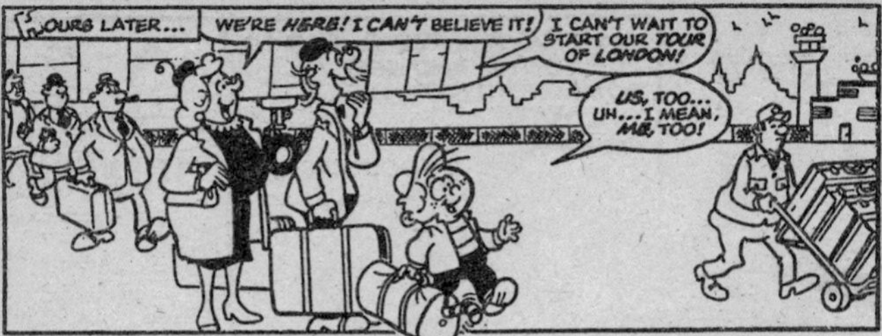
HOURS LATER...
WE'RE HERE! I CAN'T BELIEVE IT!
I CAN'T WAIT TO START OUR TOUR OF LONDON!
US, TOO... UH...I MEAN, ME, TOO!

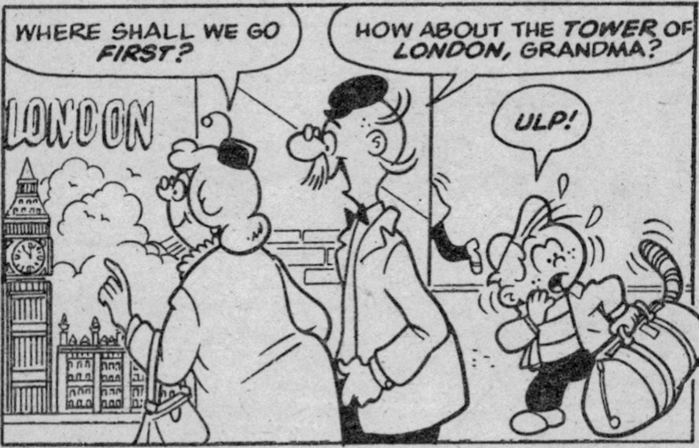
WHERE SHALL WE GO FIRST?
HOW ABOUT THE TOWER OF LONDON, GRANDMA?
LONDON
ULP!

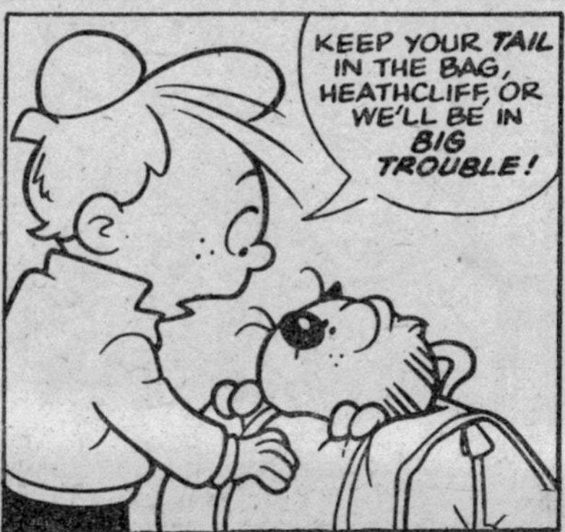
KEEP YOUR TAIL IN THE BAG, HEATHCLIFF, OR WE'LL BE IN BIG TROUBLE!

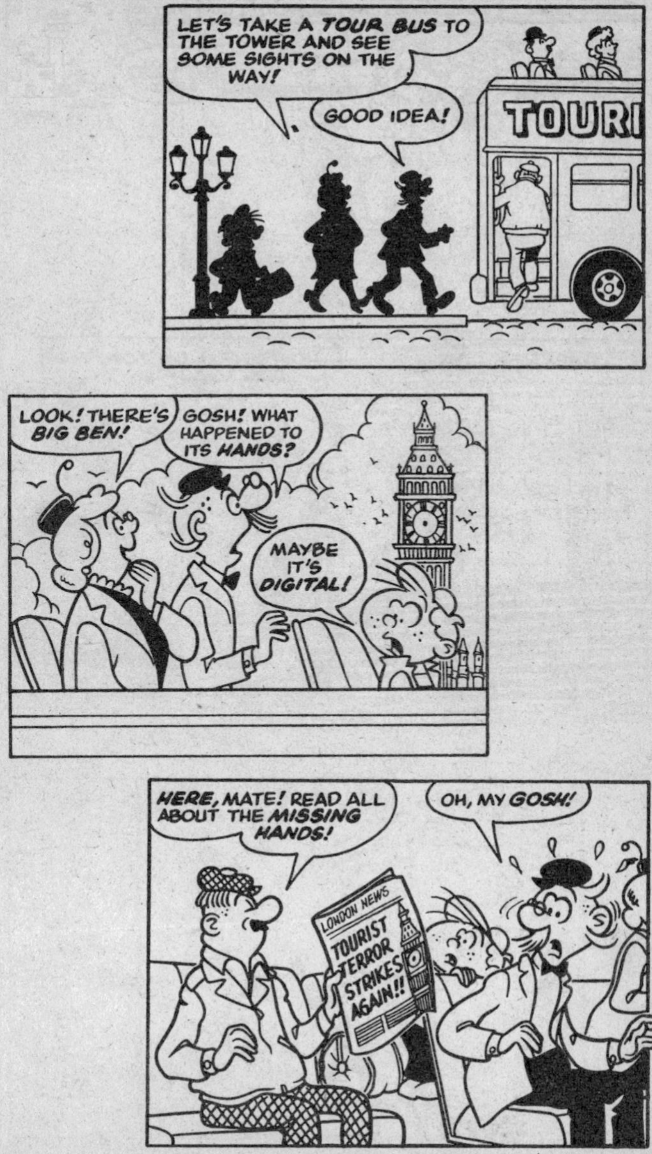
LET'S TAKE A TOUR BUS TO THE TOWER AND SEE SOME SIGHTS ON THE WAY!
GOOD IDEA!
LOOK! THERE'S BIG BEN!
GOSH! WHAT HAPPENED TO ITS HANDS?
MAYBE IT'S DIGITAL!
HERE, MATE! READ ALL ABOUT THE MISSING HANDS!
OH, MY GOSH!
LONDON NEWS
TOURIST TERROR STRIKES AGAIN!!

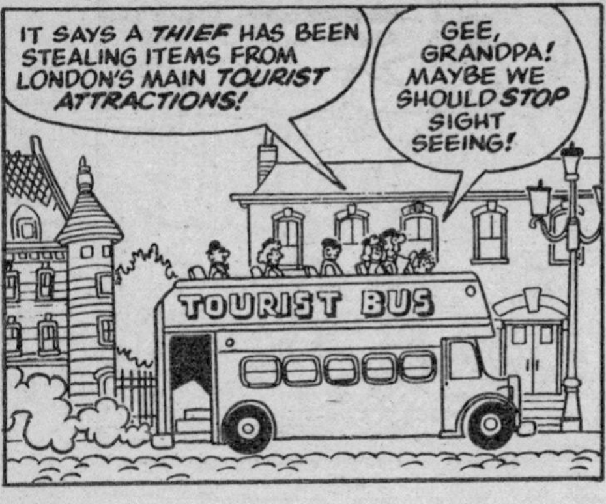
IT SAYS A THIEF HAS BEEN STEALING ITEMS FROM LONDON'S MAIN TOURIST ATTRACTIONS!
GEE, GRANDPA! MAYBE WE SHOULD STOP SIGHT SEEING!
TOURIST BUS

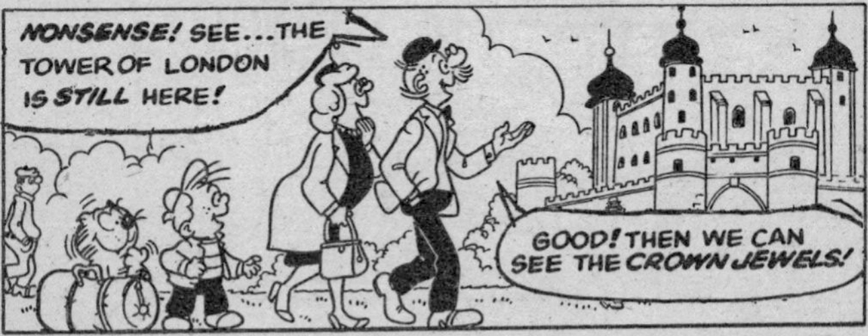
NONSENSE! SEE...THE TOWER OF LONDON IS STILL HERE!
GOOD! THEN WE CAN SEE THE CROWN JEWELS!

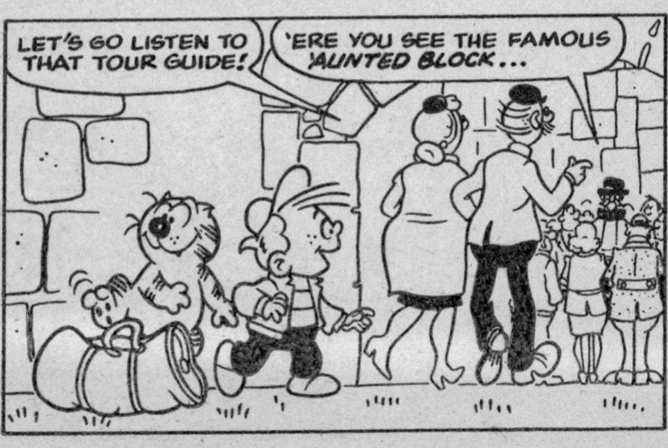
LET'S GO LISTEN TO THAT TOUR GUIDE!
'ERE YOU SEE THE FAMOUS 'AUNTED BLOCK...

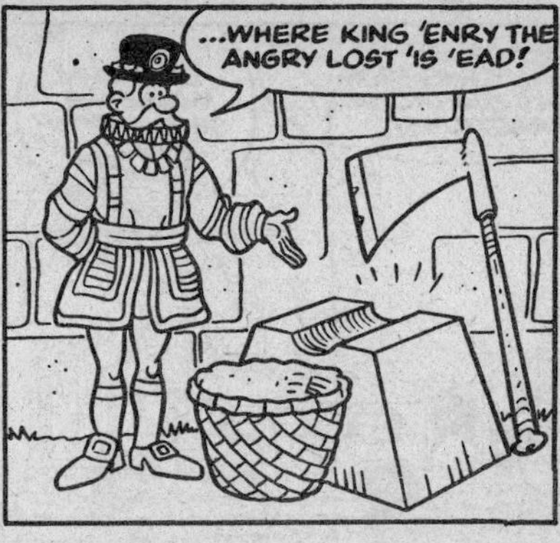
...WHERE KING 'ENRY THE ANGRY LOST 'IS 'EAD!

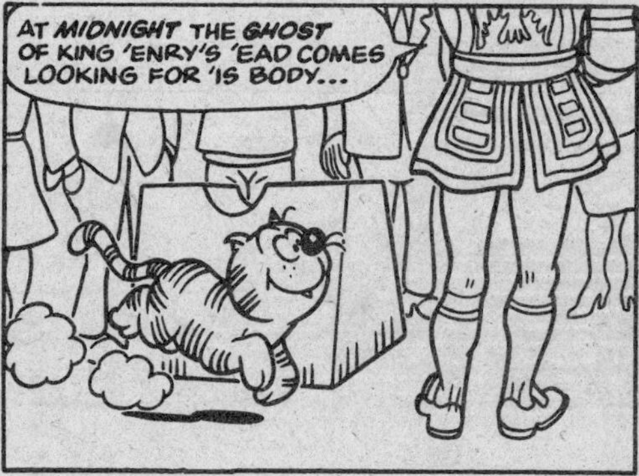
AT MIDNIGHT THE GHOST OF KING 'ENRY'S 'EAD COMES LOOKING FOR 'IS BODY...

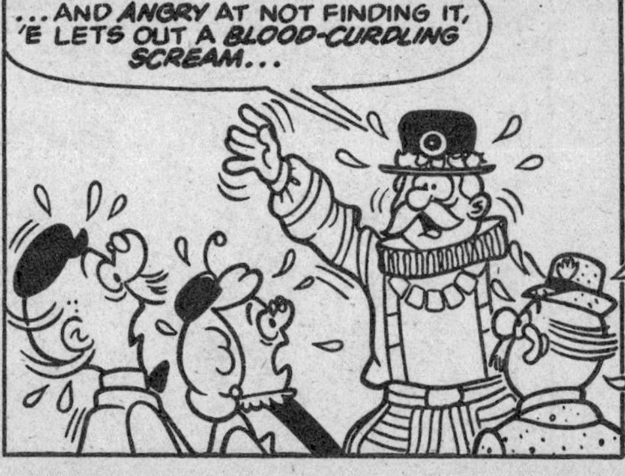
...AND ANGRY AT NOT FINDING IT, 'E LETS OUT A BLOOD-CURDLING SCREAM...

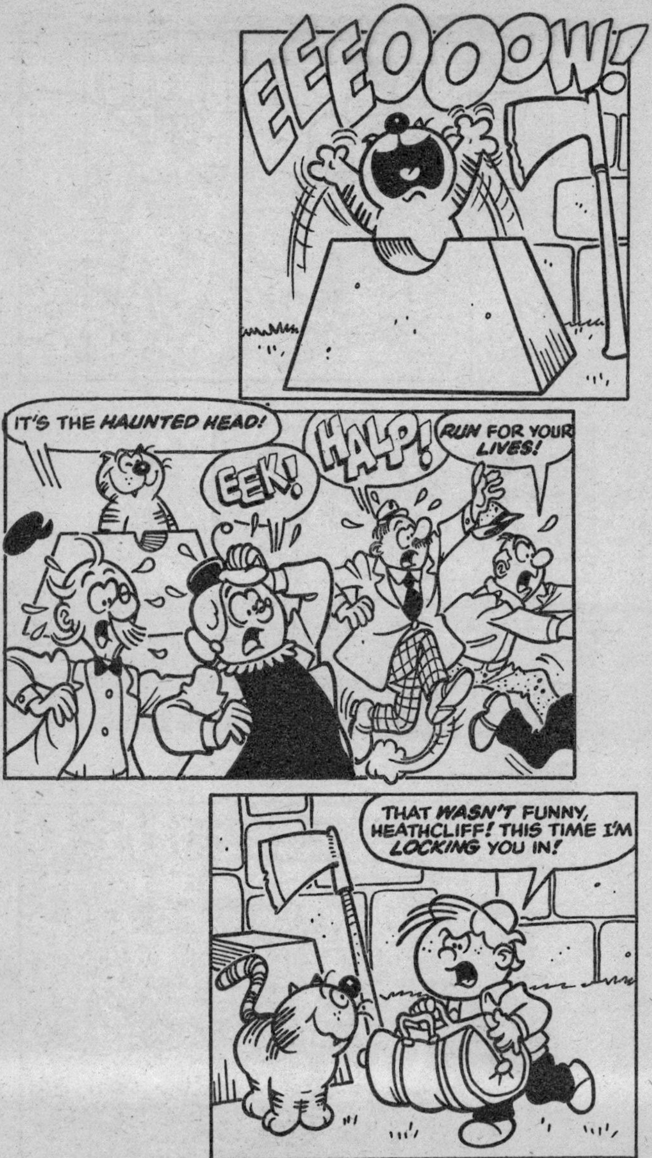
EEEOOOW!
IT'S THE HAUNTED HEAD!
EEK!
HALP!
RUN FOR YOUR LIVES!
THAT WASN'T FUNNY, HEATHCLIFF! THIS TIME I'M LOCKING YOU IN!

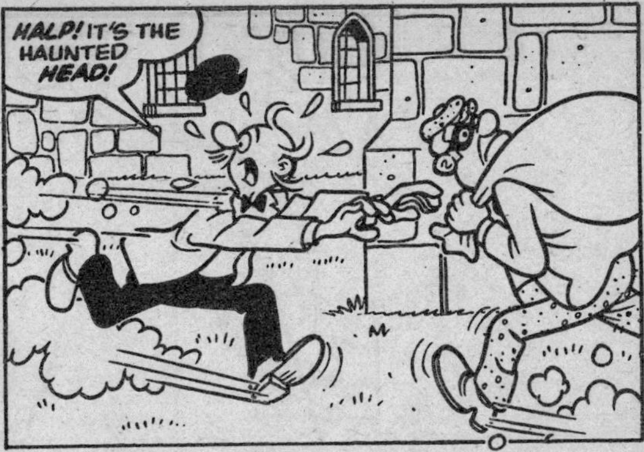
HALP! IT'S THE HAUNTED HEAD!

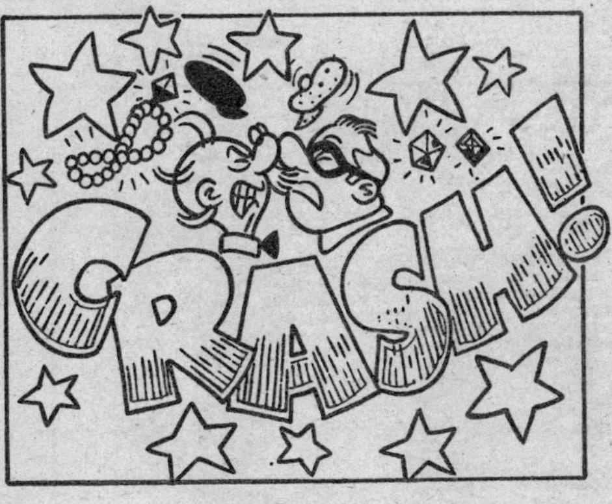
CRASH!

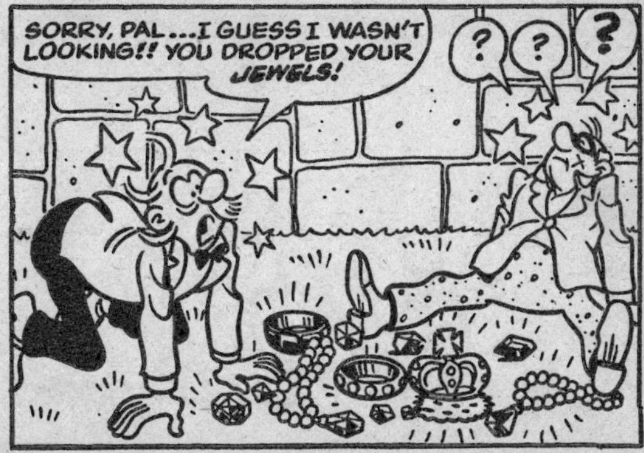
SORRY, PAL...I GUESS I WASN'T LOOKING!! YOU DROPPED YOUR JEWELS!
?
?
?

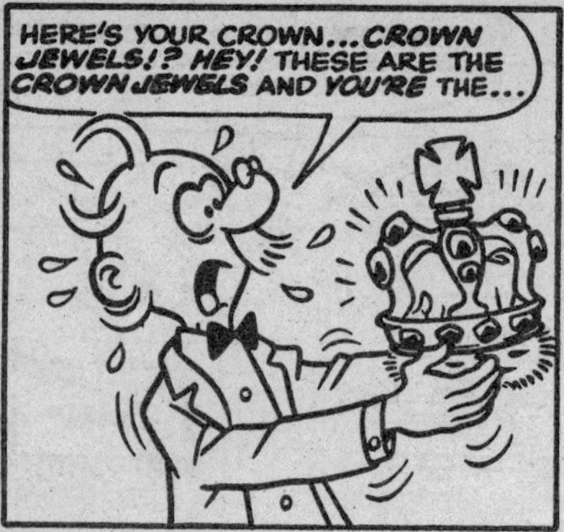
HERE'S YOUR CROWN...CROWN JEWELS!? HEY! THESE ARE THE CROWN JEWELS AND YOU'RE THE...

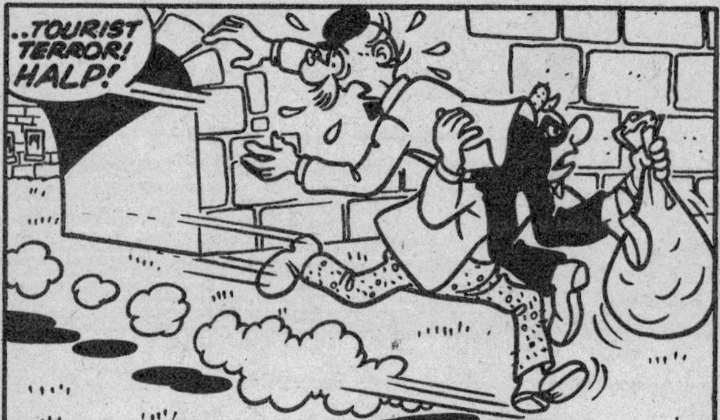
..TOURIST TERROR! HALP!

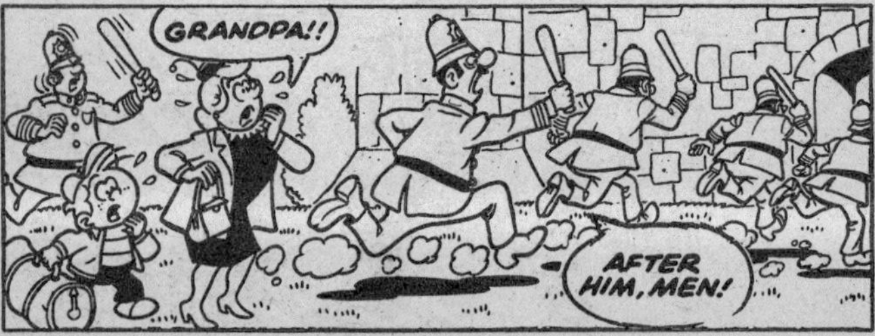
GRANDPA!!
AFTER HIM, MEN!

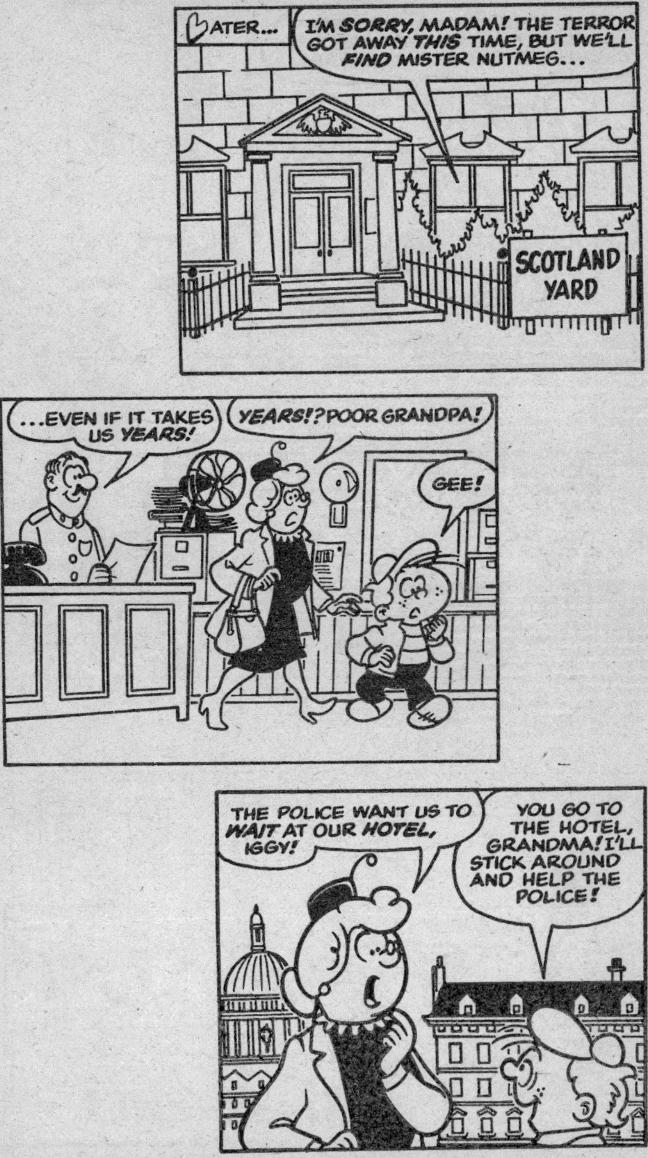
LATER...
I'M SORRY, MADAM! THE TERROR GOT AWAY THIS TIME, BUT WE'LL FIND MISTER NUTMEG...
SCOTLAND YARD
...EVEN IF IT TAKES US YEARS!
YEARS!? POOR GRANDPA!
GEE!
THE POLICE WANT US TO WAIT AT OUR HOTEL, IGGY!
YOU GO TO THE HOTEL, GRANDMA! I'LL STICK AROUND AND HELP THE POLICE!

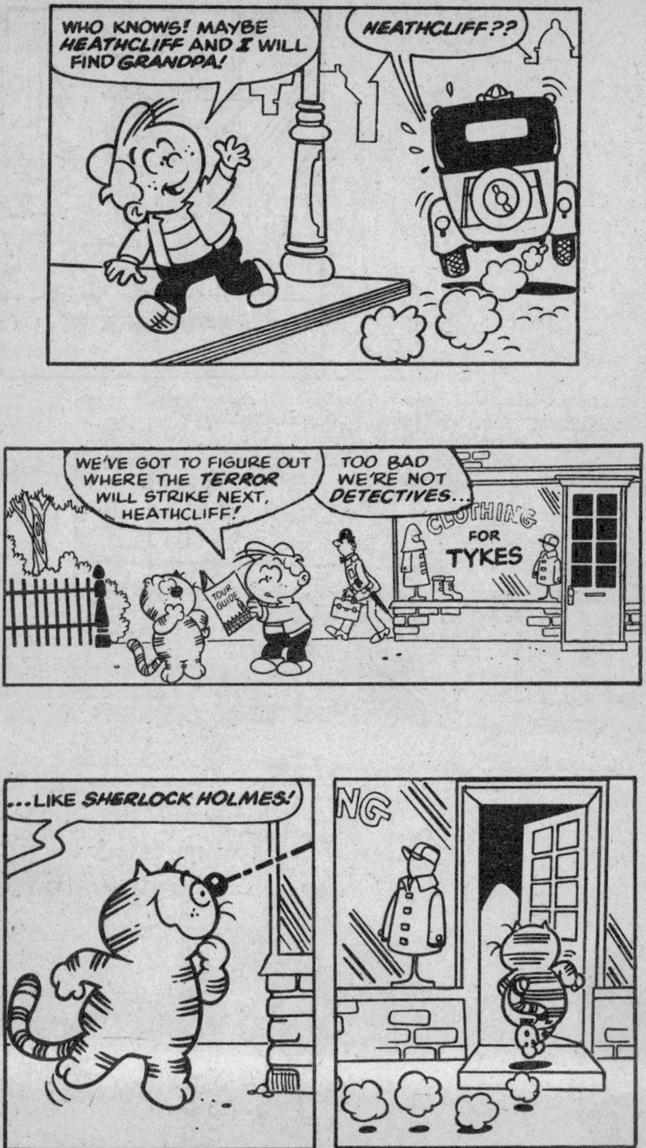
WHO KNOWS! MAYBE HEATHCLIFF AND I WILL FIND GRANDPA!
HEATHCLIFF??
WE'VE GOT TO FIGURE OUT WHERE THE TERROR WILL STRIKE NEXT, HEATHCLIFF!
TOO BAD WE'RE NOT DETECTIVES...
TOUR GUIDE
CLOTHING FOR TYKES
...LIKE SHERLOCK HOLMES!
NG

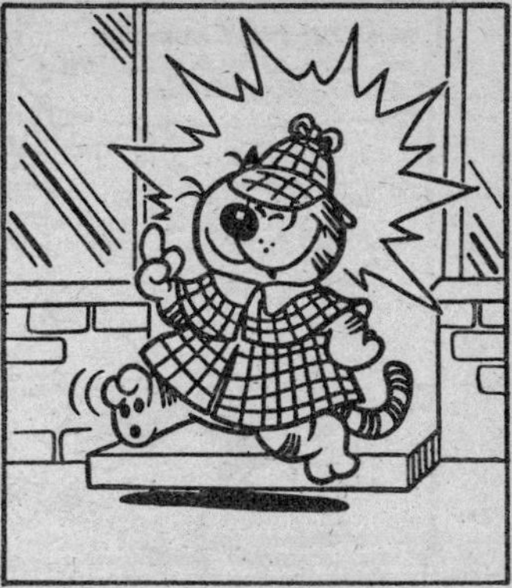

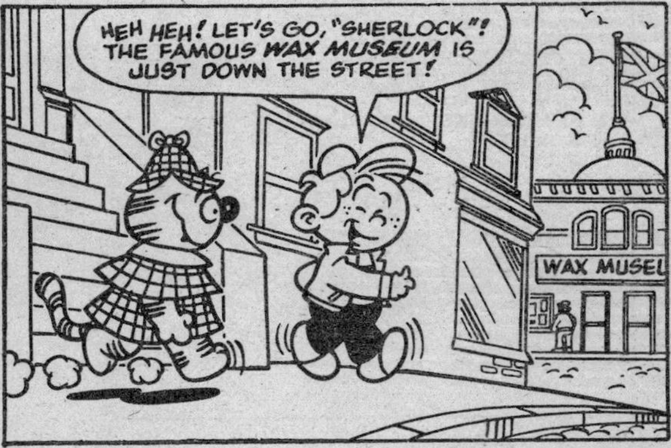
HEH HEH! LET'S GO, "SHERLOCK"! THE FAMOUS WAX MUSEUM IS JUST DOWN THE STREET!

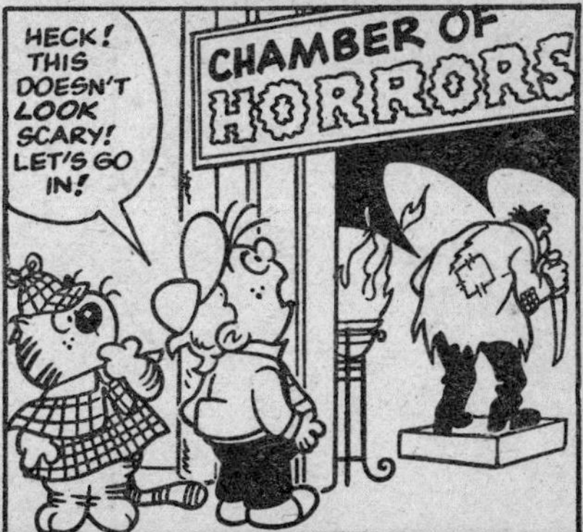
HECK! THIS DOESN'T LOOK SCARY! LET'S GO IN!
CHAMBER OF HORRORS

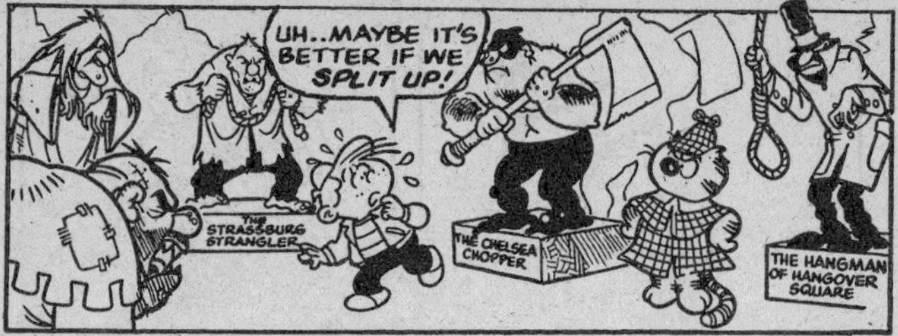
UH..MAYBE IT'S BETTER IF WE SPLIT UP!
THE STRASSBURG STRANGLER
THE CHELSEA CHOPPER
THE HANGMAN OF HANGOVER SQUARE

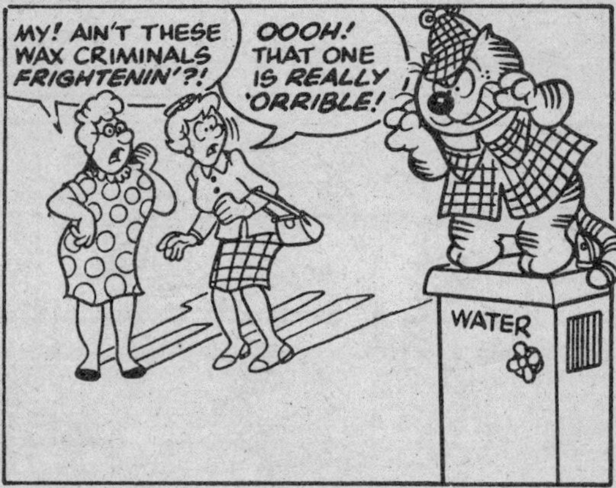
MY! AIN'T THESE WAX CRIMINALS FRIGHTENIN'?!
OOOH! THAT ONE IS REALLY 'ORRIBLE!
WATER

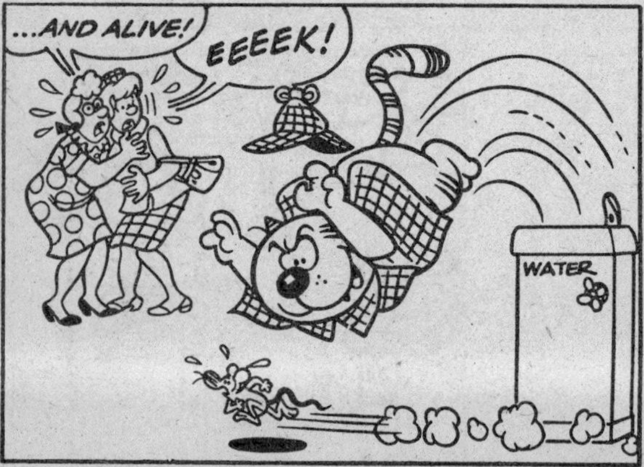
...AND ALIVE!
EEEEK!
WATER

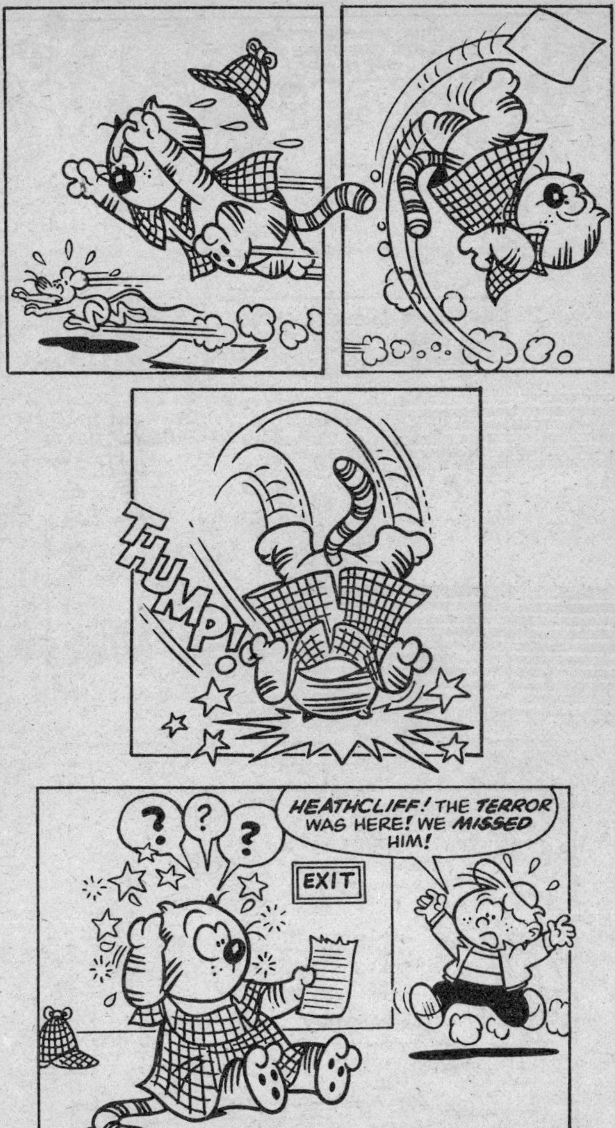
THUMP!
?
?
?
HEATHCLIFF! THE TERROR WAS HERE! WE MISSED HIM!
EXIT

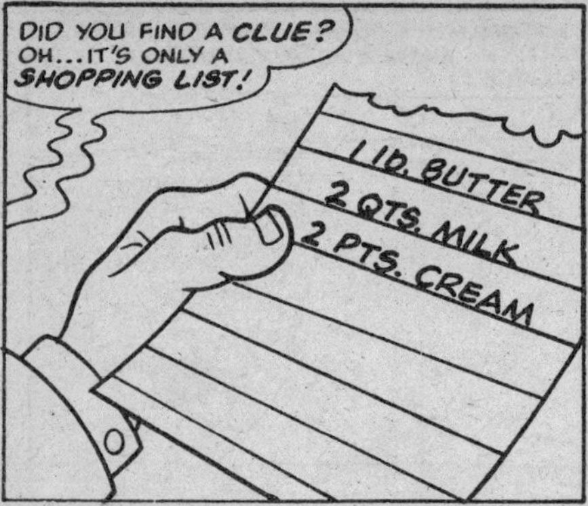
DID YOU FIND A CLUE? OH...IT'S ONLY A SHOPPING LIST!
1 lb. BUTTER
2 QTS. MILK
2 PTS. CREAM

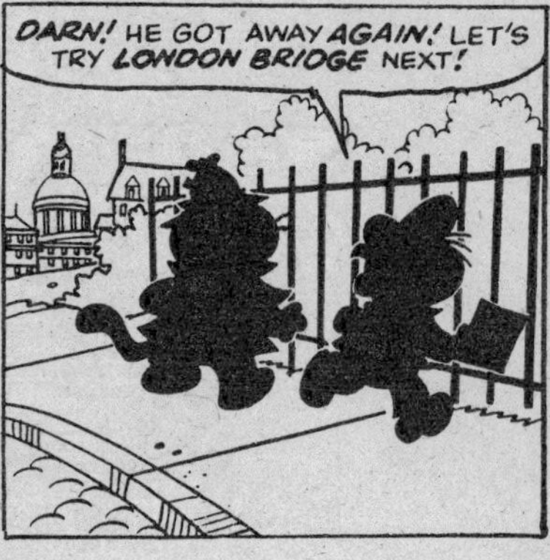
DARN! HE GOT AWAY AGAIN! LET'S TRY LONDON BRIDGE NEXT!

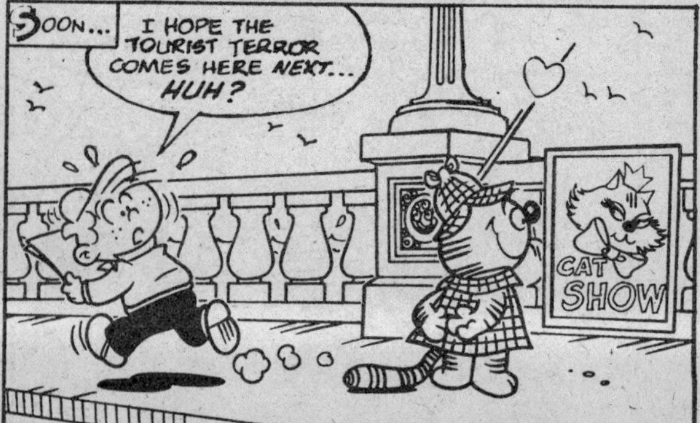
SOON...
I HOPE THE TOURIST TERROR COMES HERE NEXT... HUH?
CAT SHOW

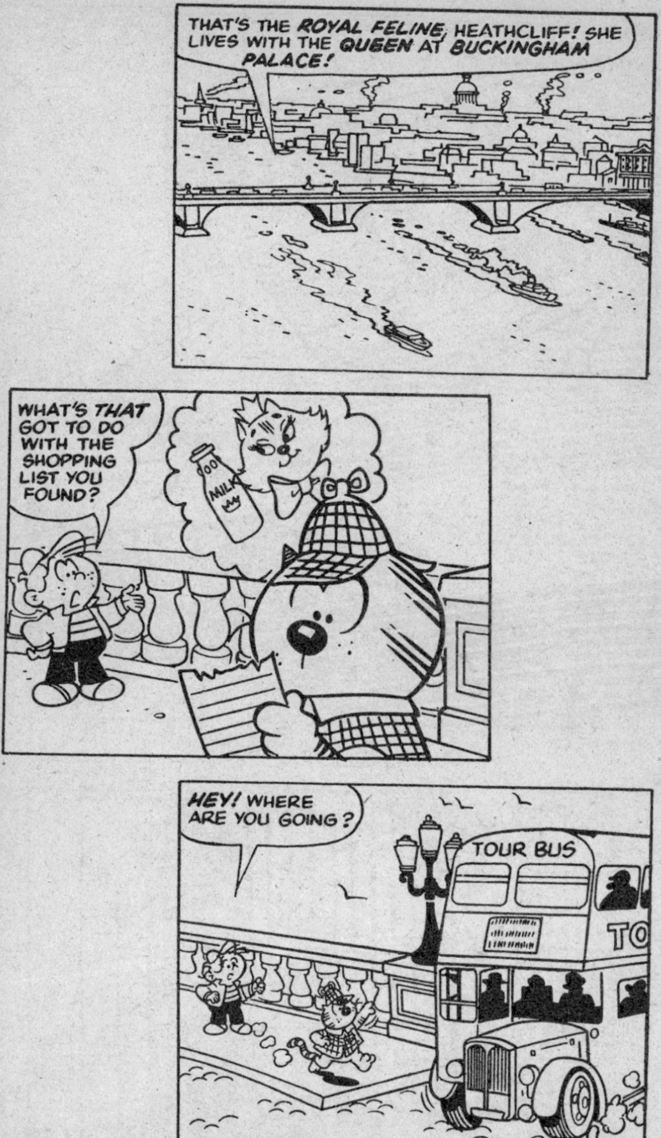
THAT'S THE ROYAL FELINE, HEATHCLIFF! SHE LIVES WITH THE QUEEN AT BUCKINGHAM PALACE!
WHAT'S THAT GOT TO DO WITH THE SHOPPING LIST YOU FOUND?
MILK
HEY! WHERE ARE YOU GOING?
TOUR BUS

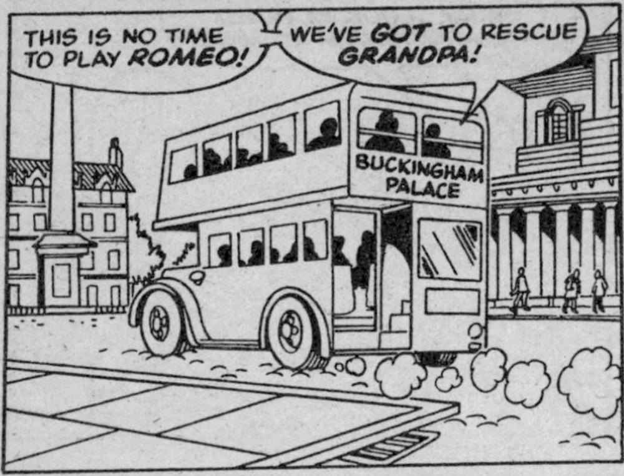
THIS IS NO TIME TO PLAY ROMEO!
WE'VE GOT TO RESCUE GRANDPA!
BUCKINGHAM PALACE

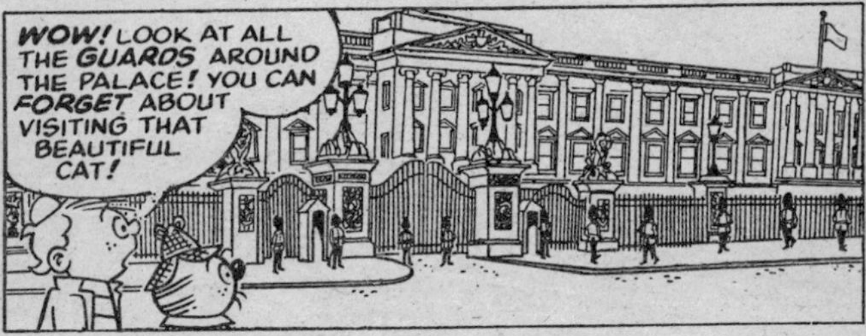
WOW! LOOK AT ALL THE GUARDS AROUND THE PALACE! YOU CAN FORGET ABOUT VISITING THAT BEAUTIFUL CAT!

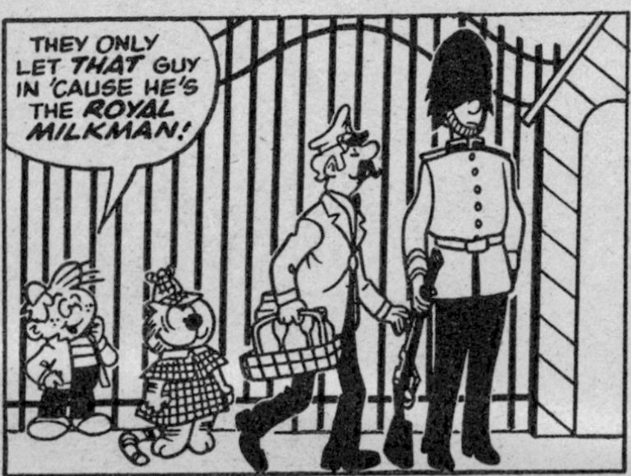
THEY ONLY LET THAT GUY IN 'CAUSE HE'S THE ROYAL MILKMAN!

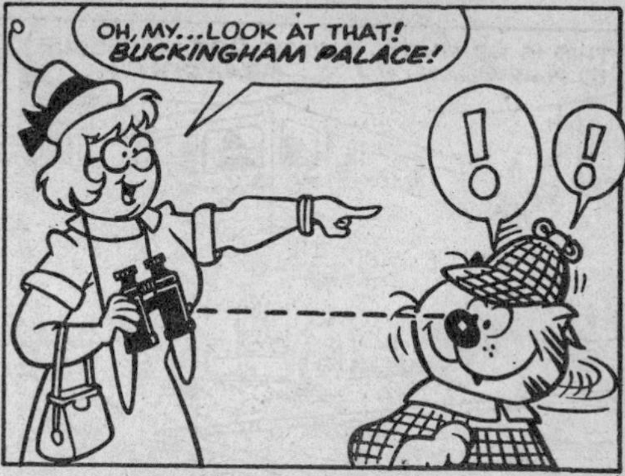
OH, MY...LOOK AT THAT! BUCKINGHAM PALACE!
!
!

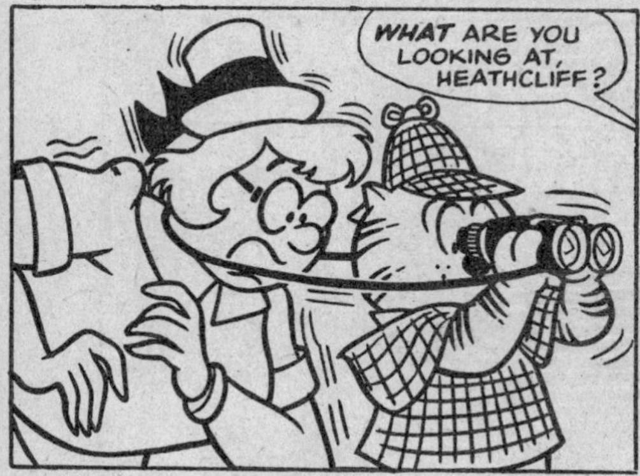
WHAT ARE YOU LOOKING AT, HEATHCLIFF?

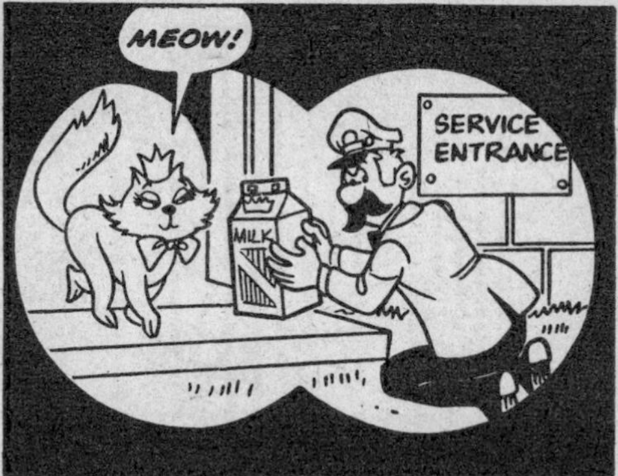
MEOW!
SERVICE ENTRANCE
MILK

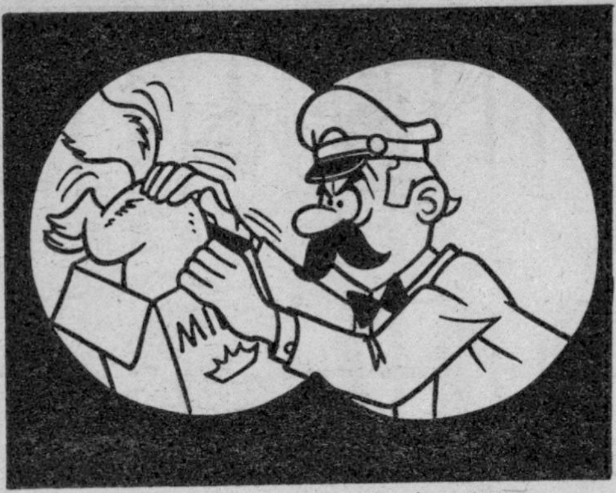

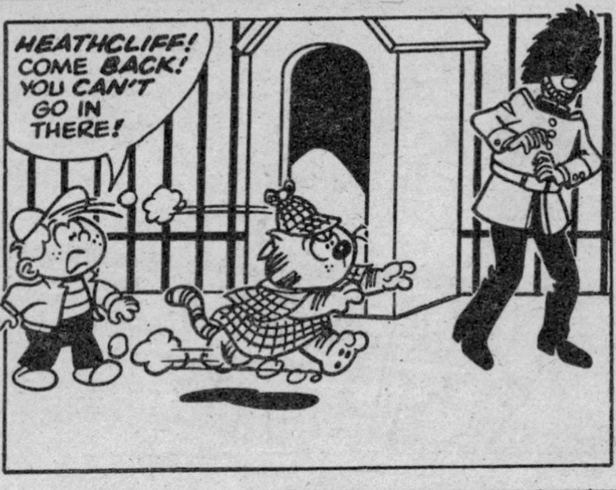
HEATHCLIFF! COME BACK! YOU CAN'T GO IN THERE!

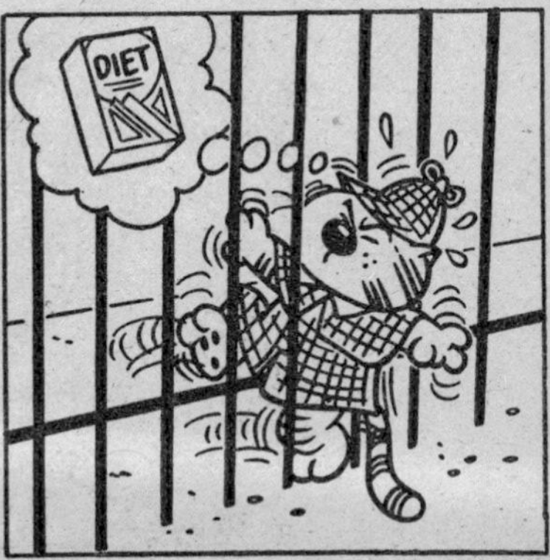
DIET

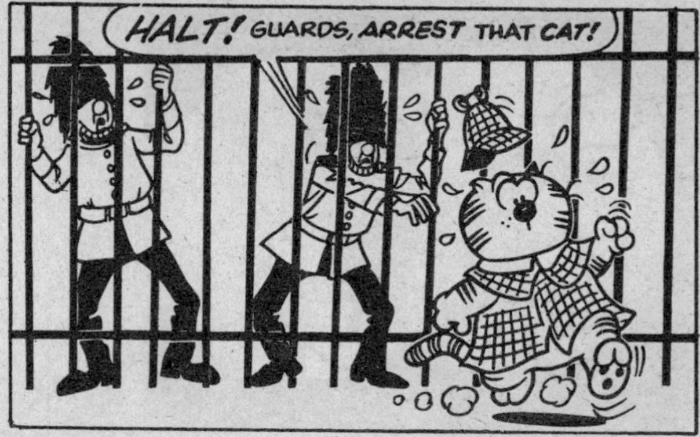
HALT! GUARDS, ARREST THAT CAT!

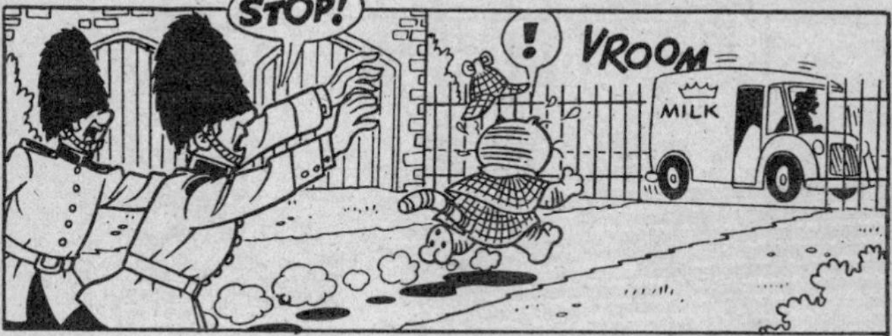
STOP!
!
VROOM
MILK

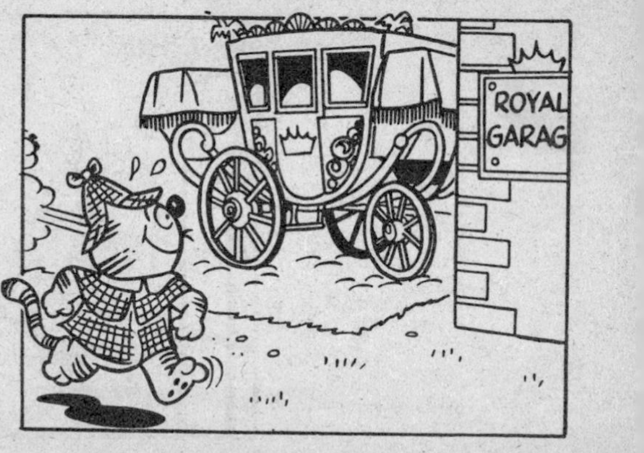
ROYAL
GARAG

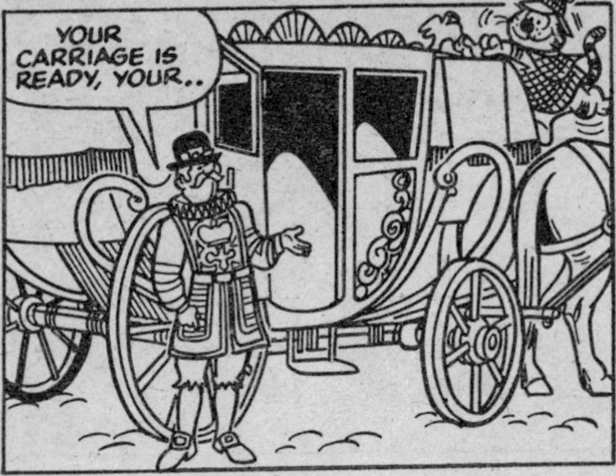
YOUR CARRIAGE IS READY, YOUR..

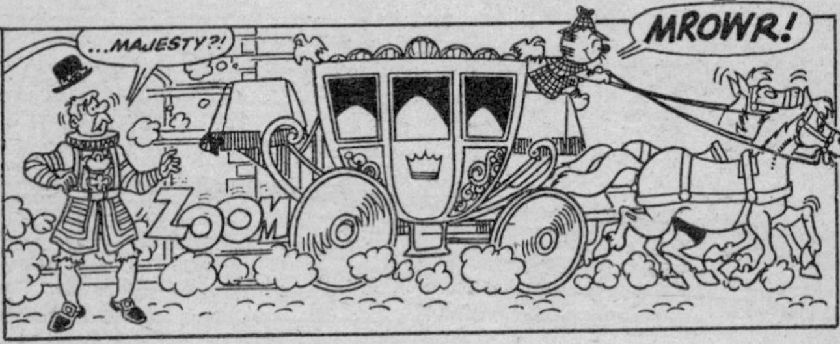
...MAJESTY?!
MROWR!
ZOOM

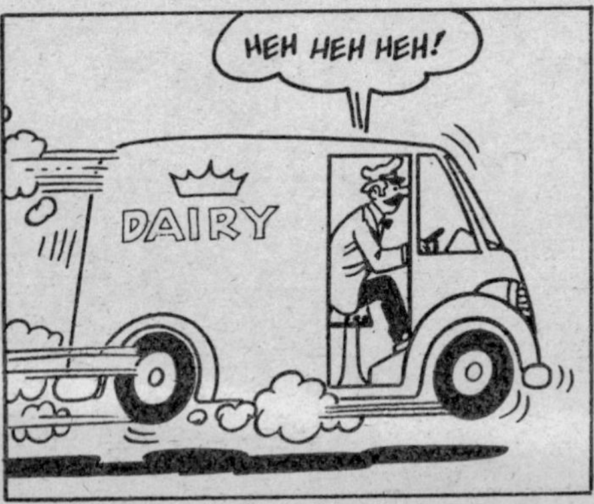
HEH HEH HEH!
DAIRY

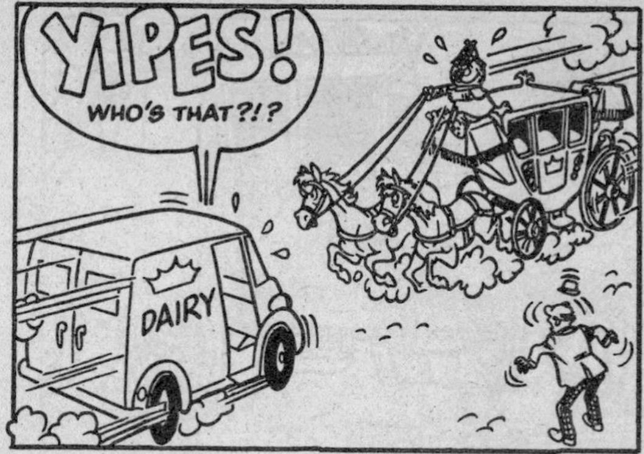
YIPES! WHO'S THAT?!?
DAIRY

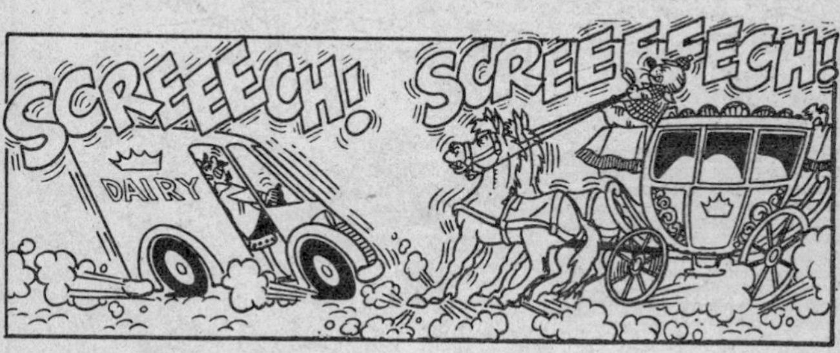
SCREEECH!
SCREEEEECH!
DAIRY

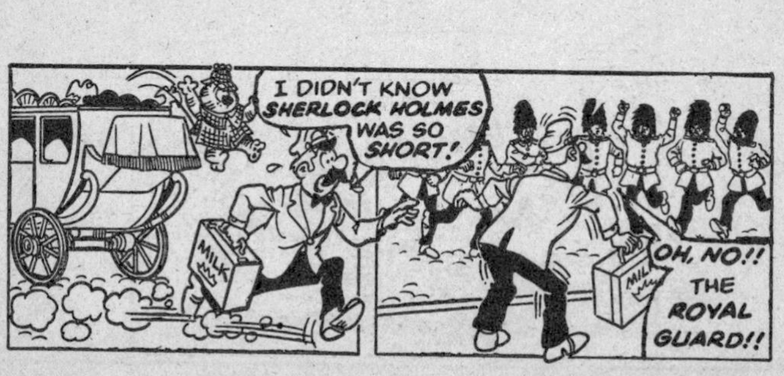
I DIDN'T KNOW SHERLOCK HOLMES WAS SO SHORT!
MILK
OH, NO!! THE ROYAL GUARD!!
MILK

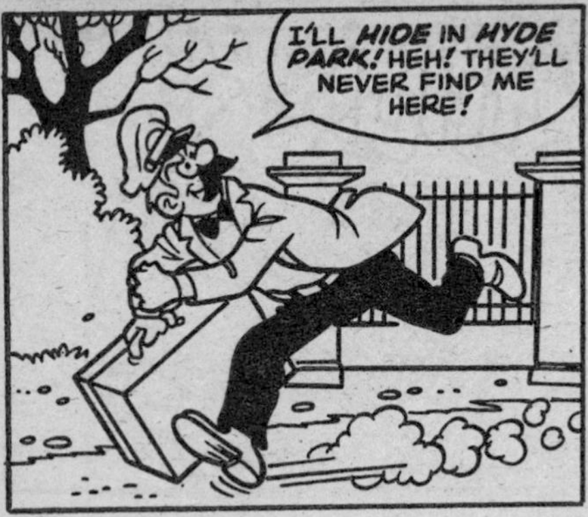
I'LL HIDE IN HYDE PARK! HEH! THEY'LL NEVER FIND ME HERE!

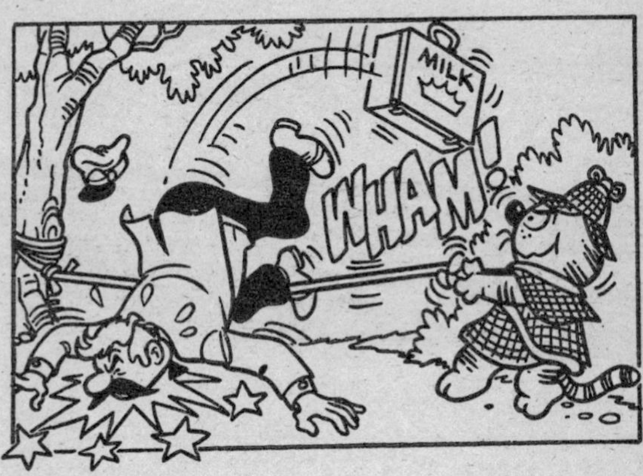
MILK
WHAM!

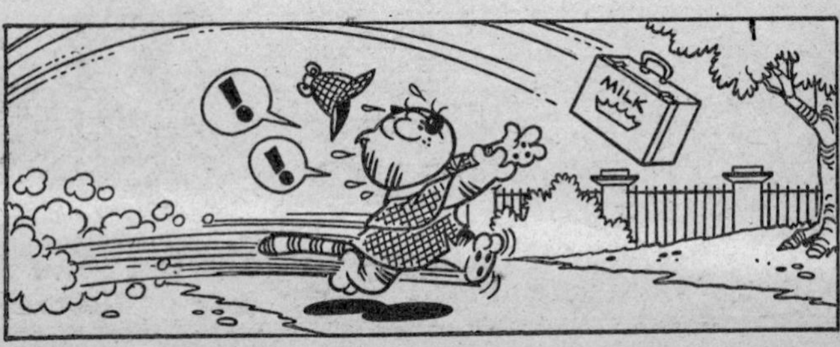
MILK

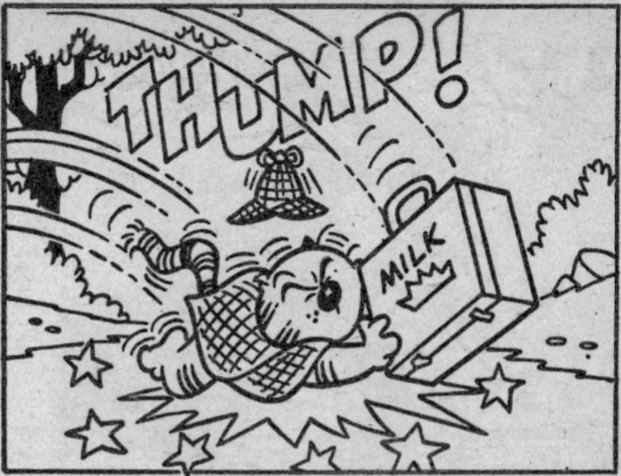
THUMP!
MILK

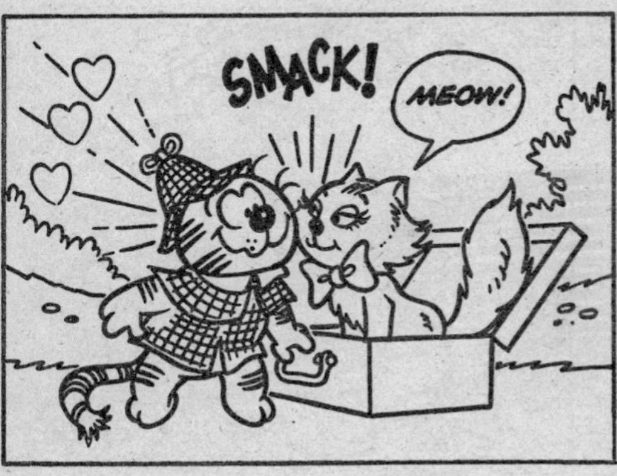
SMACK!
MEOW!

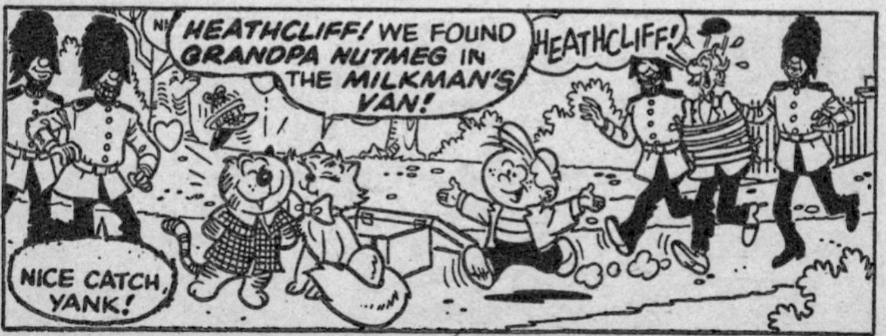
HEATHCLIFF! WE FOUND GRANDPA NUTMEG IN THE MILKMAN'S VAN!
HEATHCLIFF!
NICE CATCH, YANK!

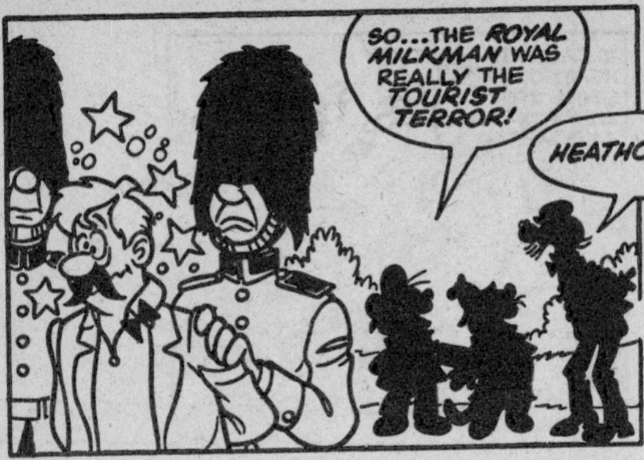
SO...THE ROYAL MILKMAN WAS REALLY THE TOURIST TERROR!
HEATHCLIFF??

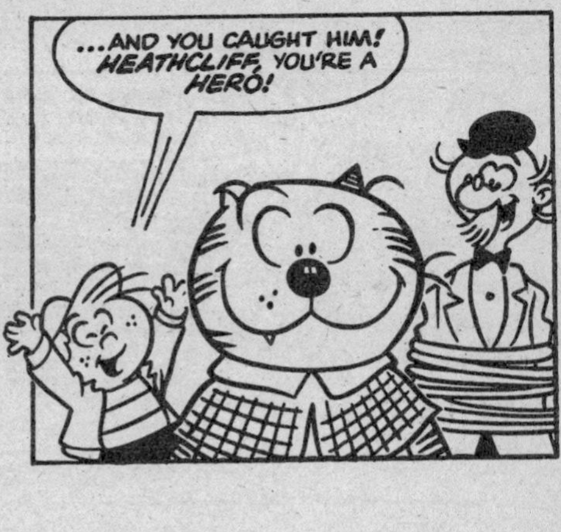
...AND YOU CAUGHT HIM! HEATHCLIFF, YOU'RE A HERO!

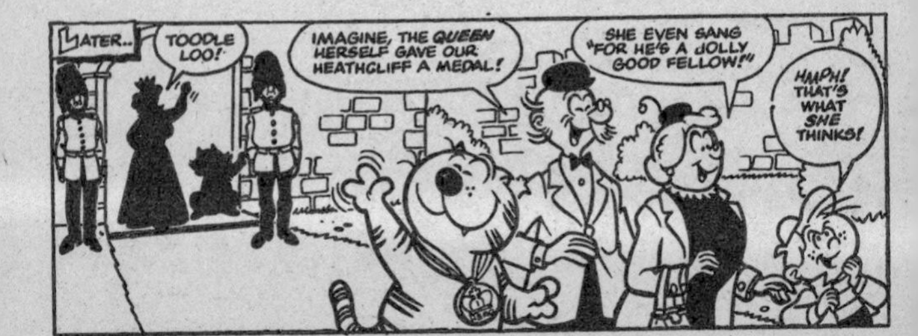
LATER..
TOODLE LOO!
IMAGINE, THE QUEEN HERSELF GAVE OUR HEATHCLIFF A MEDAL!
SHE EVEN SANG "FOR HE'S A JOLLY GOOD FELLOW!"
HMPH! THAT'S WHAT SHE THINKS!

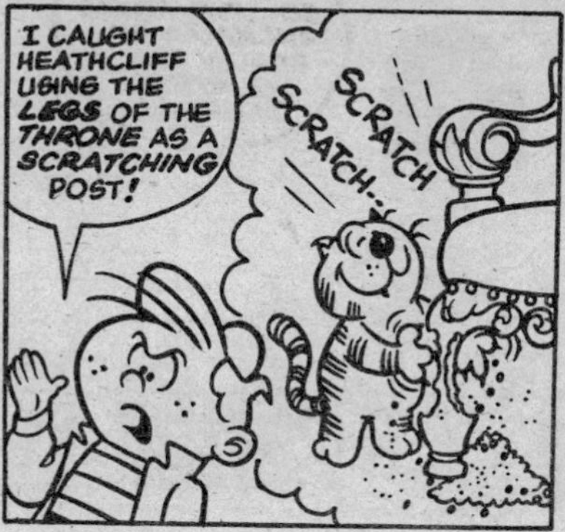
I CAUGHT HEATHCLIFF USING THE LEGS OF THE THRONE AS A SCRATCHING POST!
SCRATCH
SCRATCH...

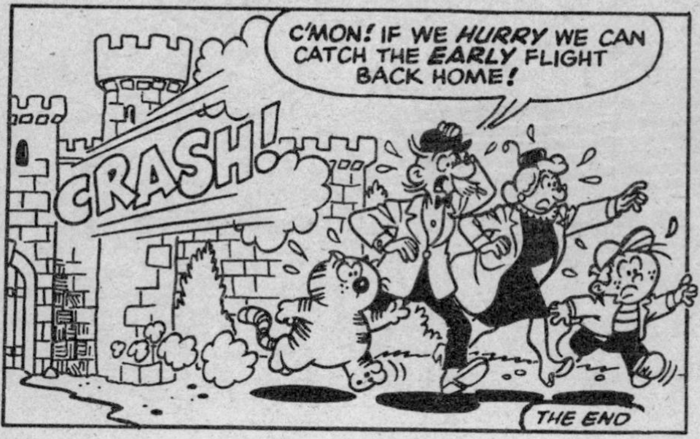
CRASH!
C'MON! IF WE HURRY WE CAN CATCH THE EARLY FLIGHT BACK HOME!
THE END

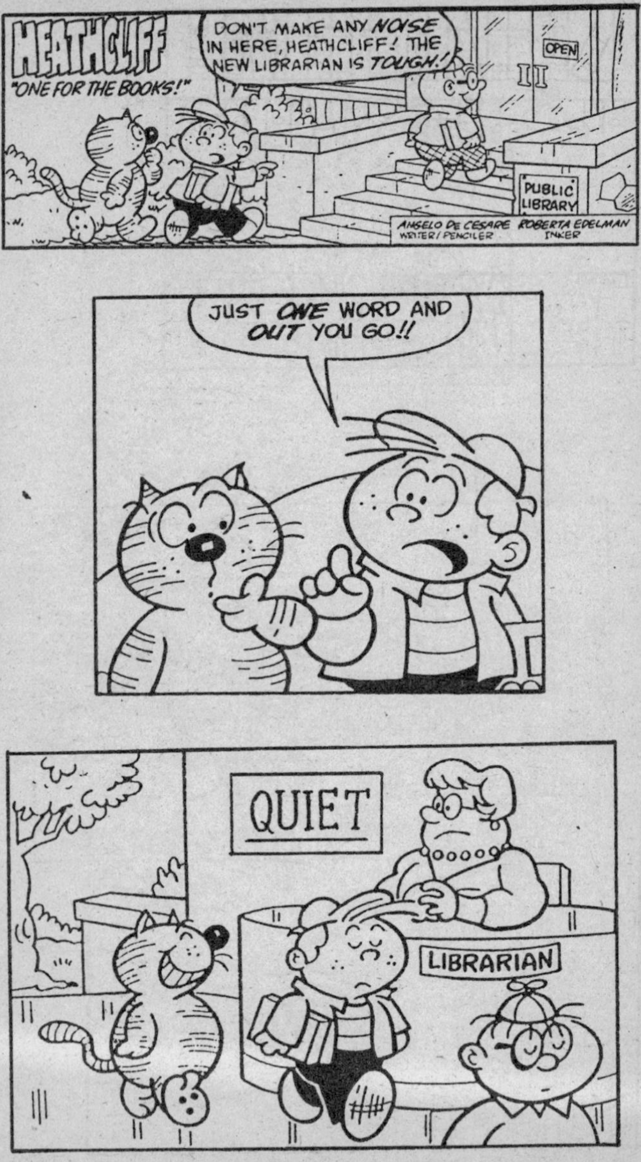
HEATHCLIFF
"ONE FOR THE BOOKS!"
DON'T MAKE ANY NOISE IN HERE, HEATHCLIFF! THE NEW LIBRARIAN IS TOUGH!
OPEN
PUBLIC LIBRARY
ANGELO DE CESARE WRITER/PENCILER
ROBERTA EDELMAN INKER
JUST ONE WORD AND OUT YOU GO!!
QUIET
LIBRARIAN

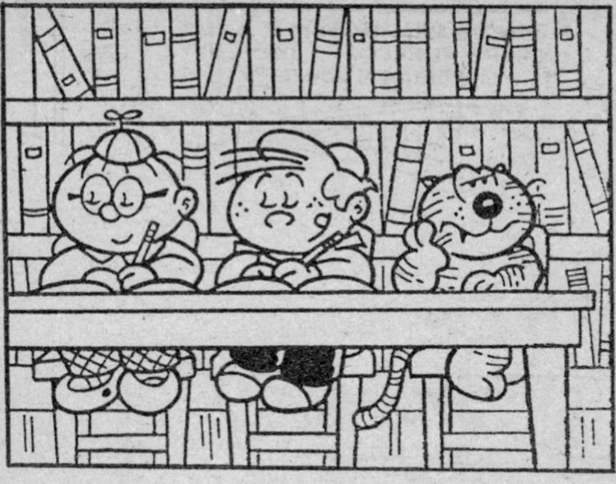

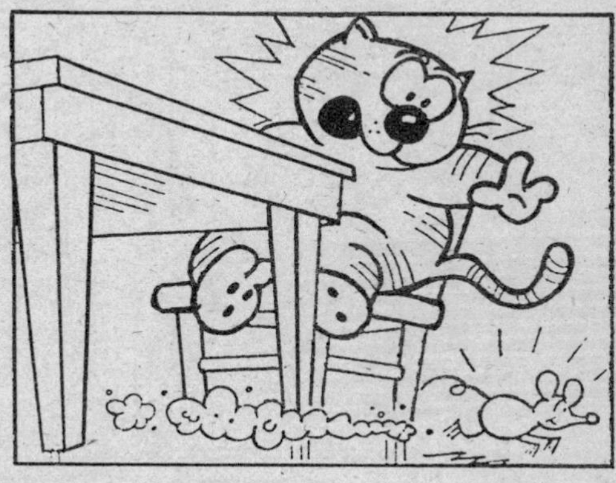

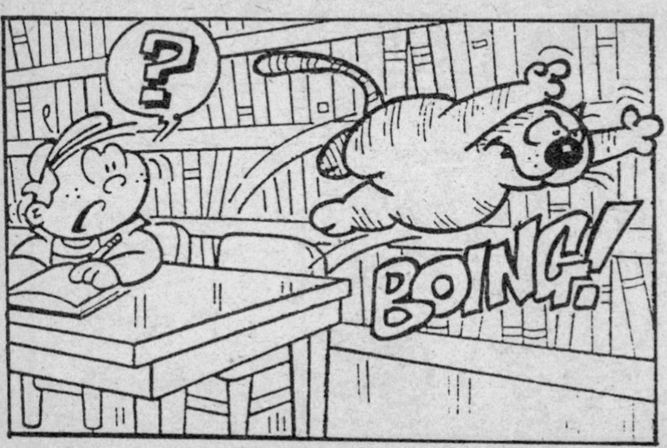
?
BOING!

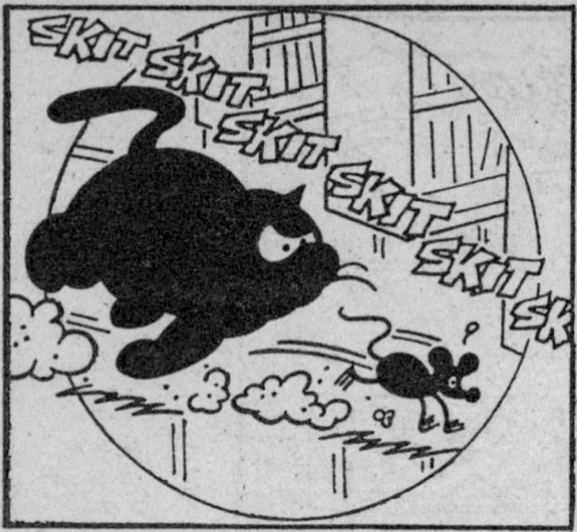
SKIT SKIT SKIT SKIT SKIT SK

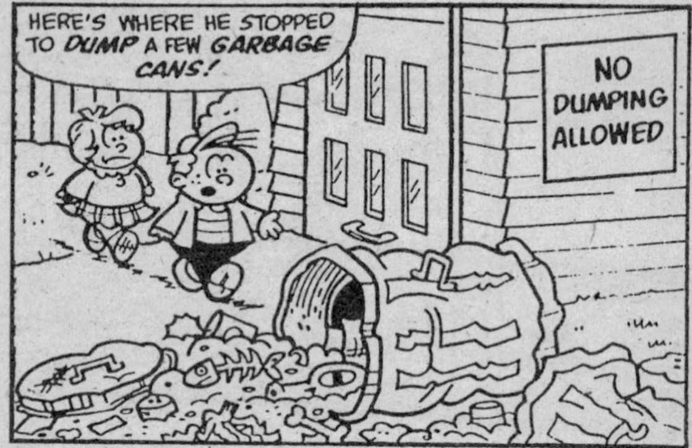
HERE'S WHERE HE STOPPED TO DUMP A FEW GARBAGE CANS!
NO DUMPING ALLOWED

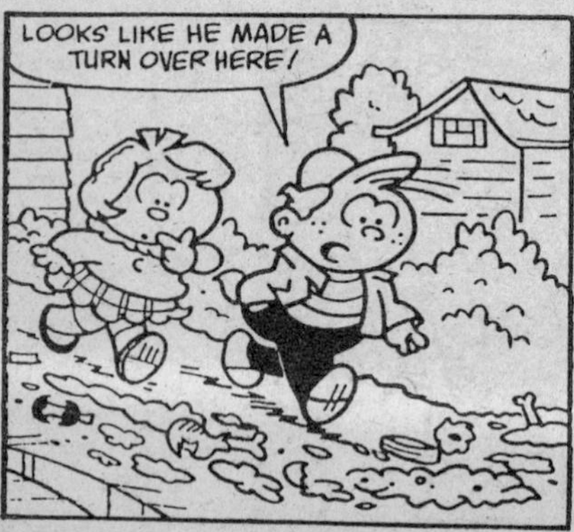
LOOKS LIKE HE MADE A TURN OVER HERE!

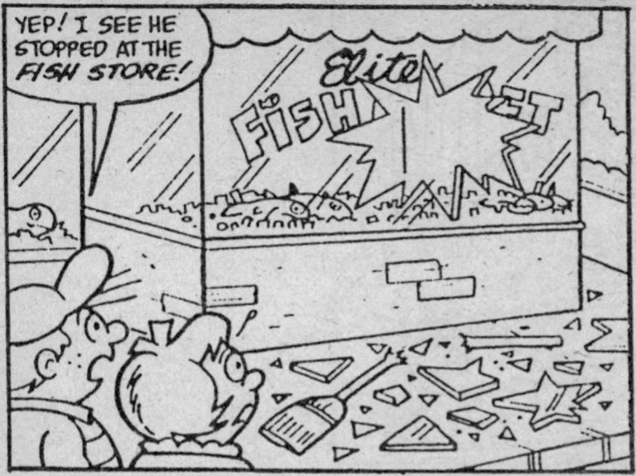
YEP! I SEE HE STOPPED AT THE FISH STORE!
Elite FISH

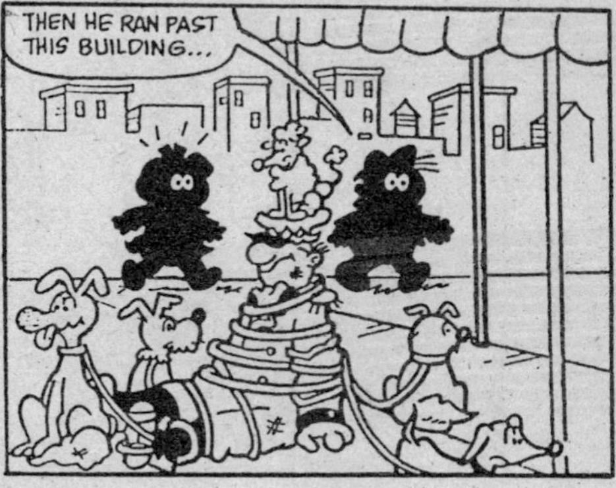
THEN HE RAN PAST THIS BUILDING...

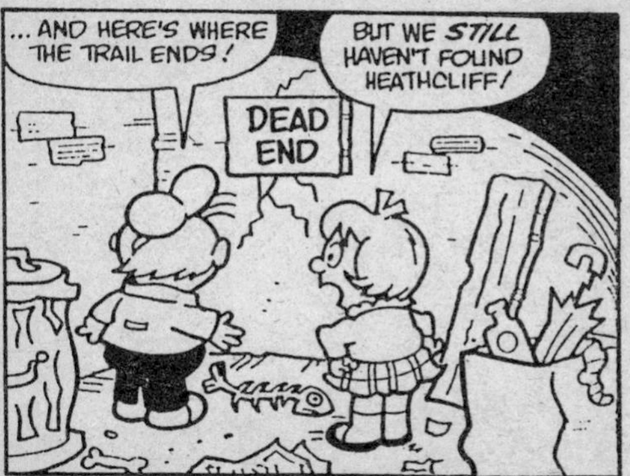
...AND HERE'S WHERE THE TRAIL ENDS!
BUT WE STILL HAVEN'T FOUND HEATHCLIFF!
DEAD END

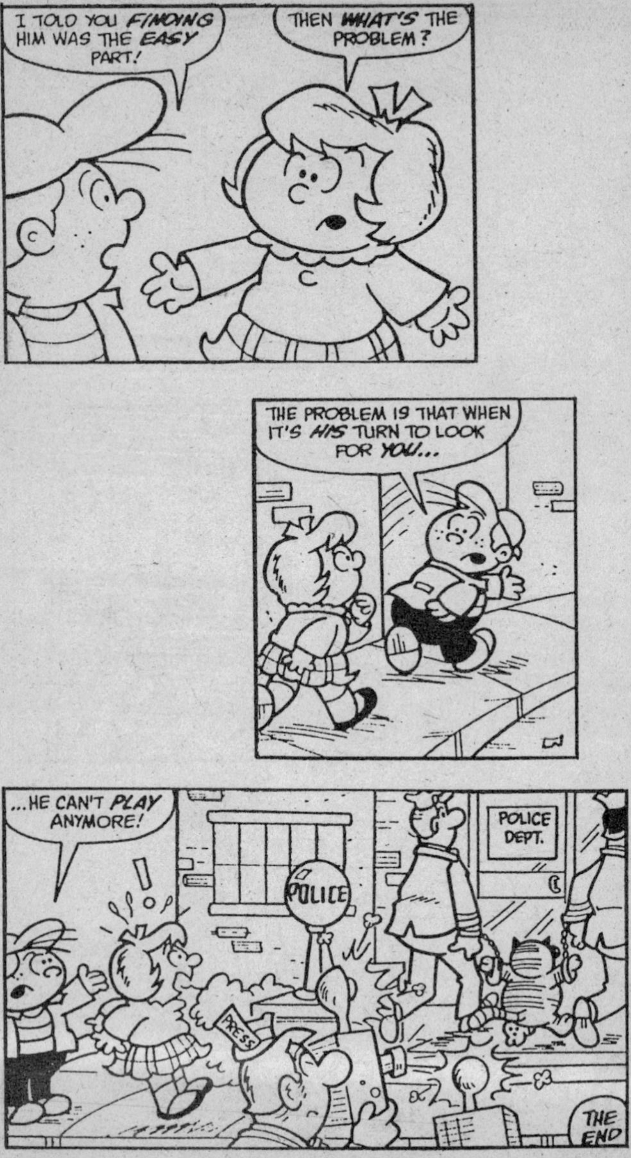
I TOLD YOU *FINDING* HIM WAS THE *EASY* PART!
THEN *WHAT'S* THE PROBLEM?
THE PROBLEM IS THAT WHEN IT'S *HIS* TURN TO LOOK FOR *YOU*...
...HE CAN'T *PLAY* ANYMORE!
POLICE DEPT.
POLICE
PRESS
THE END